THE ALTARPIECE

BOOK ONE OF THE CROSS AND CROWN SERIES

SARAH KENNEDY

KNOX ROBINSON
PUBLISHING
London • New York

KNOX ROBINSON
PUBLISHING

3rd Floor, 36 Langham Street
Westminster, London W1W 7AP
&
244 5th Avenue, Suite 1861
New York, New York 10001

Knox Robinson Publishing is a specialist, international publisher of historical fiction, historical romance and medieval fantasy.

First published in Great Britain in 2013 by Knox Robinson Publishing

First published in the United States in 2013 by Knox Robinson Publishing

A CIP catalogue record for this book is available from the British Library.

ISBN HC 978-1-908483-47-8

ISBN PB 978-1-908483-48-5

Typeset in Bembo by Susan Veach
info@susanveach.com

Printed in the United States of America and the United Kingdom.

Download the KRP App in iTunes and Google Play to receive free historical fiction, historical romance and fantasy eBooks delivered directly to your mobile or tablet.

Watch our historical documentaries and book trailers on our channel on YouTube and subscribe to our podcasts in iTunes.

www.knoxrobinsonpublishing.com

England

in the Sixteenth Century

Scotland

Havenston*

Fountains Abbey ✝ ✝ Mount Grace

York

Leeds

Doncaster

Grantham

Stamford

King's Lynn

Peterborough

Norwich

Yarmouth

Huntingdon

Stratford-upon-Avon

Hatfield Place

London

*fictional place

CHAPTER ONE

May 1535, North Yorkshire

Mount Grace Priory was cold as a crypt, despite the gold-shot tapestries on the stone walls. Sister Catherine gathered the woolen shawl around her shoulders. The candle on the oak infirmary table guttered, and she cupped her hand around the flame. When the light steadied, she stepped to the window and tucked cloths between the shutters. She placed her ear against the wood for a moment. Nothing. It must have been the wind. The soldiers had surely gone to the inn for the night. She had a few hours at least.

Catherine tiptoed to the door and peered down the long corridor, but her eyes could not adjust to the blank darkness beyond her workroom, so she turned once more to her task. She laid out her receipt books and measured them with her eyes. They could be hidden easily enough. She ran her palm over the worn leather covers and opened one. She had drawn the herbs and flowers herself, and her finger traced the bright veins she had penned into the daffodil leaves on one page. She had copied details of their altarpiece in a corner of each page. The Magdalene with her golden jar of ointment. A cherry tree with Joseph reaching to pluck the fruit. A Christ child, sitting in the crook of his Mother's elbow. The Madonna, always in the upper right-hand corner.

The script was black and firm, and Catherine read through a few of her receipts. Yes, she had them by heart. She could do without the books. For now. If only she could find a way to practice physic without losing her head. She stacked them, lifted the pile, and unlatched the door. Stepping into the darkness, she slid along the interior wall of the nuns' walk until she reached the dormitory. She hesitated, listening. An animal rustled along the garden's edge, a weasel or a rat, too low to be seen. Not a man. Not yet. She had already loosened this latch and she slipped inside without a sound.

The other nuns were sleeping under heaps of blankets, and Catherine crept to her own pallet, where she knelt and arranged the books in the hole, easing the loosened stones back into place. The last one clunked as it dropped, and she froze, her heart banging loud inside her ribs. But no one stirred as she slunk back out.

Her taper still burned in the infirmary, and Catherine took it up before she stepped softly into the walk again, turning the other way this time. She hurried around the corner to the narrow steps leading up to the reading room. Catherine's head grazed the low ribs of the vaulted ceiling, and she went straight to her knees, reaching under the scriptor's desk. Her fingers found the wrapped manuscript, tied tight with string, and she lifted it onto the small table. Her hands were icy, and she trembled as she tested the knots. The parcel was intact and she lifted the candle to go.

Voices. Men's voices. Catherine stiffened. Boots on stone pavers. They were in the church. She should have written out the will first. If Catherine fled right now, she might make it back to her infirmary unseen. But a door whined below. The door from the church into the convent. Too late. Catherine blew out the flame and sat holding the ends of the string and breathing the sweet smoke. She was sweating under the heavy woolens, but her feet were cold, and she began to shiver. They would surely hear her gulping for air.

At least two of them, right below. Someone seemed to complain, and a wisp of yellow light flickered past the steps. Her scalp prickled. Another door, farther off, at the back of the convent, opened, and the voices faded. Thump of wood against wood, a metal latch coming down. All was blackness now. Her feet went numb, but she squatted without moving. All was silence. She was afraid to show her face at the window, but after an eternity of quiet, she flattened herself to the wall and raised herself to the sill. The interior of the convent seemed at peace. No soldiers in sight. Catherine snatched up a few pigments pots and, balancing them on the pages, teetered down the steps. The door into the church, usually locked, stood open. Fear knotted her limbs, but she clenched the goods and ran back to her infirmary, where she skidded inside and bolted the door, chest thudding like a rabbit in a trap. She pulled the stopper from a bottle of perfume and inhaled. Essence of lily of the valley, said to heal the heart. She let the fragrance fill her, but her ribs still ached.

Before she set to work, Catherine lifted her skirt to wipe her damp palms. Her shift was embroidered with red and yellow birds that seemed to lift their beaks and trill from the cloth, and blue-eyed, many headed flowers that sprawled and twisted the tendrils of their stems. She could not see the colors, but she ran her fingers over the slick threads. Would they tear the very clothes from the women's bodies? She'd heard stories of worse. She sat until she could no longer hear the terror whistling in her ears, then she held the candle's wick to her bowl of embers again.

Catherine had already prepared her egg whites and quills, but when she laid the parchment open, she faltered. Latin or English? English, she decided, but still she postponed the beginning. The page lay before her like creation and she stared into its surface as she had stared up into the clouds as a child, searching for God. Her hand trembled. She must not err. It might be the last document she would write. Her fingers cramped from clutching too tightly in the frigid air, and she laid the tool aside. The sharp nib pointed at the parchment like the lean muzzle of some fiend. Like the point of a soldier's sword.

Catherine touched her breast. *Breathe.* A drop of sweat trickled down her forehead and landed on the parchment. She had copied a hundred receipts. The uses of borage for jaundice. Mint for the stomach. She had drawn saffron. Roses. *Loosen yourself to the work at hand.*

The quills continued to deride the young woman. She began again by picking one, but chose instinctively with the left hand and hastily returned it to the jar. No. She must not make a mistake. She selected again, whispered *Sweet heart of Mary, strengthen me,* and wrote out the page in perfect script with one inkhorn and one penknife, dipping and mending precisely. *This is the will and testament of Catherine Havens, twenty years of age, foundling of Mount Grace Priory, Yorkshire, England, adopted daughter of Christina Havens, Prioress of this Convent. I have secured Receipt Books written in My Hand under the Seventh Stone from the West Wall of the convent dormitory for their safekeeping. We are to remove from our Home at the order of King Henry VIII and I leave these Goods with intent, God Willing, to return and claim them. I have made and illumined the Books with my Own Hands and have tested the properties of all the Herbs listed therein. I have found them good. I have worked physic as a practice of my gifts from God. I have done this with the Blessing of my prioress and my priest and for the Good of my Immortal Soul.*

The list of contents covered the entire page, and when she had finished, Catherine switched to her left hand and signed her name at the bottom. She added a flourish of ink, as she had done in her books, and was pleased with the royal look of it. Catherine opened the jars of pigment and swirled colors into the shells of egg white and water. Closing her eyes, she began to see feathers and leaves. The birds and beasts and imagined faces of the saints filled her margins, and vines and acanthus leaves twisted themselves under her hand into ferociously serpentine windings. She bloodied her initials, adding around the text miniscule drolleries and grotesques, a monkey face grinning from a daisy head and a blue-faced clown playing a silver pipe, with canaries for ears. On the top right corner hovered the Madonna, who made all things well. She held the light over the page and, seeing the work was good, scattered sand over the words. Now she could rest her eyes for a few minutes before the storm of the morning struck them.

When the door rattled, Catherine was slumped with her head on her arms, sleeping. The candle had burned down to a puddle, and she jolted awake. The parchment lay dry before her, and she covered it with her arms.

"Catherine, are you in there?" It was Sister Ann.

Catherine's arms went weak with relief and she unlatched the door. "Come in. Quick."

Ann stood in her sleeping gown and a thick shawl, the dark nimbus of her hair disordered around her ears. She was a big woman, but she glided inside without a sound. "What are you doing out of the dormitory? And alone?" Ann took up the parchment and held it to the shrinking flame. Her brown eyes looked almost black. "Is this wise? You have put your name to it." Ann could not read, but she knew the fancy signature well enough.

"It's my will. There is nothing to shame me in it. I do not intend to be taken for a witch. And if someone else should find it, I will likely be dead."

"No talk of that now. What will do you do with it?"

"Put it somewhere safe."

Ann lifted the wrapped manuscript. "Is this the work of that Margery Kempe woman?"

"I mean to keep it." Catherine stretched to her full height. She was almost as tall as Ann, though of a thinner build.

Ann huffed out a laugh. "No one will want it. You may leave it in plain sight. That woman was lunatic."

"I will have it. It's too delicate to leave to chance."

"It may not go well with you if you are thought to be an admirer of hers."

"It will not fit under the floor. But I mean to keep it."

"As you wish."

Catherine pulled a bag from a shelf and emptied a heap of coins onto the table. "Is it enough, do you reckon?" She shuffled the gold. "I will add all the printed books. They are almost a library now."

"You could add the gift of your sweet green eyes and it wouldn't be enough, Catherine. Keep your books and stow them where they won't be burned. He will take the altarpiece, whatever you offer him. He will take whatever he wants. Hide your money, too. You'll want it before the snow falls again."

"I could make the offer. He may prefer ready coin."

"Come, Robert Overton keeps that much in his purse for tidbits. Hide your money and put your books away. He knows good and well how much that Madonna is worth. Let it go. If he is content with Her, he may not see us so clearly."

"She means more to me than all these books together. I have prayed under Her eyes all my life."

Ann rubbed her thumb against her fingers. "That money will feed you for a while. Mary will not." She palmed a gold piece and let it fall. "I tell you, save your wealth. Your Madonna is already gone."

The cock sang a few choked notes outside the window, and Catherine placed the coins, one by one, back into the bag. "Is there light yet?"

"No. Why? You're surely not eager to see this day begin."

"There were men in the church tonight. I want to see what villainy they've wrought."

"Soldiers?"

"I only saw their torches as they went past the reading room. I thought they were coming for us, but they went on through." Catherine folded the parchment twice, tied it with string, and sealed the bow with a button of soft wax. "Mother Christina says she will barricade herself in her chamber if they come into the convent."

"We'll see how firm she stands when a blade's at her throat. She's the one who has brought us to this."

A pain wormed across Catherine's forehead. "The king's secretary has done it, not Mother."

Ann shrugged. "Don't be angry. Cromwell doesn't act without the forms of law. All he needed was a word of suspicion. I don't blame her. I just say how things are."

The pain went flat. Ann was right. "You're free to go if you want."

"Go where? With the others?" Ann shook her head. "What a choice these men give us."

"Devil and the deep blue sea. I am decided. If I am not allowed to practice physic, I have no life. And I have promised Mother Christina to stand by her."

"You had better hide that parchment, then. Even the drawings could put you under a charge of dealing with the devil these days."

Catherine pushed her stool to the outside wall and stepped up onto it. A door hinge squeaked somewhere outside and Ann pinched the light to death. A flicker. A footfall, steps hurrying by. A swish of cloth. Then nothing. Catherine clung to the stone, and after a few minutes in the dark, Ann lit another candle with her flint, but she tented it with her shawl. She pushed her ear against the doorframe.

"Is anyone in the walk?" whispered Catherine.

Ann shook her head.

"Was that a man, do you think?"

"No telling."

Catherine stretched to the seam where the wall met the curve of the roof. There was a narrow gap in the corner, just wide enough. She pushed the will in as far in as it would go and hopped down. "Is it concealed?"

Ann nodded. "Now, show me where these men were."

"They came from the nave, but they went the other way out, toward the river. Either through the refectory or the garderobe." The two women inched the door open. They were alone. Catherine trotted around the walk, Ann close behind, into the dark church. It was still full night.

"I cannot see my hand before my face," Catherine whispered, and Ann raised the candle, but its small halo was lost in the vast shadows of the nave.

They skidded from pillar to pillar. The space was empty, the double front doors barred, as they always were at night. Catherine pulled at the latch, but the bar was solid. The rooster tried out his morning song again.

"Are you certain they came from the church?" said Ann.

"I thought so. I was sure so. But perhaps my ears deceived me in the dark."

"I see no way a person could have entered this way."

"They went out the back. Maybe they came in that way."

"Did they have a key?"

"I saw nothing but the light as they passed by."

"It makes no sense." The flame trembled in a sudden breeze and went out. They felt their way across the nave to the sanctuary, where the air was still, and Catherine held the candle while Ann sparked it to life once more. The flame cast its circle of gold as high as the carved angels above them, who threw long winged shadows across the arches, their slender arms grasping at nothing. The saints stood, palms clasped together, in their niches, and the stained glass of the windows winked.

Catherine said, "All seems well, thank God. For now."

"If all is well, we should go back. Perhaps it was only the sexton."

"That was not the sexton in the walk just now."

"Come on to bed." Ann tugged Catherine's sleeve. "We will need our strength soon."

Nodding, Catherine turned, but she glanced up and the candle dropped from her hand. Flames splattered and bubbled across the pavers. "My God," Catherine cried out, leaping backward.

Ann gasped. Even in the dark, they could see the gap above them, a great blank space. Their altarpiece, with its blue Madonna and Child, was gone.

CHAPTER TWO

A freezing drizzle had begun again, and though it was past time for lauds, the nave was still dark. It had been raining all year. Thank God for the cold, Catherine thought, peeling wax from the stones in front of the altar. Not even soldiers relished an interrogation in bad weather.

No one had appeared to pray. Most of the other nuns were leaving, and they had elected to spend the morning packing their belongings. Catherine's knees hurt, and she sat back on her heels just as the convent door opened and old Sister Veronica hobbled over with a couple of kitchen knives.

"These will make the work easier." Veronica eased herself down and they scraped in silence for a few minutes. "How is your arm?"

Catherine held out the bandaged wrist. "Mother wrapped it for me. She still has all her skills."

"She does." Veronica lifted bits with her fingernail and thumbed them into the basket at Catherine's side. "As do you. You know you are not to display such knowledge when we are removed?"

"I know." Catherine looked at the closed convent door. "Is anyone else up?"

Veronica shrugged and sat on one haunch. "The cold never leaves my bones these days."

"Let me do this. You should be in your bed."

"No sleeping for me. Not today. I would like it done, whatever comes."

Catherine stood. "Enough of this." She took up the basket and offered her hand to the old nun. Veronica heaved herself to her feet and brushed her tunic and Catherine picked a few stray nubs of wax from the wool. "I have made a mess for us all."

"It wasn't you who made this mess." Veronica ran her foot over the greasy spots on the pavers.

"You will not go with the others?"

"Not for the world." The old woman studied the naked pins where the Madonna had been. The altarpiece had been fastened to the wall when Catherine was a small girl. "We had it nailed up there to keep it safe," Veronica said. She hacked out a noise that might have been a laugh. "Have you an idea where it has gone?"

"I think the soldiers must have come in during the night. What I heard had to be men."

Veronica nodded quickly. "Ah, yes. You must tell the constable. That you heard men. In the convent. After dark. They will have much to fight for among themselves, then. Well. I will go set out some victuals to break our fast." Veronica shuffled into the convent, pulling the door closed behind her.

Catherine made a circuit around the windows to the door, a fresh candle before her. If there had been bootprints, they had dried to smudges, and nothing else was missing. If there had been any signs in the sanctuary, she had likely smeared them when she dropped the taper. She had been a fool to think she could buy it, Catherine determined, climbing the ladder to the room above the porch. And fools were often hanged these days. She felt sick, and her burned wrist throbbed. She rested her face against the cold wall. Without the Mother of God, there was no place to send her prayers anyway.

Catherine put her eye to the narrow window. The stars were barely bleached into the early light, and the shower had become full rain, but she could see them plainly enough—a clot of dirty men sprawling with their daggers out in the barn across the road. So that was what soldiers looked like. And now, coming from the south, up the long hill into the village, was a wagon and two men on horseback. One of them had to be Robert Overton, coming for his sisters and whatever else he could carry off. He probably already had a buyer for the Madonna. His Madonna, he would claim. He probably already had the lease papers for the property, signed and sealed.

Break a wheel, she thought. *Tip over.* She knew how it ended with nuns who resisted, even those without charges against them. The priest had told her. They were arrested or whipped down the road, even if they had nowhere to go. They would call her a witch, make her kneel to that fat King Henry as head of the church. They would turn her down the road or, worse, force her to become a servant in Overton House, scrubbing their linens or dumping their piss pots. *Slip into the ditch.* Catherine watched steadily, and the wagons seemed to keel sideways as they rounded a bend. Her heart lifted giddily for a second, but one of the soldiers' horses nickered

15

below, lifting its ears toward the approaching caravan. The vehicle righted itself. The wagons were coming. This day had been coming toward them for months.

The door linking the church to the convent creaked open again, and Catherine descended, her skirts gathered in one hand. Mother Christina waited in the sanctuary, and she reached for Catherine's hand. "How are you, Daughter?"

"Barely a scald." Catherine held out her arm. "Your wrappings are as neat as ever."

The prioress smoothed the linen bandage. "This is what comes of carrying flame with the sinister hand." She checked Catherine's fingers and palm, then faced the altar. "And now, what shall we do here?"

"Robert Overton will have someone's head, Mother."

Christina regarded the dark spot. She spluttered, and Catherine bowed her head to avoid seeing the prioress weep. But Christina was laughing. She doubled over, slender hands on her knees, and the sound echoed through the nave.

"Mother?" Catherine heart slid a little. "Mother, what is the joke?"

The prioress wiped her eyes. "Daughter, we are saved."

"Saved? How can you say so? Mother, if we do not produce Her, Robert Overton will be in a passion. He will not rein in those men. And you know what they are. We are finished when he discovers this."

"You said it yourself. It was one of those thieves of his. You can swear it before the constable that you heard men in the church. You may swear it before the Justice of the Peace. Robert Overton will have no one to accuse but his own men. You will see, child. They will begin to fight like the wolves they are. It is always the way with such people. His interest in us will burn off like an early fog."

"They will whip us down to the gaol. They will hang us for traitors or sorceresses."

"Nonsense. They are sniveling cowards, afraid to come in without Robert Overton. This proves it. And he knows who I am, however he has puffed himself up. They will seize this convent when my corpse is cold in the ground. If he wants that altarpiece, let him search his men for it. He will not lay a finger on me. Or on you, Daughter."

"You loved that image. I thought you did."

The prioress fluttered her fingers. "The world will be as it is."

"I meant to buy it. I have coin." Catherine's voice dropped. "I have my books. I was going to trade them all. I thought it was dear to you. It was to me."

"It was, Catherine. It is. But we must see to the hours ahead now." The prioress squeezed Catherine's hand and pulled free. "Now stop your fretting. All this noise

16

of the king's will blow by like a spring wind and Robert Overton will have to go home with his tail between his legs." Her eyes brightened. "I have it. We must take down the portrait and put it here. We can do it together."

Christina hurried off, and Catherine followed, plodding. The painting of King Henry was alone on the south wall of the nuns' walk, though the stain where Queen Katherine had hung beside him was still visible. Katherine now resided in the prioress's private chamber. They lifted the king from his place and wobbled him to the altar. He was made of thin boards, and they easily hoisted him into place.

It was a bad painting.

"I could have done better myself," muttered Catherine.

The prioress giggled like a girl. "Smile, now, Daughter. Those men will be so busy blaming each other, they will forget we exist. They want a reason to leave us be. You mark me. We are Christ's brides, and they know the queen will return. The rightful queen. And when she does they will answer for all these troubles and we will have our authority once again."

"How can you believe so, Mother? We've had no word from the queen in years. Nor no donation."

"Trust in the Mother, Catherine. She never changes." Christina stared briefly at the new image scowling down on them, then pinched Catherine's chin gently and swooped away into the convent.

"We must find that Madonna," Catherine called, but the prioress was gone. "Or somebody will die," she said to the closed door.

Catherine spit at the foot of the new portrait. The old altarpiece of Mount Grace was widely known for expressiveness and depth. It was rumored to have come from Flanders, the work of Hugo van der Goes or even Hans Memling. This Henry was full-length and vulgar, round-bodied and red-faced with a huge, shiny codpiece. To see him hanging in the nuns' walk, fading in the wind and rain, was one thing. But over the altar. Good God.

The dawn light spangled in broken colors across the stone floor and Catherine trudged to the south window, but the green and grey glass that made up the grass and parts of Jesus's feet prevented any clear vision. Through the eye slit she could see one of the soldiers. He was on the porch, and he'd pulled a dagger to dig at his boot. He looked like the gentlemen who came through the village to stop off at the Hare and Hound or to buy wool. The weapon glinted, even in the dull light. The other nuns shuffled in, stretching and yawning, and Catherine lingered at a distance.

17

Someone gasped, "Our Mother is gone!" The women all began gabbling at once, and Catherine ran up the aisle.

"Be quiet, will you? The king's men are on the porch. Do you want them to hang us where we stand? Someone has taken the altarpiece."

"No one will hang us," a voice said from the back. "It belongs to Robert Overton now."

"All the more reason for them to arrest us when it is found to be missing." The nuns fell silent, glancing sullenly into each other's faces. "Were any of you up last night? Up at all?"

"No one was up, Catherine," someone grumbled. "Where is Robert Overton? We mean not to be molested."

"He is on the road," said Catherine. "You may come see for yourselves." She tried to lead them to the porch room, but they huddled together at the altar and she went up alone. The rain had been relentless and cold for weeks, and the soft road sucked at the horses' hooves. It would not improve the mood of the soldiers. The approaching wagon crawled up the incline. But they were coming.

Ann called her name from below, and Catherine climbed back down the stairs, where her friend stood, heavy arms folded across her breast. She was gazing across the nave at the king's portrait, her mouth twisted into a wry grin. "You didn't happen to see our altarpiece out that window?"

"They must have hidden it someplace before dawn. Someone let them in, but no one will admit to it. The twins, maybe? They think everything's theirs."

"Maybe. If they could be bothered to get out of their beds. You had better hope it was them. If we are accused of secreting it, they'll use torture."

"Don't say that. Mother is sure they won't harm us. She says the queen—"

Ann shot a doubtful look, and Catherine broke off. The words sounded desperate, even to her. There was a new queen these days, and everyone knew she wasn't friendly to nuns.

Mother Christina came tripping back in and the little band of women fell into attitudes of prayer, but the prioress failed to notice. "We will hang Jesus beside him," she announced to no one in particular. "It will fill the space nicely."

"What Jesus do you mean?" said Catherine, striding across the nave with Ann.

"The one from the refectory, of course," said Christina.

"He is horrible," said Catherine. "You can't mean it."

The prioress stood, hand on her chin, contemplating the flimsy king. "You will mend your speech with me, child. You're not so tall that I can't show you the hand of God, much as I love you." The other nuns tittered, and Catherine bit the tip of her tongue.

Ann said, "You will drive him beyond himself, Christina." She pointed southward. "Robert Overton is on the road. He is almost upon us. Catherine has seen him with his men and wagons."

"That weakling," said the prioress. The words sizzled, and in the wake of a brewing argument, the other nuns fled the sanctuary, leaving Catherine and Ann alone with Christina. "If that man had not made his bargain with the king and his lapdog, those men would not be here and our Madonna would be right where She belongs. Everything would be just as it has always been. Isn't that so? That altarpiece was a gift to this priory from my family. It is Havens property. If it has been removed, let him worry his damned king and all his court for it. Robert Overton owes *me*. There is much he owes me." Mother Christina turned at the squeak of the convent door. "There you are," she said, brushing past Catherine and Ann. "Bring it here." The white-haired sexton, Nicholas Hale, and a carpenter were hauling the Christ toward them and they chucked it at the prioress's feet. Catherine had always thought he looked famished, hanging on his gnarled cross, and the two big men who carried the painting made him look even thinner.

The sexton growled, "Where does he go?"

Christina lifted her arm to the space behind the altar. "Up there. Let the old red bull be his saint if he wants." She watched them heft the skinny Jesus into the air. "Have you repaired the dining table?"

Hale frowned behind his thatch of beard, looking in the direction of the king's portrait instead of at the prioress. "Yes. Let me finish this and we'll get it."

Veronica entered from the convent and watched the men fix the new image into place. Her face hung in folds, and her hands shook these days, but her voice was still strong. "You think this will trick him?" she said to the prioress. "You think this will satisfy him? You think he will be amused by this?" She flung up a hand to indicate Catherine. "Ask your daughter there whether she trusts that this will keep us from violence. She's the one with the genius, let her tell you."

"I could give a fig for what he thinks," said Christina, raising her fist, "and Catherine knows that she is safest in the lap of the convent. With me. As she has always been." She nodded approval of the placement and shooed the men toward the refectory. "Now, my daughter in mercy and love," she said, smiling at Catherine, "go bring out some of the books and some small pieces of silver for those heathens to paw over. Arrange them on the far side of the nave."

"Robert Overton will not tolerate provoking," said Veronica. "He will give those soldiers their freedom. My God, Christina, will you listen to no one?" But Christina was already whisking through the door.

"You waste your breath, Veronica," said Catherine. She looked about her. "Ann, can you pull down the big tapestries?"

"They're heavy," Ann said, pushing back her long sleeves. She was well-muscled, the strongest of the sisters, from her years as the wife of a mower. "But they might be bright enough to entice a soldier's eye."

"I'll get the silver from the kitchen."

"I see no reason to make their thefts easier with everything. Lay out a few of the bent pieces."

"A good thought." Catherine headed out.

Veronica hobbled along behind her. "Christina is working there. Let me help you."

"Mother is in the kitchen?" said Catherine. She hadn't known Christina to bother herself with cooking in years. But Veronica was right. The prioress was bent over the fire, poking at something in a pot.

"Porridge for the sexton," she said, glancing up at Catherine's entrance. "I will take it to him when he and that carpenter finish. A small gift of thanks in this time of our crisis."

"Mother, we need Father John," said Catherine. "Do you think you might bring him to us?"

"He is no help anymore, and he tells tales to frighten you." Christina stood and aimed the spoon at the rafters, her tall figure thin as a quill. "The four of us will remain firm. We will be as we have always been. This is my family's land. This is my home." Her voice was high and tight. "If the king wants it closed off from heaven, he should give it to me."

"Mother," Catherine blurted, "the king doesn't care whose land it has been and he is not going to deed it to a prioress." She added in a whisper, "Especially one who refuses the new succession." The porridge began to burn and Catherine yanked it from the fire. "I can take this if you prefer not to be on the road."

The prioress grabbed the pot. "I will do as I please when I choose, as always, child. If I mean to take porridge, then I will take it. I am still a Havens and this is still

Mount Grace. There will be no new heir in England. It's a lie." She marched out, bearing the porridge before her like a relic.

Sister Veronica had loitered beyond the doorway, and after the prioress passed, she leaned against the jamb. "No one has ever told Christina Havens what to do, not in the forty years I have known her. Not even the priest." The old woman laughed. "Not even God. She still imagines Queen Katherine is going to ride up with an army to protect us."

"Yes," snorted Catherine, "and perhaps she will spirit me down to Greenwich and make a lady of me, as long as we're dreaming." She knew she wouldn't have said it in the prioress's hearing.

Veronica said nothing.

"Would those soldiers dare to take that altarpiece out from under Robert Overton's very nose?"

Veronica tucked a rogue strand of white hair under her coif. "It is a large nose."

Catherine couldn't help but laugh. "They had better hide it well if they want to keep their heads."

The old woman hacked out a sound, either a laugh or a cough. "It will be their heads or it will be ours."

CHAPTER THREE

The big dining table in the refectory screeched as the sexton and carpenter slid it into place. One of the carved legs on Christina's end had cracked, and she had asked them to replace all six with plainer work. The prioress was bent by her chair, examining the table's underside, while Catherine and Veronica watched. "You braced it all the way across with boards?" The pot sat on the floor by her feet.

"Yes, madam," said the sexton coldly. He crossed his arms and waited.

Christina fingered the seams in the top. She grabbed the edge and tried to shake the whole thing. It barely moved.

"Good enough for you, madam?" said Hale. His eyes had gone dull and resentful.

"It will do. Where have you stashed the old legs?"

He pointed to a pile covered with canvas in the corner. "There. They are still solid if you will find a use for them. Master Overton might like them. Are you done with us, then?"

"For the moment." Christina wiped her hands on her tunic. "Here, I have made you this. It will warm the dampness from you."

The sexton sniffed and nodded. The carpenter was already out the door.

"Now, have you laid out a few things to tempt those villains?" said the prioress to Catherine.

"Going just now, Mother." Catherine went to her infirmary and, setting aside the expensive volumes, gathered a few tattered old books into a pile. She had copied the receipts from them that she wanted, but they might look valuable enough to put out for bait. She took a couple of small silver-plated bowls, too, and headed for the nave.

The twin Sisters Mary were sitting side by side in the north aisle when Catherine came through, fair heads inclined together and small white hands neatly folded before them, like slim patient icons. They were Robert Overton's younger sisters, and they had entered the convent at fifteen years of age, after their mother's death and Robert's betrothal. The fiancée had died of sweating sickness shortly thereafter, but, having paid dowries, their father left them at Mount Grace. The two had always maintained their superior position, since the Overtons had already bought almost all the old Havens property by the time of their arrival. The convent would be simply the latest acquisition. The Marys, still shoulder to shoulder, blocked Catherine's way.

Mary Frances glanced at Mary Margaret. "You may move what you want of the convent's goods," said Frances, "but they will belong to the crown. That means they will belong to our brother. I don't mean to be cruel, Catherine, but your time would be better spent making up your mind to confess your faults and submit to the new order. With your many *talents*, your great *scholarship*, you should be able to secure a position somewhere or other." The twins smiled at each other wickedly. "If you will stop making potions and casting spells, I mean to say."

"Since you lack a family, after all," added Margaret.

Catherine bit her cheek. "Any physic I have made has been done under the eye of God, as you well know. And I am setting these things in plain view to make the men's task easier." She held out the pile.

The twins scanned the pile of books dismissively and brushed past, into the convent.

Ann came in as they disappeared. "Chilly in here," she smirked.

"The little bitches," Catherine murmured through her teeth.

Ann shook her sleeves down. "Nothing new under the sun," she said. "Put a silk skirt on a dog, she's still got a hairy snout."

"And Mother has had the dining table repaired," Catherine said, still glowering at the door where the Marys had gone. "Now, of all times."

"As I said. Get Veronica to move the smaller pieces of plate. We might as well hide a few of the better things. Our Lord and Master Overton might be so angry he doesn't notice."

John Bridle, the priest, burst through the side door, his rosy face redder than usual. His white hair tufted his head like a spiky cloud and though he rubbed it down, it sprang again to its glory. "Who barred the front door? Did Christina do it?"

"We never unbarred it this morning, Father," said Catherine. "We have been robbed."

"How could that happen if the door was barred?" The priest didn't bother to ask what was missing. "Today is the day, you girls. The men are out in the road and Robert Overton is almost upon us. You must decide for the king and have done.

23

They will leave you be then. It is an easy enough decision. And Christina, too. That woman will put a noose around all your necks if you listen to her." He walked up the center aisle and threw the bar off the door. "Christina!"

The prioress appeared from the convent. "What devil is calling my name?" She met the priest in the middle of the empty nave. "John Bridle, we are occupied this morning and you must entertain yourself for once. Catherine, bar that front door."

"Occupied? At what?"

Catherine slid down the side aisle to obey Christina's order.

"Preparing our home for assault," said the prioress.

The priest clenched his fists at her. "Do you not see, woman, that there is nothing left to fight for? You've been spoken foul at court. You will go. You will acquiesce or you will be gaoled. I will see that you are awarded a pension. I will. But you will relent."

Christina waved him away. "John Bridle, you have ever had a vile temper and you should say an Our Father and a Hail Mary to relieve your soul of its burden. And brush your hair, man."

"You will be regular old Christina Havens again, and you must resign yourself to it," he shouted. "Don't you care that you're leading these others into danger? You will no longer be the sovereign you think yourself," he said, pointing a finger in her face. "Do you want to see them string Veronica up? Catherine?"

"They will do no such thing. You talk and you talk. They will never touch us."

"They will, Christina. They will question you. They will demand answers."

She blew through her nose and pointed to the southwest. "No one has removed the monks from Fountains, and they're corrupt as a pile of plague corpses. You send for the news from them and see."

"They haven't gone down yet, but they will. Mark me, Christina. All the houses will be closed. You hear me? All of them. You had better accustom yourself to it."

Christina batted at him and turned away. "This reform is a hobby-horse of the king's, and he will tire of it. And I will still be in charge of Mount Grace when he does. This is my land, John Bridle, and you would do well to remember it."

The priest raised his hands as though he meant to go for her throat, but he just flailed at her retreating form. "I will set you on the damned road myself, Christina," he said, but she was gone again, long hands over her veiled ears, her sliding walk never slowing. Veronica followed.

Catherine joined Ann at the sanctuary and he turned his sermon on them. "You, then," he said, taking them each by a shoulder. "You must listen to reason." His gaze rose to the altar as though to petition God on their behalf. His eyes were blue as ice in the morning light. "Jesus Christ," he said.

"Indeed," said Ann.

"Where is it?" said the priest. "Who has taken it? Tell me."

"It must have been the soldiers," said Catherine. "I tried to tell you. There were men in the building last night. I heard them."

"Robert Overton will stretch someone's neck for this, despite what Christina believes." He pulled on his beard, then gripped the two women again. "You want to lose your home or lose your heads? I can take a few things to my house. Not too much and nothing too costly. I will do my best to keep them for you. But you must hurry. Go now." He looked once more at the altar. "My God."

"No, I believe that's your king," said Ann. "And I have nothing but my person and a few knives. Some of the linens are my work, I suppose." She shrugged as if they were of no importance.

"My manuscript," said Catherine. "And some of the printed books." She lifted her skirts and ran for the infirmary.

Veronica was seated at the small table, her head on her arms, and she looked up mournfully at Catherine's arrival. "Have you got a draught for a sour stomach?"

Catherine pulled down a crock of mint as the priest walked in.

"You must talk some sense into these girls," said John Bridle. "You won't sit here and let them cut your throat, I think. And, Catherine, you must stop this work. You will not be allowed to continue."

Veronica nipped at a leaf of the mint and ground it between her front teeth. "And who would miss me if they did kill me?"

"I would," said Catherine. "And Mother Christina would."

"Yes. Christina would." Veronica poured herself a draught from the pitcher of ale Catherine kept on the sideboard. "You want me to be Robert Overton's chamber maid? Maybe wipe his arse for him when he shits?"

"Such talk," said the priest. "And in front of the girl."

"You may sheathe your sanctity, John Bridle. Catherine is no child and I am a tired old woman. Now leave me be, will you?"

"I want you to keep Catherine from throwing her life away for nothing."

"Catherine's skills are not nothing. She and I will stay with Christina."

"And I will stay with Catherine." It was Ann, at the door.

"Are you all gone out of your heads?"

"You may say that, John Bridle," said Veronica. "You have your sturdy house. And the king will let you keep it, whoever he marries. You may keep your pulpit, as well. It is not so pleasant an alteration for women."

"Plenty of others have gone over to reform. Women. Even old women. Even headstrong women."

"Yes," said Veronica. She tore off another bite of mint. "And what has become of them?"

The priest chewed his lip, then turned to Catherine. "You say soldiers were in the nave last night?"

"Men. I heard men's voices. They came through the convent. And someone came down the walk later."

"Alone? A man?"

"I couldn't tell. Ann was with me."

Ann shook her head. "It was too dark."

Catherine dug through her baskets. "Take these." She handed over the pliers she used for pulling rotten teeth and her small surgical knife. "And these." John Ardenne's instructions to physicians, Trotula on the conditions of women. Hildegard's *Causes and Cures*, Dioscorides on medical procedures and instruments. "And this." She dropped the bag of coins on top.

"Is this everything?" said John Bridle, tottering backward.

"No, one more." Catherine balanced the wrapped manuscript on top.

"Is this the leavings of that Margery Kempe woman?" He glared down on the linen covering.

"I mean to copy it, Father."

"She was gone full lunatic."

Ann laughed and Catherine blushed.

"They had her before the bishop," said the priest.

"And she was released." Catherine put her hand on the manuscript. "I want it."

"No one else will. You may consider it secure wherever it is."

"Keep it for me, Father. I beg you as your ghostly daughter."

"Very well, Catherine," he sighed. "No one is going to wage war over it, of that you can be sure." He settled the pile in his arms. "Arguing with you is like arguing with Christina. And now, this is all I can carry."

"Many thanks, Father," said Catherine and he humphed down the walk toward the back door, muttering about mule-headed women and nooses knotted by the king's own hand.

CHAPTER FOUR

The reading room contained some valuables, and Veronica gathered more books while Catherine stacked shells for mixing pigments and a handful of gallnuts, like small gnomes' heads, for making ink. She lifted down the earthenware jars and bottles of dry color, the purple turnsole, the chalk for whites, the vermilion and verdigris, the precious tiny stores of lapis lazuli and gold leaf. Her first receipt book, a tiny one, the size of a girdle book. It had been illuminated by Veronica with vines and flowers. She closed her fingers on the embossed cover. So easy to conceal. Like a belief. She tucked the book into her pocket, under her tunic.

"Are you going to keep that?" Veronica said.

Catherine raised her eyes. "It is worth nothing to anyone else."

"They will search you," Veronica warned. "If they find that, they will think you still practice. They will call it a book of spells."

"I will keep it." She tightened the knot on her belt. "One way or another."

They backed down the stairs and almost bumped into Ann, coming from the dormitory burdened with plate and small drinking vessels, a purse of hand knives at her waist.

"Have you got the tapestries down?"

"Two of them," said Ann. "They are heavy as mattresses, Catherine, and dusty as any hayrick." She led them into the nave, where the tapestries, rolled and tied, bulged against the north wall like a miser's moneybags. A body would trip over them walking up the aisle. "Do you see? If they see those they will know there are more. Let them believe that we have no better sense and take the damned things. Robert Overton won't want them."

Catherine lifted the edge of Lazarus at his tomb. "They are all moth-eaten anyway. Come, I have the floorboards in the porch room already loosened."

The space upstairs was small but dry. Catherine wedged in some of the better books, and her hourglass went onto its side on top. "Give me a couple of those knives," Ann said behind her. "We can't predict what might need cutting." She tucked one of the blades into her pocket and slipped the other down her boot.

The cups were fitted into hollows, and a few of the pigment jars went inside the cups. Three more trips down the ladder secured a stack of plates, more cups, a handful of quills and brushes, Ann's large silver crucifix and Veronica's three gold bracelets, along with a handful of rings, which Catherine poured into a leather pouch and wedged into a corner. At the last minute, she tossed in the small girdle book.

It was all the hollow would conceal, so Catherine lowered the boards and pounded them back into place with a stone. She scattered old pieces of board and unused wooden pins and swept her footprints away before leaning the broom against the wall. Three old psalters and a breviary she left in a neat pile near the door, as though they had been brought there for storage and forgotten in a disused room. She scooped some wood shavings that she had collected and tossed them across the threshold, artlessly she thought, and backed her way out and down the steps, wiping each with the hem of her tunic. She landed on the pavers with a thump. She went to the window and saw a soldier staring back at her. He scratched at the glass with a metal point.

"God's foot," she wailed, suddenly cold with fear. "They aim to pull down the walls around us."

Veronica, standing by the front door, blanched and their eyes met. "You may go with the others if you will," the old woman said. "You could make something of yourself."

A few moments of silence hung between them. Outside, someone laughed loudly, and the heat returned to Catherine's breast. "I won't take any oath that makes the princess a bastard," she said. "I won't be Robert Overton's servant. Mother Christina won't and neither will I."

Veronica's face relaxed. "Nor will I."

Ann had gone to get the linens, and she pushed through the side door with the prioress, her arms full. The cloths were fully decorated, ready for sale, and fell like a bright soft bouquet when Ann tossed them into an empty tomb beside the altar. "These are worth good money, and they're small enough for us to take along." She glanced up at Catherine and Veronica. "In the last resort, I mean to say."

She had barely slid the heavy lid back into place when the Marys glided in, wearing heavy silks. The pleats in their skirts glistened in the morning light and their bodices sparkled with small gems.

"We would like to pray before we depart," said Mary Frances. "In a reformed manner."

"We are engaged here," said Ann. "If you're so reformed, you can pray somewhere else."

"You will do as I say, widow-woman," said Frances. "You think yourself better than you are because this old cow has protected you." She tilted her head toward the prioress. "She and her little *orphan*. After today, you are nothing. They are nothing. This place is nothing. You will all cease your business and behave like the spinsters and servants you are. Do you understand me or must I have the constable make it clear to you?"

Christina had gone three shades of purple and she heaved for air. She opened her mouth and closed it again.

Ann's jaw muscles twisted. "I see no gentlemen breaking down the doors to marry you. You're older than I am. I think you hit thirty last year. And I would rather be dead than lick your slippers in Overton House."

"You will be licking more than my slippers if you live through this removal," sneered Frances.

"I will not. You will never see me your servant at Overton House. Your brother's minion, that's what you'll be. The only reason he comes to fetch you at all is that he has nowhere else to stuff you anymore. He never asked for you home before he was forced to it."

Frances's blue eyes narrowed. "We will pray now. And you will leave us. Widow."

"What do you need God for? You have a brother. Your loving brother. You have a king." Ann lifted a pearl pendant that hung from a thick gold chain around Frances's neck. "You have this."

Frances's face went ashy and her fist came up in a blur. She wore a ruby, foiled high in gold fretwork, on her forefinger, and the faceted stone caught Ann on the cheek, tearing a gash. "You may get yourself to your washtub, Ann Smith. It is all your dirty hands were meant for."

"You little heathen," breathed the prioress. "How dare you raise a hand to your sister in God's house."

"It is my brother's house. And I will dare do whatever I like, Christina Havens. No old bag tells Frances Overton her place. And you," she said to Ann. "Get out of my sight."

"As far as your reformed law is concerned, I may go where I please from this day forward whether it is in your sight or no." Ann swiped at the wound.

Catherine stepped between the twins and Ann. "Let me make you a dressing for that. I have root of agrimony. It will soothe the skin."

"It's only a scratch," said Ann, dabbing the blood with her napkin.

Frances took Margaret by the hand. "Oh, and now we must hear more of the great *learning* of the miraculous foundling Catherine. I wonder that no one has gone to the constable to ask about the source of your powers. There has always been a demon in you. I cannot endure you any longer." Frances stomped to the front door, dragging Margaret. She heaved at the bar, but she wasn't strong enough to lift it off. "You, Ann Smith. Come here and open this door."

Ann sauntered up to them, examined the bar, and yawned. "I think I will not. I will let the soldiers break it in."

Frances snorted. "Soldiers. Don't flatter yourself. They are just men Robin has paid."

"Paid men at arms make an army. Men in armies are soldiers," said Catherine.

Frances simpered. "Such a child. The *soldiers* will break nothing without my brother's orders. We are to be out before they come in. We have it in a letter." She checked her nails at the window.

"Was it you who removed the altarpiece then?" said Catherine.

Margaret sniffed. "That old thing." She went to Frances. "Robin has probably already had it taken home."

Catherine took her by the arm. "Did you let them in? Was it you?"

A commotion started in the road, and Margaret jerked free. Catherine warily peered again through the 'eye slit. "He's arrived," she said, and the sisters clapped their hands and ran off, calling for the others to get ready to go.

Robert Overton was marching up the path to the door, whip in hand. She could see the wagon behind him, several men in the blue Overton livery jumping to the ground, and the younger brother, she thought his name was William, who had been away for years. Robert looked directly at her. He was short-sighted but too vain to wear spectacles, so his dark eyes were always screwed into a squint. "Christina, is that you?" He tried the handle. "Open up and let me bring my sisters out. The way is pure mud, and we must get back on the road." He pounded on the wood with the side of his fist.

"Robert, it is Catherine. Are the soldiers about?"

"Soldiers? For God's sake, I see no soldiers, just some men I have gathered to help you remove." Overton backed a few steps and turned his head this way and that. "The road is empty as Christ's cave. Open the damned doors, will you, woman? These are just the king's servants. We're not going to eat you."

Catherine lifted the bar away, and Robert Overton, followed by his brother, entered the church with an air of ownership, throwing back his cloak to show off the scarlet silk lining. Robert was thick and fiery-haired, a few years past thirty and growing a small paunch, while his brother was tall and brown.

William Overton stopped at the door. "And have you summoned me all this way, through plague and sickness, to seize upon this? These women? Is this all?"

"Brother, no complaints. These women have been spoken against at court. This is already as much as ours. You might want to have a look."

"It's yours, I think you mean to say," said the younger man. "And I have seen all that interests me." He remained at the door, gazing over his shoulder now and then at his horse.

Margaret came tearing back in. "Robin, thank the saints you finally arrived. We thought you had been detained." He allowed a sisterly kiss on either cheek. "You have brought men to carry our clothing? And you have brought little William!"

Robert bowed with his usual display. "I have come to collect you and anything of yours," he said gallantly. He turned to his brother. "You will see that William is somewhat grown."

Frances came in, more slowly. She smiled indulgently at her sister, and the twins flanked their younger brother, leaning in on either arm as though to absorb him between them. William worked himself free, bowing and kissing the Marys' hands, then he moved to Catherine and stared straight into her eyes when he raised his head from her awkwardly outstretched fingers. The fire rushed her cheeks and she pulled back. William returned to his post by the front door and leaned, gazing outward, against the frame.

Robert busied himself appraising the condition of the ceiling and glass. He ran a hand down the nearest pillar and gave it a quick rap with its knuckles, and when Catherine started to swing the doors shut, he called, "No need for that."

"Your soldiers mean us no good," Catherine protested.

"You see what the pope has done to you. Stuffed with notions of devils. There is no threat here."

"Not as long as you are here," muttered Catherine, but Robert Overton had not heard her.

"William can stand watch to see that you are not molested. He is strong enough for that." The brother did not turn around to answer. Every so often, he rubbed his forehead.

Out in the road, a soldier grinned at Catherine. He kissed the air toward her, then wet his lips slowly with his tongue. His right hand was on his scabbard.

CHAPTER FIVE

The four servants trotted in, each dipping a little bow as they laid eyes on the nuns. One of them crossed himself at the door and his knee wanted to bend, but he cast a frightened look at his master, straightened quickly and crumpled his fingers against his chest.

"Wait there," said Mary Frances, "while we bring another load."

Robert Overton grabbed his sister's elbow and she almost fell backward. "How many men do you require? They are at your service."

"But our things are in the convent," said Margaret.

"God's blood, you act as though it's sacred. There is no need for you to behave like pack animals, sisters. Just take the men across and let them empty your rooms. You must instruct yourselves again in the bearing of gentlewomen, sisters, or you will dishonor me."

The twins looked at each other, and Frances nudged Margaret.

"Robin, there is another subject which we must raise with you before we depart." Mary Margaret glanced at Frances, who nodded.

"Well, out with it. You see me standing here. I haven't all day."

Mary Margaret took his arm in hers and leaned into him. "There is a matter of our companions here. Other sisters who wish to reform. Dear women. Hard working. They had dowries that will be restored to them, if you see to it."

Robert was frowning and Mary Margaret rushed on. "They wish to be our tenants. In some of the cottages. If you will have them. They are only six in number and we wish it. They want to use their pensions to stay together. They can keep the poultry. Some of them are excellent cooks. They could be of great benefit to us."

Robert Overton squeezed his eyes shut. "No, sisters, I have enough mouths to fill as it is. Let them make their ways as they can. Do you want to ruin me before I begin?" He opened his eyes again. "No, I am resolved."

"Robert." Mary Frances's face was set, though her small nose twitched at its delicate point. "We have almost extended a promise to the poor girls. And what will we do for lady's maids?" She took Mary Margaret's arm in hers. "We can share them between us. We have already prepared new clothes for them."

Catherine turned her back.

"Let us bring them out and show you," said Frances. Margaret ran for the convent door, and the six nuns filed in and arranged themselves before Robert Overton, heads bowed and hands folded demurely before them. The looked like a string of well-behaved puppies.

"Well." Robert Overton walked past them, lifting a chin here, studying a scrubbed hand there. He stroked his gold beard. "They could do with more beauty among them. They will take the oath of succession?"

"Without delay," said Frances.

"You have spoken to them all about this matter? They understand that the king is head of the church?"

Frances rolled her eyes. "Many times, brother. They have made the decision themselves."

"Any of them carrying seed?"

Frances punched him. "Don't be vulgar."

Robert toed the stones, worrying an invisible crack. His lips pursed and sagged. He raised his eyes, screwed to wrinkled knots, in the direction of the angels above his head. He looked like a fat fox. "Yes," he said finally to his sisters. "It will do if you wish it. They may take the old cottages down by the milking barn."

"Go now," Frances said, "and pack your things. Go." She herded them off, Margaret gliding along after her.

"This is the first time in my life I have wished I had a child," Ann muttered to Catherine.

"Why?" Catherine whispered.

"I would have someplace to go where I was wanted."

By midday, the nave and porch were crowded with chests. Piles of linen and silk, a few scattered books, jewels, combs, and mirrors lay amassed, while the servants toiled away at them. Catherine chose a green silk skirt and pulled it to her just long enough to feel how soft it was.

"Where in the world did they keep all of these?" said Ann. She pulled the hem out sideways, and the gathers unfurled like feathers.

"In our chamber." Frances had walked up behind Catherine and Ann, Margaret at her side. Catherine jumped and dropped the skirt. "Oh, Frances." She looked at the heap around her feet. She was at fault. "Forgive me."

"You have ever had a probing mind." Mary Frances picked up a pair of yellow sleeves. "We knew we would need fresh things. You aren't the only one here with aptitudes."

The few belongings of the other nuns, some items of black clothing, the underthings that Veronica had embroidered, their psalters, and some pots and pans, were in a tidy stack against a pillar. The Marys themselves were walking around the side aisles, noting which of the icons would look well at Overton House, but Robert busied himself with cleaning his dagger. "We have got rid of these ideas, Frances. We will not display images of saints."

"Not even in the chapel?" asked Frances. "Not even if we could sell them?"

He seemed to reconsider, and Catherine could almost see the calculation of their possible value in his eyes. "No one will want them. Just stone. Leave them for the pleasure of the men." They were not crudely done, however, and he walked over to S. Etheldreda and ran his hand down her throat. "The carvers had some skill," he said, peering at her. "We don't want to seem like Lutherans, after all. Let me consider it. Perhaps they could be stored away in the cellar until I can find a buyer."

The wagon was full, and the servants were tying the load down, slinging the ropes across to each other and looping them through the rings on the wagon's side. One of them rocked it back and forth, testing the stability. The load rocked as tenderly as any cradle and the servants gave a private cheer.

The Marys were by now in dark green cloaks, and they wore French hoods, Anne Boleyn's style, netted over top with small pearls. They had about their waists girdles woven with gold thread from which hung velvet bags for their fans and ivory combs. Mary Margaret carried coarser brown skirts over her arm. "I will just take these back to the dormitory for our women."

They had not yet brought out the Marys' large pieces of furniture. One enormous carved cupboard could not be made to fit, however they arranged the smaller items. Their downy mattresses and the frames for their beds were all too unwieldy.

Mary Frances said, "It is no matter. We will return for the other things as we need them. When the weather warms and the skies are clearer. Be sure your men know to stay out of our room, Robin."

"They are no bandits, Frances. They are men like all men. Come, we must make haste. I have left business unattended and the damned rain could begin again any minute. I will ride ahead and order a second wagon to be made ready to come again tomorrow or the day after. No one will bother with your things."

Mary Frances, suddenly radiant, clasped her hands before her. "I believe we are ready?"

"It is past midday," said Robert, checking the sky.

Margaret cleared her throat. "But brother. We've not et today." Margaret had never missed a meal in all her years at Mount Grace and she had not tasted a sip of wine all day. She squinted down the long sloppy road, looking like her brother. "We could sit once more at our old table?"

"Margaret, do you think of nothing but your face and your stomach?" said Frances, stamping her foot.

"There is a cold joint of mutton from yesterday," said Margaret, pouting. "A good fat one."

The mention of meat seemed to change matters for Robert. "I could do with a bite, I suppose."

"And a bottle of claret," said Margaret.

Robert looked again at the heavens. All was still dry. "So be it. Just keep the others from nattering in my ears, will you?"

Passing by the sanctuary, Robert stopped at the altar. "Before God, where is the altarpiece?"

Catherine's stomach lurched. "It has been stolen."

Robert grabbed her arm and whipped her around to face him. "You lie. When?"

Catherine shook him off and raised her nose as she thought the prioress would. "We found Her missing just this morning. Someone was in the buildings last night. Men. The same night, I might add, that your men arrived in the village. Mother Christina has placed our Jesus in Her place. As you can see. Your sisters knew it."

Robert strode to the convent door and flung it open, bellowing for Christina. The prioress appeared almost at once.

Christina held her hands before her, fingertips matched together. "What do you want of me?"

"You know what I want. You want me to rattle it from you?"

"The altarpiece is gone and I am no watchman. You are the one who brought soldiers into Mount Grace with their sneaking ways. Look to them. You have likely given them a key to the buildings yourself."

"I have no key to the buildings. By God, woman, I will tear this convent down stone by stone and I don't care if you are under them as they fall."

"Look to your men, I say."

"My men know to put a watch on that piece. They are not fools enough to steal it."

"I cannot speak to what sort of fools they are. It was Havens property, I might remind you."

"It was the king's property and now it is mine. I want that goddamned painting, woman, and you had better produce it. It's the only thing in this whole place worth the time to haul it away."

Christina narrowed her eyes. Her face was as white as her wimple and her voice fell to its menacing octave. "Then I suppose you had better put your great wit and your massive fortune to finding it." She slid back through the door and let it fall shut behind her.

Mary Frances said, "Robin, it is old and smelly. We can have better paintings made. We might have this portrait of the king if we like?"

"Are you completely empty-headed? I can shit a better likeness of the king than that. I thought you had been given an education in this dungeon." He grabbed Catherine again by her injured wrist and shook her. "Where is it? You're Christina's little favorite, aren't you? Have you sold it from under me?"

"I have sold nothing," stammered Catherine. Her knees trembled. "I wanted to buy it from you."

"Buy it?" Robert laughed in her face but he wasn't smiling. "With what? Your cross? Your leaves and sticks? Your great *learning*? Your *virtue*?" He held her away from him and looked at her body. "You might do for an entertainment, but you're not worth that altarpiece."

Ann slung his hand from Catherine's. "Leave her alone. She says she doesn't have it."

"Who the hell are you to tell me what she does or doesn't have?"

"Don't mind Ann," said Frances. "She's just a bitter old widow with no place to go. Nobody wants her."

Robert turned to his sister. "Is there anything in that head of yours that's useful?"

Frances's lips crimped. "There have been workers in the church this morning."

"Who?" said Robert. "What are their names?"

"It was the sexton. Nicholas Hale. He had that carpenter with him. Thomas. We saw them in the refectory."

Robert turned again on Catherine. "You. Lady Heir Apparent. You're the convent's great prodigy and you have an interest in this. I know your sexton. He's a reformed man. He has been public in his allegiance to the new order. What would he want with my altarpiece?"

Catherine tucked her hands into her sleeves. "You know as well as I that men's minds and mouths do not always correspond. There were men in the church last night, I tell you. The door was barred. Do you not think it strange that your soldiers come and our altarpiece disappears?"

"You mean my altarpiece." He reached for her again and Catherine backed away. "You had better not have done anything to it."

She raised her arms. "You see room to hide an altarpiece here? You may search my pallet in the dormitory if you like. What, do you think I would destroy it? And to whom would I sell it? If you want to ask the sexton about it, summon the man and question him yourself."

"Where is he?" said Robert.

"God knows," said Catherine.

"Has he got keys?"

"Of course he does."

"Christ, what a man has to go through to put a piece of property to rights," said Robert. "Send someone to bring that sexton. Somebody have a look in Christina's chamber and make sure she hasn't stuck it in with her jewelry. William can fetch the constable to search the men. And lead me to some food now, will you?"

"I will go look in the prioress's room," said Frances. Margaret took Robert by the arm and guided him toward the refectory.

Ann moved closer to Catherine. "I would rather be worm's meat than that man's servant."

Catherine murmured, "Is it possible that the Marys have that altarpiece somewhere?"

"They would have to be stronger than they look. And brighter."

"Someone could have helped them. For a fee. In the back of that cupboard?"

"Why hide it from their brother?"

"Maybe they know a private buyer. Maybe they know more than they let on." Ann was silent a moment. "Have the others really gone over?"

"Yes."

"They will accept that Boleyn woman as queen?"

"Yes."

"May it do them some good." Ann shook her head.

"He will take every penny they have and make them do the dirty work." Catherine slumped backward. "I will not go."

"It is as well as it can be. Your self-rule will be called treason, you know that."

Catherine looked at her hands. The long fingers were white but calloused from work. "Robert's men will get them all with child if the Marys do not see to them. Perhaps Robert himself."

"And if they are put on the road alone?" Ann said. "What then?"

The two women looked at each other for a long second. Catherine dropped her eyes again and said nothing.

Ann patted her hand. "Not to worry. I will stay with you and the old ladies. I need someone to mend me when someone tries to tear a piece of my face off."

Catherine looked up and laughed, putting her fingers on Ann's cheek. "The cut is not severe. I will make you a salve for it if I am still allowed to make balm for a wound without being arrested."

"I will never bow my head to an Overton," Ann said, serious now.

"To the refectory, ladies?" They both jerked around. William Overton was in the nave, sitting silently on a bench on the other side of one of the pillars. "I was not eavesdropping," he said as he pushed himself to his feet and came into view. "I can barely hear my own thoughts in this cavern." He walked toward them with his hand on his forehead. "I have had no appetite for two days. Perhaps your prioress has a remedy for me." He glanced up at the hanging Jesus. "I hope she can find one for my brother's ailment, as well."

Robert was already at the table, sitting astraddle one of the benches and cleaning his nails with his hand knife. The meat and bread were laid on the table, and Christina, followed by Mary Frances, came to sit at the foot, leaving Robert the head. "As the usurper here you will no doubt want the seat of honor," the prioress said stonily. "And I will thank you to keep your sisters out of my chamber."

Robert pointed at the canvas in the corner. "What's this here?"

"The old legs to the table. One of them was cracked and I have had them replaced with a simpler design." Christina poured wine. "I supposed that you would cry up the constable if we did not leave the carved ones for your taking."

"Well enough."

The nuns assembled themselves, and Christina regarded them all. "Girls. Daughters

I might have said. I hope you have considered what the decisions you make today will mean for the disposition of your souls."

They all exchanged frightened looks.

"Enough, Christina. Will you terrify these women with painted demons?" said Robert Overton.

"There will be real demons enough to torment them when they come to their ends."

Robert snorted. "Oh, we shall have a moral play now, shall we? Please, let me call up some players and have them bring us a Vice to be subdued by this paragon of virtue. William, you can see to that, can't you?" Robert waved toward his brother. "Our William was right ready to train for a priest himself when the reform came, weren't you, brother?" William didn't answer, and Robert laughed. "Our brother will turn shepherd now, methinks, and stand on the green hillside reading books and making verses to his lady love. He is a solitary soul, he is. The court has not suited his temperament." Robert slammed his hand on the table to punctuate his opinion, and William, who had sat on his brother's right, made a noise and put his palms to his temples. "Are you still down, William?"

"What is the matter?" said Christina. "Are you ill?"

William Overton waved his hand. "My head feels as though it will float off my shoulders. Perhaps it is this constant rain. I have ridden for days almost without sleep. You might see to a remedy for me if you have one."

"Catherine has possession of the infirmary these days," said Christina. "I have instructed her myself. She has great talent as a healer."

"Oh, yes. Ask *Catherine*. She can do anything," said Frances. "She can surely find some ointment or other for you." Her eyes glinted with malice. "It is almost as though she has learned magic somewhere."

"I believe I have a wormwood infusion for that green cast in your complexion," said Catherine between her teeth. William Overton guffawed, then groaned and held his head in his hand.

"Daughters," snapped the prioress. "Stop this. You have all been healed under Catherine's hand and not a one of you has complained of her knowledge when your stomach troubled you or your head gave you pain. Catherine, have you a cure for the young man or not?"

"Do you feel fever?" asked Catherine.

But before she could get an answer, John Bridle ran in, shouting, "Christina!

40

Come at once." He leaned on the door frame, heaving for breath. The prioress and the Overton brothers stood, and Christina motioned for a mug of water. The priest slugged down the drink and ran his hand over his face. "The sexton," he said, gasping. "Bring physic. He is dying in the road."

CHAPTER SIX

Nicholas Hale lay on his back in the middle of the muddy high road, surrounded by the small group of soldiers. One of them was poking at the downed man with the tip of his sword, and another toed his side. Hale did not move, and the Overton brothers shouldered the crowd aside to get closer. Behind them, Christina picked her way from stone to stone, a basket on one arm, and Catherine followed her, but the prioress took a quick look over John Bridle's shoulder and entered Hale's small cottage instead of stopping. William Overton lowered himself to the man's side and peeled back his eyelids. The sexton's face shone with sweat, and he had vomited on himself. A wad of the sudsy mass still clung around Hale's mouth. He did not move.

"This man is dead," said William. "See here, Robert. Tell me if I am mistaken."

The older Overton squatted beside his brother and put his hand near the man's nose. "I sense no breath." He rocked back onto his heels. "What do you make of that?" He pointed at the remains on Hale's lips.

"Witchcraft," muttered one of the soldiers, and everyone backed away except for the Overtons.

Catherine stepped into the breach. "Come, be sensible, we are not children here," she said, kneeling beside William. She leaned over the man's face and swiveled it from side to side. "Did he say anything?" she asked, looking from soldier to soldier, but no one answered. "I will look at his cupboard," she said with disgust, rising and shaking out her soiled skirt.

"Someone see to the constable," said Robert Overton. There was some shuffling, but no movement. "I said, someone go."

"I am here already, man. Give me some room." The constable waddled and elbowed his way to the front of the crowd and stared at Nicholas Hale. "Well, damn me for a toadstool. Did someone run him down?"

"He fell dead in the road," Robert Overton said. "And this after my altarpiece has been stolen."

"Say you so?" The constable cast a squint over the soldiers. "And you villains. What have you to say for yourselves, riding in as you have? Which one of you has felled our sexton?"

"We are no villains," said a scrawny young soldier. "We come here in the name of the king. There's reports made against the convent here."

"You will speak with them," said Robert Overton to the constable. Then he waved his hand over the heads of his men. It looked like a benediction. "You hear me?" he shouted. "Not a soul moves from here until I have some satisfaction in these matters. You there, stop. No murmuring, neither. You will go. All of you. Constable, do your office and lead them to the gaol."

Catherine backed to the edge of the circle of grumbling men and hurried into Hale's cottage. She found Christina in the front room, bent over a large bucket, rinsing her hands. "You'll find nothing here," said the prioress firmly. "He had washed his dinner dishes already." She motioned toward the wooden table, where a bowl and spoon lay, clean and damp.

"These are still wet." Catherine glanced around the small room. The shelves held a few clay cups and one tin mug. Two plates, a bowl, a knife, and another spoon sat beside them. The hearth was burning low but it was empty of pots. "Robert Overton has set the constable upon his own men."

"Perhaps he knows them better than he will confess." Christina tossed the water from the bucket out the back door and surveyed the garden. "But Nicholas could have picked any number of weeds from that mess to kill himself," she called, and Catherine followed her back. "There is a world of venom out there and the man was a half-wit. Look there," Christina said, in her testing voice. "What is that, right there, just showing itself?"

"Nightshade," said Catherine. The line between cultivation and woods was impossible to see, and the rainy spring had caused a riot of growth.

"Very good, Daughter." Christina patted Catherine's arm.

"Surely he knew better than to eat that. You saw nothing doubtful inside?"

"Everything about that man I found doubtful," said the prioress, "but I believe whatever killed Nicholas Hale is inside him. Whether one of Robert's men helped him along I cannot say."

"But Nicholas wanted reform. Why would they kill him?" Catherine lifted a few of the dishes, smelled, and replaced them. They all seemed very clean.

"I think when our altarpiece is recovered, we will have an answer to that." Christina shook out a cloth and hung it near the fire. "I cannot worry my mind over the man. He certainly was not worrying himself over us when he went over to the king. He probably sent informations against us to Robert Overton."

Catherine looked out the back door again. "It is still a horrible death."

Christina wiped the bucket and set it by the fire. "Every death is horrible, Catherine, but it is the valley we must travel through to arrive at our reward. I hope he saw his errors before he passed, or his reward will be a bitter one indeed." She dried her hands on her tunic. "If the man knew no better than to eat plants without knowing their properties, then I cannot help it."

Catherine lifted one of pots. "This is the one you gave him. With the porridge."

"He was probably afraid I put the pope's piss in it. It has been washed, as you see."

"Yes," Catherine mused. She walked into the back garden again and turned over some leaves. She could barely make her way over the tangle of vines and rotting wood. "I see no porridge out here," she called to the open back door.

Christina came out, tightening her wimple. "Perhaps he got one last meal in him before Robert's men got to him." She took the pot from Catherine and set it among Hale's other dishes. "Leave it. If they see this in my hand, those men will have their paws on it, cheap as it is."

They went back out to the road, where Father John had given Hale the rites and still knelt beside him, head bowed. Some people from the village had gathered, the younger children tucked against their mothers' aprons. The soldiers posed in angry knots of two and three down the road by the gaol. Christina called out, "Where is the carpenter? Thomas Aden. They often dine together. Send a boy to find him."

John Bridle collared a nearby child and sent him off down the road. Two soldiers came swaggering back toward them, their hands awkwardly on their swords. They glowered at Robert Overton.

"What would you have me do?" said Overton. "Ignore you? Favor you?"

"You will answer for this insult, Overton," said the taller one.

Robert Overton bristled and his hand twitched toward his hip. "Would you challenge me?"

The soldier took a step back. "There are more serious matters at hand."

Christina said, "The sexton's sister should be found. The woman is mad, you know. She and Nicholas have ever been at odds." She went among the people, speaking more softly to each in turn and pointing to the threatening sky, and they began to disperse, crossing themselves and nodding to the prioress.

Robert Overton hauled the priest to his feet. "Who is the sexton's sister? Is she one of the nuns?"

"No. A cunning woman. Lives in a hovel at the edge of our sheepfold when she's not wandering the woods." John Bridle shook himself free. "She hasn't shown her face at the mass in ten years. I will see if she is to be found."

"Very well." Robert Overton looked up and down the road, slapping his leg with his glove. A few drops of rain splashed down. "I have these blasted women to attend to, William. God's wounds, women and more women, is there no end of them? I must get that wagon back before the clouds open up on us again."

"I will stay," said William. "And as things stand, I believe I need to rest before I travel again." He laid his palm on his forehead. "I feel a bit of fever on me, brother."

"Well, then. That settles it." Robert pulled Catherine by the arm. "You get this pretty little sister here to fix your head. And you find that altarpiece, while you're at this business, hear me? Make sure that damn constable speaks to everyone. No one excepted." William nodded painfully and Robert Overton ran his eyes over the dead man. "Poor devil," he said scuffing his heel. "Dust to dust," he said, checking his boot sole. "Or should I say mud to mud."

The boy came flying back up the road, splattering himself as he came. "Carpenter is gone, sir," he gulped, halting in front of Robert Overton and ripping the cap from his head. "Wife says he's not been home this three days. Says he's helping the sexton fix the ladies' table." The boy rubbed some of the dirt around on his face, then held out one grubby hand.

Robert Overton dropped a small coin into it and the boy scooted off. "Does your carpenter own a cart?"

The priest turned to Christina. "Does he?"

The prioress pursed her lips. "Why would I keep accounts of what Thomas Aden owns? You know the man as well as I."

"A cart perhaps large enough to haul your altarpiece away?" said Robert. He turned the question to Christina this time.

"Good Christ, he had better not. And now, I must return before your highwaymen are freed to rob us blind." She turned on a heel and headed back toward the convent.

"You will have to go, you understand," Robert called after her, but Christina did not look back. "Eh, what is one nun more or less?" he murmured as she disappeared into the side door. He glanced at Catherine, who pretended not to hear. "You will depart or you will hang for your sins. It is of no matter to me."

Catherine quietly knelt again at the head of Nicholas Hale. William Overton lowered himself on the other side of the body. "What are you thinking?" he said.

Catherine looked into his eyes. William's face looked flushed, she thought, dangerously so, but he met her gaze steadily. "I think this man has died of a poison. And I don't believe he did it himself."

CHAPTER SEVEN

The lettuce was fresh and sweet, with green onions sliced onto it, and the wine was pleasantly strong. Catherine had added rosemary and orange peel to a pot of cool sage water for the hand wash before she brought it to the refectory, and she and Veronica laid soft bread and trenchers out with the pewter spoons and salt. There was the joint of mutton, still uncarved, and old apple-Johns with figs and almonds. But no one could eat.

Nicholas Hale lay alone in the nave. He had no family but the one sister and now they had no one to dig a grave. William Overton had taken his leave for the afternoon, pleading the headache, and Robert had taken his wagon, pleading the lateness of the hour and the impending bad weather. They had barely had time for a wave goodbye to their old sisters.

The prioress sat drumming her fingers at the chief place of the board. "How dare those girls enter my chambers. Robert should get control of them. And that William should get out of the bed." She sniffed and lifted her wine goblet to her lips. "Next we will have the soldiers upon us, I suppose," she said, mostly to herself. "Let them try to make me kneel to their king without their nobleman at their head. They will see the hand of God, by Christ. I will show it to them."

Catherine sat on Christina's left. "Someone will have to seek Thomas Aden." She waited until she had everyone's attention. "I do not believe he murdered Nicholas Hale."

"What leads you to believe anyone murdered him?" said Christina, reaching for the bread. "The old clown likely tainted his food himself. We should bury him in the crossroads, not in the graveyard."

Catherine said, "I'll wager my soul Thomas Aden is no killer. Nor no thief, either."

"Then why did he flee?" said Veronica, adjusting her hips on a cushion.

Catherine shook her head. "I have no answer for that. Maybe he had a journey planned."

"How very timely," sneered Christina.

"How far can he go with something as large as the altarpiece in his wagon?" asked Ann.

Veronica laughed. "A carpenter can take things apart, you know," she said. She glanced at Christina, who frowned at her.

Catherine imagined the painting being dismembered and felt a scowl come onto her own face. "He would not be so stupid as to destroy it if he meant to sell it."

"It may still be in Mount Grace somewhere," Veronica continued. She poured more of the Spanish wine and drank deeply.

Ann clanked her spoon against the pewter dish a few times. "How can we eat with that man lying in there and no one even to dig him a hole?" She threw down the tool and picked up a few leaves of salad with her fingers.

Catherine stopped her friend's hand. "Father John will say him a decent mass. Even in these times."

"The church is locked up. And we have thrown the bolt ourselves. Who will come to bid him farewell in an empty building?"

"No one, with Thomas gone," said Catherine quietly. "But Thomas's wife is going to give birth within the month. He will surely not leave her alone. He will come."

"Not today, he won't," said Ann. "Nor tomorrow, you mark me."

"Men," said Christina, cramming a chunk of bread into her mouth. "They do what they will, the women be damned. From carpenter to king, they're all the same."

Veronica dabbed at her food and drank, her eyes seeming fastened on some invisible portent hanging in the middle distance. Ann tore at the edge of the meat with her hand knife.

"Robert might at least have taken his soldiers with him," said Veronica. "He could have them questioned at his own house."

"What of William?" said Catherine. "They will need to mind him as they mind his brother."

"What of him?" said Christina. "A younger son. You think they will listen to him when they find a church full of goods before their eyes?"

"He will oversee them," said Catherine with as much authority as she could muster. Ann snorted. "If we can wake him long enough to get his attention."

"He is ill," said Catherine. "I saw it in his countenance. Perhaps the soldiers will make a plot for Nicholas if we give them the spades."

Ann laughed again, but she was not smiling. "If they dig any graves, we are the ones they will bury."

CHAPTER EIGHT

The nuns had just cleared the table when the pounding began. By the time they entered the nave, John Bridle had opened the door. "There they are, gentlemen, and they are no doubt shaping their minds to the new world. Ladies, no more delay. Christina, I have a glass of wine for you. You may join me at my table. Please come away from this while you may do it in one piece. Catherine, come."

"John Bridle, you old Satan," shouted the prioress. "You will open the house of God to men of the sword? How did you get in?"

"I came through the convent. I have a key." He dangled it by its string for her to see.

Christina clenched her fists. "You are a white-livered coward. You are a spineless worm."

"Of that I have no doubt, Christina," said the priest, "but I will be a live one."

"You will stand at the throne of the devil to answer for this," she called, but the priest was walking out, one hand raised in farewell. Christina gathered her skirts about her and stalked up to the men, who were already surveying the statues and decorations, assessing what could be moved. "You are not allowed here without permission. You must give your testimonies to the constable. You must confess where you have concealed our Madonna. You must take yourselves out until William Overton wakes or until the church doors are open."

The tall soldier in front stepped forward. He wore a silk shirt and he smoothed his beard with one hand. His breeches featured an enormous embroidered codpiece, and he positioned himself wide-legged to show it off. He had clearly been recently at court. "The church doors *are* open, madam. And we have all been before your damned constable and he has seen fit to leave us free men." His other hand was on his dagger, and Catherine and Ann stayed where they were. The rest of the soldiers hung back. "You women are reputed to be immoral. You may perhaps save yourselves from the scaffold if you will take the oath of succession and admit your many faults."

"My oath has been given to God and it goes to no man. Nor no court piece and her bastard, neither," said Christina. She glanced at the addition to his clothing and, with a slight smile, lifted her eyes away dramatically. "I see it is the fashion to brandish your daggers these days. Well, gentlemen, you may keep your weapons where they are and leave this place."

A few of the men sniggered. "I may, may I?" the front soldier said. His face tightened and he turned to his men. "Who tells me I may leave this place? The Whore of Rome?"

Christina's face bloomed red. "To what have we come when the house of God is not safe for the people of God?"

"God had better show himself quickly," said the tall soldier, raising his hand. "Be speedy about this, friends." The knot of men, dressed in various colors, began to loosen. Two of them were almost in rags, and went skulking up the side aisles like hungry rodents. Two stayed by the first soldier's side and acted like his companions, dressed, as he was, in soft light shirts and gold. One wore his beard in a point. A ruby twinkled in his ear.

One came by himself right up the center of the nave to where the other three nuns huddled. He had a ring on his thumb with a large pearl at its center. "Ladies," he said, leaning back as though he meant to bow. But he was looking them over. "Those costumes will have to go to the players now. You may be able to ask a good price if they are in need of sluts' robes." He fingered Veronica's wimple, and she shrank back. "Oh, particular, is it? Dainty, is it?" He called over his shoulder, "We have us here a delicate one, so old she might blow away without these weeds to hold her in place." He moved closer. "And what else has she got that's keeping her fastened to the earth?" Veronica was wearing no crucifix and her rosary was made of simple wooden beads. He yanked them from her belt, raised them to his eyes, then cast them aside. "You old girls have something better than kindling, I think."

Another had joined him, less richly dressed and wearing no gold. His beard was thin and spiked, like the whiskers on a terrier. He was young, dressed in brown woolen, and deferred to the other, showing his broken teeth in an obsequious grin. "William Overton will be here soon," Catherine said, trying to draw his attention from Veronica. Her face was unmoving but her eyes had gone liquid and soft. "You will need him to sort out what you may take and what of these things are Overton goods. *Their* goods."

"And good they are," said the soldier. He lifted Catherine's crucifix with his dagger. "Silver. Very pure." He stepped closer and she held her breath. He had a grip on the chain and she braced herself for the pull. When it came, her head bounced forward and back, and the crucifix dangled in his big fingers. "And a silver chain to match. Very elegant." He placed the crucifix inside his doublet and looked at her more closely. "You are not the prioress here." He glanced over his shoulder at Christina, who was glaring around. "Why do you wear the only silver?"

"We have so little these days. We have sold most of our valuables to keep ourselves fed." Catherine caught Veronica's warning eye but went on. "The changes have brought us to think that to keep such idols will only harm our souls and we have turned our attention to more substantive goods. Those we lay up in heaven."

The soldier eyed her narrowly, then turned his head without moving his body to look at Veronica and Ann. Catherine was put in mind of a boar, swishing this way and that through the woods to snuff out some edible morsel. "Surely the king does not begrudge us our small portions of meat?"

"The king begrudges no one nothing," the soldier growled, turning his eyes back to Catherine. His doggy partner chugged out an unctuous hoot. The dagger was still in his hand. She forced herself to stare into his eyes.

"You three may take your places there." The soldier indicated the south wall bench with his dagger. "Which of you knows physic?"

"I keep the infirmary," said Catherine. "I tend the medicinal plants in the garth."

"And where do you keep your poisons?"

"I know nothing of poison."

"You women all know of venoms. You will have to cease your black magic in the light of the new order. You have done your last poisoning, lady."

Christina was coming across the nave like a hot horse, nostrils flaring as she approached. "This child is no poisoner," she said, yanking the man by the sleeve. He pulled back and she gave him a light slap. "The jars in the infirmary are all labeled. If you have ever learned to read." She arched her eyebrows and crossed her arms.

The startled man glared at the prioress for a few seconds, then reverted his attention to the three on the bench. "We will have more conversation by and by." The soldiers fanned out, a few headed for the altar, and Christina followed the one who had spoken.

Ann gripped Catherine's hand. "You do know something of venoms," she whispered. "They are looking for someone to saddle with this murder. Is there a chance we can get there before they do and destroy your store?"

"They will not know what sits before them if it does not glitter." Catherine nodded toward the prioress. Christina was following the soldier who had taken her cross, chattering in his ear. "I am more worried about her."

"I am worried for us all," said Ann.

Veronica rested her chin on her chest and closed her eyes. "Where is your William now?" she said under her breath. "They're going to steal our goods, then they're going to try us and find us guilty. It's already finished."

The soldiers were gutting the church, tearing through whatever they could reach. The shabbiest one had found little to carry off, but his dagger was out and he was chipping off the noses of the saints. His eyes were glazed with lust for his task, moving with methodical precision from statue to statue, as though he were walking the stations of the cross. S. Catherine's wheel was battered and notched where he had tried to knock it from her and it now looked like a wheel of fire. S. Christopher's shoulder was now empty and forlorn, his feet pointing into the broken waves. He sliced at S. Etheldreda's neck, and left the gallant profile of Thomas Harrington a bedraggled pile of crumbles on the flags. He ended at the bench, where Catherine and Ann sat.

"And what have you got upon you, pretty lady?" He advanced on Catherine, the blade lowered to his side but showing in his hand.

"Nothing. I have nothing." She raised her palms to him. "You may search me if you like. That one has taken my crucifix already."

He looked her up and down, then side to side. "You're a young one. You might be able to find you some husband to take you in." He grinned savagely and kneaded his groin. "I would take you on right here if you want breaking in."

Ann rose, a head taller than the scraggly man. "You boys finish your games here and go. We do you no harm and when William Overton arrives, you are likely to face charges along with us. I will bring the constable myself. A body lies just there," she said, pointing at the covered form, "and you disturb his rest. I wonder what your men were up to before he died."

Catherine almost laughed, it was so bold.

"I have done nothing unwarranted," said the soldier, looking around for his fellows. They had gone and he was alone with the women and the dead man. He put on a hearty voice and grinned. "We have license from the king, woman. What will you do? Wrestle me down? You look like wench enough to try it."

Ann sat. "I would not dirty my hands on the likes of you. You are the ones making violence here. I serve the church. I do not tear it apart."

The other tattered soldier came through the door. "Found me some good things." He showed his long yellow teeth and hefted a small canvas bag. "I am going to take the upper floors."

"There are no upper floors to speak of," said Catherine. She was shaking, and she hid her hands in her tunic. "Just some small rooms." She pointed in the other direction. "There is the vestry, and you will find some of the plate there, but John Bridle may object to your taking his vessels. There is hay in the tithe barn, as well. And apples. Some cabbages buried in the hay for keeping. There are fine birds in the dovecote." There were also jugs of wine in the kitchen pantry but Catherine did not mention them.

"You think we rode from London for cabbages and birds?" He walked away, swinging his dagger. It didn't take them long to discover the steps to the small room over the porch and she could think of no other story to distract them.

"They'll find their bliss now," Ann whispered.

They could hear it all well enough. The boards being ripped up, the splintering cracks. Wood being slung against the wall. "Heigh ho, what have we here? The little sisters have been hoarders for God."

First came the books down the steps. The soft tumble of their pages told Catherine everything that would follow. She heard a call as one of the two came to the door above. "Michael! Coz, are you there? You must see what we have discovered here." But Michael must have been the one busy on his knees at the altar, his head in the table, or one of the absent ones, because no one responded. "You will be sorry when you hear what we have found," the voice said. The soldier who had been defacing the icons angled down the steps and walked over to Catherine. "Where is your purse? I have need of a bag." He had one of Veronica's pigment jars in his hand.

"I have no purse." Catherine held out her open palms again. "You may see for yourself."

"Steal what you can carry and go," said Ann.

The soldier held it up to his eyes. "Steal? No, no. We clean in the king's name. Have you not heard? The church is to be purified." He winked at Catherine and pulled her to him. She struggled to free herself, but he held on. "You might need a bit of swabbing, too, lady." He breathed in her face and, laughing, released her.

The soldier in the altar table tossed the linen corporal out flat and examined the sewing on it. He lifted the edges and held each one close to his eyes, like a trader expert in stitching. He rolled it again and shoved it aside. He brought up the platen next, along with the monstrance and chalice. The chalice he stuffed into his waistband. Catherine shouted, "Father John Bridle will need those for the Eucharist, whoever owns this building."

The soldier looked at her as though she were an unruly hound that had intruded on the building. He looked down at the goods again, and weighted them, each in a hand. Then he pulled a leather bag out from under his cloak and stowed them inside. "The priest can get him more," he said, not exactly to Catherine.

"I will call the watch, if you steal what belongs to the reformed order," said Catherine, approaching him, "and they will have you before the court when next it sits in session." Her words came out shaky and she feared her knees would give way.

"Watch? The watch?" He laughed out loud now, and Catherine could see the black teeth at the back of his head. "Woman, do you not see which way the wind blows? We *are* the watch now. Your Robert Overton has gone, and we take what we think fit. I will take *you* if I decide you might be worth the having." He came around the altar table to have a better look at her. Catherine snugged the wimple tighter around her face and backed away again. "He is not our Robert Overton. He has never been for us."

Ann was right behind her. "Catherine, please, do not persevere in this." She led Catherine back to the bench. "They have their head and will take it all. Don't let them take you as well."

Six of the men were now walking around the nave. Two had unrolled the tapestries and were debating their relative worth like a couple of traders haggling over a price. Then they walked away, bored, leaving the tapestries rumpled and splayed on the stones. No one took note of the still form of Nicholas Hale.

A young man descended from the porch room with various chains and one large crucifix—it was Veronica's—slung over his shoulder. He had a bulging bag over one arm and a smirk on his face like a cat at a milk pail. Catherine's hourglass swayed at his belt, the time inside it sloshing as he bounded down the last few steps. He kicked at the pile of breviaries and psalters, one copy of *The Legend of Good Women*, and the Gospels. Catherine went to gather some of the volumes, but the soldier booted her back. "You won't be needing no reading anymore, sister. You were better to study up on your roasting."

"May I stack them for Robert Overton?"

The soldier thought a moment. Catherine could see the effort of his attempt to determine whether this could be some sort of trick. She put on her most inoffensive expression and waited while he sorted through the grueling logic of it. He finally could determine no reason to prevent her, so he assented with a grunt and strutted off. Catherine straightened most of the volumes, though she tucked both of the Chaucers and a new Ovid onto the bottom of the pile lest their titles and decorative covers attract the eyes of another, more perceptive, of the soldiers.

Ann came to help, and Catherine sat back on her heels. "I can stand this no more," she said. The soldiers were coming and going through the church doors, stopping to urinate against the wall. They had smashed the south window, and one was relieving himself in the pieces of the Virgin that had stood outside, swinging around so that the stream would hit her square in the face. "William should have been here ages ago. I will run for Father John, while they are drunk with their success."

"Go now, or you will be the next thing they take."

CHAPTER NINE

John Bridle was sitting at his table with a book and a glass of wine. "Daughter," he said gently when Catherine knocked and entered. "Have you brought your Mother Christina?"

"She bides at the church, Father. You must help me fetch William Overton before those soldiers tear it down to the very stones. Good God, they will heave Nicholas Hale into the ditch before they finish."

"Sit." The priest laid a new oak leaf on the page and closed his volume. "How many times have I told you this day was coming? I have watched you learn physic, watched you learn to make your letters. You will be a fine wife. You must settle your mind on marriage."

"And who would you have me marry, Father? You, of all people. It has not been so many years that you told me to settle my mind on my vows. To put my wits to study. I have done so and I do not mean to throw it all over for marriage. I have seen how marriage treats women. You yourself have taught me to see. You said I was bound for greater things. Called to do more."

"The world has changed, Catherine. I was born in Mount Grace. I buried my parents and a brother here. I buried . . . well, it was before you were born." He looked up and combed his beard with his fingers. "I have never told you this, girl, have I?"

"No, Father."

"My parents' graves have no stones. It was a plague time, and we buried people by the dozens. I thought it was the worst I would ever see. But I was mistaken. Pride. It was pride in me." He stood and gripped her shoulders. "You must accept the reform with me. You will be forced to accept it. There is a new arrangement in the world, and we must bend to it as we have always bent to God's will. You are fair and fine, Catherine, and you will be seen." He pushed the wimple back from her face and, taking her by the chin, turned her to the window. "You look just like . . . you have a face like an angel." He suddenly kissed her on the cheek and sat again, laying his face in his hands. "You will put away your learning now."

The priest had never touched her in such a way, and Catherine was stopped as though he had struck her, the cheek burning. "But what of our vows? What of our Father in Rome? What of my skills?"

"The king has defied the pope and under his rule we must live." John Bridle spoke from inside his palms. "I have said yea to it and you will, too. It is done, Catherine. The head of the church in England is Henry. The reform is no longer in question. It is treason to say otherwise."

"Mother Christina will bow to no earthly king, whatever is demanded. And I will stand by her, as she has stood by me."

The priest muttered, "It will mean hanging for her to refuse it. She has been too free in her ways. I did not curb her, and that is my sin. But she will be the one who pays, do not doubt that."

A fire rushed into Catherine's face and her voice rose. "It's easy for you to say it. You are a man and will have your church. How will it be for the women? At least our father in Rome let us be as we thought best. This . . . this *king* will have us making shirts for some clod or other." She stopped, blinking back tears. "He will have us ignorant as dirt."

John Bridle looked up. "You have been conversing with Veronica."

"I have been conversing with Veronica my entire life. With Mother as well. They cared for me, though I had no one. You yourself have smiled on it."

"You had best prepare yourself to become a woman like other women." There was sadness in the words and they came without conviction. "Though you are not like other women." He stood again, tottering a little. He slicked back his hair. His blue eyes were bright on her. "Now where is that William?"

They walked together to the Hare and Hound, where John Bridle called, "Where may I find a William Overton? Is the noble young man refreshed to the point where he might stop a pack of knaves from knocking down God's house?" His voice rose to a shout, and Simon Stubbe, the owner, came to the front door.

"Father John, I beg you. Lower your voice."

"I will lower my voice when the young man lowers himself to come to us." The priest cupped his hands around his mouth and shouted again. "Or can the younger brother not be bothered to come to our aid? Shall I send word into the neighboring parishes that I have some women in need of the yoke and no one will relieve me of them?" He chuckled strangely and murmured to Catherine, "That should get the boy out of bed."

And sure enough, William Overton, hair standing in wild clumps and face swollen, appeared at the sill above them, buttoning his breeches. "What is it, old man?"

"Your serving men are busy knocking down the church and stealing from poor women," said Catherine.

John Bridle added, "If you have completely restored yourself, perhaps you could see to assisting us?"

William shook his head as though he did not recognize them, but finally he rubbed his face and said that he would come. Catherine and Father John waited in the road. "If you will not get you a husband, you must plan to take refuge in Florence or Rome, if we can figure a way to get you to Yarmouth and on the right boat," he said to her quietly. Then he shouted again, "Here is your savior now." William was coming through the front door, tucking in his shirttails and waving them on. His hose were loose and bagging about his knees, but he trudged after them, back to the church.

The soldiers had sorted through the old altar corporals, broken candle ends, bits of paper and thread and utensils and the rejected goods were piled on the altar. The small pyxes were salvageable, and the men had found the feretory, which held a shred of the bloodied robe of Thomas à Becket. Men seemed to be everywhere, searching corners and digging into cubbyholes.

Veronica was resting on a bench. "Thank God. Finally you have come. Christina is in full armor. She has gone back into the convent to stand guard over her chamber. I did not think a mortal woman could make such noises. I believe I can make out something about God's will and the obedience of soldiers to their true King. I am put in mind of an angry falcon. Perhaps you can manage her before someone sticks a sword in her?"

A soldier stormed into the church, Christina shouting behind him. Another man, younger and less muscled, was prying at the lid of a tomb with his dagger's tip, trying to gain some purchase, and the prioress turned her fury on him. "What now?" Christina shook him by the arm. "Taking the building down by its foundation stones, are you?" The man was slight and he fell under the prioress's grip. "Get up from the floor, and behave with some dignity. Mark me, I will show you the face of God if you wreck that tomb."

Catherine hurried up the side aisle. "Mother, I have William."

Christina pushed with her narrow foot at the downed man. "Daughter." She glanced up, smiling, but her face hardened like soft soil under sun at the two men. "Well, well. John, you have finished your dinner? And Master William. I do hope you're feeling refreshed. There are your men. Perhaps if you cannot direct them with your tongue, you can succeed with a blade." She gave the groveling man another little shove with her toe.

"Christina, how many times must I warn you? You will end up on a gallows if you go on this way," said John Bridle. The soldier climbed to his feet and slid past them, retreating to the first window, where he tried the solidity of the lead seams.

"You will not," Christina said, pushing the priest aside, "make a mark on those windows. Leave off. You will obey me, or I will make you see the hand of an angered God."

"Mother Christina," said William. "You should let me sort these men out."

"Let the men handle it, is that what you mean? You have done a fine job of it thus far." She glared at him. "We are the victims of a perjurer at court, and now we are at war and the army has come to do battle. What shall we do for weapons against them when you desert us? Shall we swing pots at their heads? Jab them with needles?"

"Calm yourself, madam. You will need no such weapons." He clapped his hands and shouted, "Come on, have done now. You, and you, gather what you have. No more today. These ladies need some relief. Yes, you. Halt now. Now, I say. Where you stand." He sent the cowering soldier into the convent to round up the others. "Bring them all here and let me see that everyone is out." William touched the face of a stone knight who stood in a shallow niche carved into a nearby pillar. The effigy had been cracked by a blade and a chunk of the noble chin came off in William's hand. He shook his head. "I fail to see the need for this destruction."

The soldiers were assembled in the nave within a few minutes. The tallest one stepped forward. "We have not searched the private rooms adequately. That one," he indicated Christina, "bolted her door against us. These women should be carried to the gaol this minute and sounded as to their faith. A report will need to be made as to their conduct. And we must conclude our search. We have found nothing in the infirmary of the poisons that felled the sexton."

"Perhaps the poisons are not in the infirmary," said William. "You looked through the physic Sister Catherine keeps?"

59

"The witch no doubt keeps her provisions hidden from men's view. I will take her myself before the judge."

"Leave it for this day," said William, waving his hand. "And leave her. Go with what you have and I will look further into the sexton's death. Did you find aught of the altarpiece?"

"Nothing but that one there," said the tall soldier, motioning to the thin Jesus. "We left it for your brother." He sniggered at the painting. "Not to my liking no how."

"Then I suppose you are done," said William. "Come, man, there's a body here. Show some respect for the dead, will you?"

They had goods in bags, goods stuffed at their waists, goods in their pockets. "Are they allowed to take so much?" Catherine asked.

William surveyed them. "They have the king's warrant and Robert's permission. There is nothing more I can do." The men shuffled and strode toward the door, and he shouted after them, "No one is to take any personal goods of these women." A few of them nodded as they left. "You will leave the Eucharist silver," he added, and one of the scabbier men reluctantly produced the items and handed them over. William followed them out to the street, the priest at his side, and Catherine watched them confer with the tall one. William pointed south, down the high road, and after some argument, the soldier turned away, smacking the air with his palm and gesturing to the others. Catherine closed the door.

"Did they miss anything?" she asked Ann.

"They seemed to have no use for the linens." She picked up a few that had been thrown to the pavers. "Not even ripped. They must have thought they were cloths for our monthlies."

"Perhaps." Catherine laid fast the heavy bar. "We may thank the stars that William is sick. If he must stay behind, he may stand between us and those men. And mark my words, they are not finished with us."

CHAPTER TEN

The four women gathered again in the refectory and Christina poured wine. She never poured the wine. "They will know better than to steal from us now." She filled her own goblet and drank. "You see? They would not dare lay hands on us. They were afraid."

"Mother, they left because William sent them away," said Catherine, "and they were not gracious about it."

Christina punched the table top with her forefinger. "And wherefore has he done it? He knows, I tell you. He knows the queen will put a stop to this war against the church. He means for us to speak well of him."

Catherine grabbed the jug. "William is unwell, Mother. That is the only reason."

Christina sniffed and turned to Ann. "How is your cheek?"

Ann touched the scratch. "I'll live."

Christina nodded. "Frances was ever a spoilt girl, but you see what this reform talk has done to her. She has become a monster. We are God's women. We do not kneel to mortal men. They will not touch us."

"Has anyone gone into the Marys' room since they left?" said Catherine suddenly.

"Why would they do that?" said Ann. "They have taken everything of worth."

"The cupboard," said Catherine, pushing back from the table. She ran around the walk and entered the bare room. Little was left but the beds and a few rolls of decayed fabric lying discarded on the floor. The cupboard was large enough, but when Catherine opened the doors she felt it wobble. It was empty and the boards it was made from were thin. She easily dragged it from the wall but found only spider webs and dust. She got on her knees and searched underneath.

"You think they buried it under the floor?" said Ann behind her, sitting on one of the mattresses. "Is there a secret passageway down there?"

"You should be on the stage you are so comical," said Catherine, brushing her hands. "There is nothing here." The entire room was visible. The altarpiece was not in it.

"They have no reason to steal it," said Ann. "You will not find it, I think. Whoever has taken it has taken it far away."

"Nicholas Hale had no reason to take it either. And the soldiers have been questioned. I cannot believe it of Thomas Aden. I will not."

"We should find Nicholas's sister."

"What would she do with it? How would she even move it?"

"She's mad but she's not stupid. She'd sell it if she could."

"But kill her brother for it?"

Ann picked at a cuticle. "She hates him. She hates us. What more motive does she need?"

Christina appeared in the doorway. "What do you find?"

"Not a thing," said Catherine. "I am going to speak with Maud Peters. There is still plenty of daylight."

"I wonder that she hasn't come looking for her brother," said Ann. "It might mean she is gone off into the woods. We will never find her if she has."

"Stand at the crossroads and call for Satan," said Christina, pursing her lips. "You might just conjure up Maud."

"She has not favored me since I took my vows," said Catherine.

"Maud Peters has never favored anyone," said Christina, "and your vows had nothing to do with it. You're her superior in physic. The sick ask for you instead of her. She is outside herself with envy." She put her hand on Ann's arm. "But if you aim to go, you had better take a companion along with you." She smiled. "And if you find our altarpiece, bring it home."

Maud Peters lived in a croft surrounded by large oaks behind the Mount Grace sheepfold, and Catherine and Ann took the wide path around to avoid the animals and the vines at the woods' verge. "Do you think Maud really believes I have been her undoing?" asked Catherine as they walked along.

"Maud is volatile," said Ann, "and she has always sought a scapegoat for her troubles. The pestilence did not improve her."

Maud had lost both husband and children in a winter of plague, and her reputation as a healer had suffered, in the same years that Catherine's had grown. Sometimes she visited her brother at the sexton's cottage and the whole village could hear them shouting. She had somewhere taken the notion that he would find her a position with the convent, and she would scream for all to hear about how he abused and neglected her, though it was Christina who had more than once slammed a door in the woman's face. At those times, she stood at the convent gate and shouted that Catherine was a witch and a thief, that Christina was a whore.

A stench blew over them before they could see the cottage. Catherine covered her face with the edge of her wimple. "Great God, what is that?"

Ann was holding her nose, her palm over her mouth. "The mouth of Hell. Or Maud has failed to wash herself."

The door stood open and an ancient mangy dog was guarding the threshold. It struggled to its feet and barked when it saw the two women on the path and Maud Peters appeared behind it. She fondled its narrow skull and grinned at Catherine and Ann. It smelled rank enough, but the rotten air was all over them now.

"Maud," called Catherine. "We come to have a word with you. Christ's wounds, what is that smell?"

Maud never washed herself or her shifts, and she had taken in the last few years to stealing men's breeches from hedges and wearing them until they gaped holes. She had on a man's jacket, too, and heavy gloves, too long for her. She grinned at them. Her teeth were tiny and stained, and she looked older than her years. It was a wonder she hadn't been dragged before the court. "Don't like the smell of me, you can get out of my yard," she sneered.

Catherine and Ann hesitated at the broken gate, watching the dog. "Does he bite?" asked Catherine.

Maud let forth one of her cackles and sauntered toward them. "Couldn't keep brother Nicholas alive, could you? They'll turn on you now, you wait and see, even if you are the daughter of the prioress."

"We are all daughters of the prioress," said Ann.

Maud hooted again. "But this one. This one is the paragon of wisdom and virtue. Come from God, are you, girl? Wonder your feet will settle in the mud at all."

"Listen to me, Maud. We seek a word about your brother," said Catherine.

Maud's gnarled fingers closed on the edge of Catherine's wimple. "You'll have to lay this off now, unless you mean to make your church in the forest like me. If you aren't too refined for the world of men."

"Maud, Nicholas is dead," said Ann, "and the altarpiece is missing from the sanctuary. There are soldiers in the village, and Robert Overton is in a rage. Your brother was in the sanctuary this morning."

"I heard. I saw the commotion in the road. What has all this to do with me?" said Maud. There was a glint of madness in her sky-blue eyes.

"He is poisoned, Maud, do you understand?" said Ann. "He is murdered, and you are his sister. Everyone knows how you dispute with him. Everyone knows that you don't come to the church. And everyone knows you keep herbs."

Maud's eyes sparkled. They look glazed. "My brother threw in his lot with Old Harry. Maybe God has struck him down." She opened her mouth and laughed. "Does his cottage belong to me now?"

Ann almost took the woman by her filthy cap but stopped her hand. "Have you taken our altarpiece, Maud?"

"What? Your old Virgin Mary?" Maud bent over laughing. The dog trotted up and licked her nose. "Prince here knows as much of your church goods as I do." She lifted the dog's chin and pointed its muzzle at them. "Ask him where it is."

"Maud, this is not to be laughed at," said Catherine. "They will come here. They may be here before nightfall if someone tells them where you live."

The woman thought this over for a few seconds. "You want to see my house? Come see my house." She waved backward and they followed her in.

The cottage was dark and low, with bunches of dry flowers and leaves hanging from the rafters. Catherine had to shove them aside to get all the way inside, and Ann sneezed. Three cats lay near the hearth-fire and one of them shot from the room at the entrance of the intruders.

"See any icons?" said Maud, opening the shutters. "Do you see any images?"

"Is there another room?" said Catherine.

"You see my realm complete and whole," said Maud, falling backward onto a stool and spreading her arms wide. "I'm as clean of art as any reformed woman in the village."

One table, the one stool. Hard earth floor. A cupboard with shelves but no front, filled with dirty jars. A pile of rags on the end of a straw mattress in a corner. They were probably Maud's clothes. Catherine asked, "May I look under your bed—just to be truthful when I say that I have looked over the cottage?"

"Look where you please." Maud tilted the stool backward.

Catherine peeled back an edge of the mattress. It sat on packed dirt and was hardly bigger than Maud herself. She took a quick peek behind the cupboard, but it was nailed fast to the wall. "I see nothing out of order here."

Ann was still in the doorway. "Then we will trouble you no further." She was already backing into the sunlight. The smell was liquid inside the cottage, like rotting urine and old cabbage.

Catherine followed and they retraced their way, hearing the fading sound of Maud's weird laughter behind them.

"You believe her innocent?" said Ann, when they were out of hearing.

"She has the whole forest for hiding places. She has juniper and belladonna and monkshood enough to poison an army of men. But there's nothing in that cottage fresh. I would wonder any of her herbs keep their potency."

"I pity her, horrible as she is." Ann looked back. "That could be any one of us, if God were to turn His face away. But that stench! How can she bear the smell of herself?"

Catherine shook her head. "A body can accustom itself." They reached the high road, and she said, "You go on. Tell Mother that I have gone to speak with Elizabeth Aden."

The Aden cottage lay within sight of the church, and Catherine was rapping at the front door within minutes. Richard Mundell, Elizabeth's father, pulled her inside. "Catherine, is it true what they are saying?" His pale eyes were bright spots in his wrinkled face, and his white hair looked shocked.

"What are they saying?"

Elizabeth, enormously pregnant, heaved herself from a back room. "That Nicholas Hale is murdered in the road and that Thomas is named in the crime." She pressed her hands over Catherine's briefly, then sat, easing her belly down to her knees.

"The death is true. I saw the body myself. It looked like poison to me."

"My God," said Richard softly.

"The altarpiece is stolen, as well, and Thomas was in the church this morning. He was seen by all of us. Elizabeth, I must speak to him."

The woman's eyes were on her belly. "He is not here."

"A boy said he has been gone from here three days," said Catherine. "We both know that he was here this morning."

"I spoke to the boy," said Richard. "I told him that I hadn't seen Thomas in that time. And, truth be told, I have not."

"And I affirmed it," said Elizabeth, "though I saw no need to speak further about who had seen him."

"Where did he go?"

Elizabeth's eyes went cold. "My Thomas is no poisoner and he has got no altarpiece."

"Where is he? Why has he run away?"

Elizabeth worried a thread on her apron and glanced up at her father. "He said he was forced to go. That he had to go. He told me not to fret and that he would return as soon as he could."

"Where did he go, Elizabeth? Who would force him?"

The other woman sat silent for a moment, rubbing her sides. "He left without saying."

Her father said, "Go to, Catherine. You can't expect a man to seek him a hiding spot and then yell out where it is."

"You can trust me," said Catherine. "Before God."

"I can't say where he's gone." Elizabeth tightened her lips.

Catherine thought for a moment, chewing her lip. It had to be said. "This makes him appear guilty."

"And if I should point you to him? What then? The Overtons would swing him in a noose before he could prove anything else. How guilty would he look then? And my trust in you would do nothing for that." Elizabeth choked on the words. "You know he has taken nothing from the church. And he has not killed no man."

"I believe you. You must know I do. Let me speak to the younger Overton and see if he will hear reason." Catherine's eyes traveled the room but it looked as it had always looked. "Neither of you must leave the village. Make sure of it."

Elizabeth patted her belly. "I have a burden here weighing me to the soil of Mount Grace. And the altarpiece is not here." She was following Catherine's gaze. "You may examine the house more closely if you want," she said tartly. "Shall I open the baskets for you?"

"It may need to be done. And mind me, Elizabeth. If the soldiers come to the door, stand aside and let them do their searching. Now I must return to the convent."

"I will obey you," said Elizabeth, but her eyes were dark with anger. "I gave you sweets when you were just a little thing, Catherine. I can't believe you mistrust us this way."

Catherine took up Elizabeth's hands. "It is not mistrust, Elizabeth. I have seen these soldiers at their pleasure and they are not to be thwarted. Believe me, if Thomas stays away, he will be charged in his absence and arrested the moment he sets foot in Mount Grace again. They will use his flight against him. They will set down the days he has been in hiding. And then no one will stop them from hanging him."

"Just as I said." Elizabeth wrenched back her hands. "If my husband hangs, there may be others who hang with him. He will not die alone, of that I assure you. There will be others swing beside him. Now go, back to your convent. Leave us by ourselves. In what little peace we have for now."

CHAPTER ELEVEN

The next morning, the four nuns lingered as they broke their fast. They were too few for lauds and no one could bring herself to say the prayers anyway. Their habits would not leave them, though, and they were up so early that the constellations hung, bright as ice chips, in the sky. The days were still cold enough for the earth to breathe frost across the young leaves at night, and Veronica had come in from turning the sheep out blowing on her nails.

Catherine ripped a chunk of bread from the warm loaf Ann set before her and washed it down with a cup of ale. "Does Thomas Aden have kin anywhere nearby?"

"He is the only living child of his parents," said Christina. "I watched them bury the others. He was the last."

"He might have gone to Norwich," said Ann, settling herself to eat. "Easy to hide there."

"He might have gone to the devil, for all we know," said Christina. "I know you gossip with his wife, Catherine, but you may find he is guilty as Lucifer, when it comes to questioning. Then what will you do?"

Catherine threw down her crust. "I have known him since I was a child. He is no thief nor no murderer. I do not believe he is any guiltier of this than we are."

Christina raised an eyebrow, but she was smiling. "And what if a jury believes otherwise?"

"Some men would sooner throw an innocent man to the dogs than worry themselves over questions of truth," said Catherine. "We must uncover the answers before the constable finds Thomas."

"We must all answer to God for something, child," said Christina, yawning. She plucked an apple from the bowl and polished it on her tunic. "Elizabeth is likely concealing him."

"Where? Under her dress?" said Catherine. "Their cottage is no bigger than this table."

The prioress said nothing, wholly taken up with her fruit. The convent bell suddenly sounded, and Simon Stubbe the innkeeper was yelling. "I need the doctor nun! Physic! I need physic right now."

Christina went to answer, the others behind, and she wrenched the rope from the poor man's hands. "Whatever is the matter that you tear our bell cord to shreds?"

"Master William is sick to death," Simon Stubbe panted. "He is hot as a devil in hell, and he cannot rise from the bed. The sweat runs from his face in rivers. He will not take a drink. He does not see my face when I stand before him."

Christina's face whitened and she turned to Catherine. "He is useful to us just now. You must see to him. Your skills are fresher than mine. Call on John to go with you."

"I will get some necessaries." Catherine ran to her infirmary and sorted quickly through the herbs. Rosemary. Sage, good for colds and chest complaints. Garlic. She gathered a basket full and followed Simon Stubbe, who ran down the road ahead of her. "I will need to ascertain his condition first," Catherine said when she caught up to him at the eating room. "Go get the priest."

"Yes, yes." He was wringing his hands.

"I will examine William's situation," she said, adjusting her headpiece. "Be off, Simon. Now, before the young man goes to God."

Five of the soldiers sat at a table, pewter mugs in their hands. One of the them was the tallest, the one William had spoken with on the road. He was probably the king's man from the Court of Augmentations, he moved with such self-importance. Thomas Cromwell's man. Lapdog of a lapdog. He rose at Catherine's entrance and stood between her and the stairs. "Here you are, among us again. How is it that you women maintain you are nuns and yet are not cloistered?"

"Cloistered?" Catherine sniffed. "Tush, we have never enforced a cloister here. Not in my memory. We serve God by serving the village."

"You serve yourselves, I say. Others say it, as well." He propped his hand against the wall to stop her passage. "I have heard of the nuns in Rome. They do not venture out to show themselves to men's eyes. They show their faces to no one. It seems a goodly system to me."

"This is not Rome. This is England."

"And the English have an English head to their church whom you refuse. You want to submit to no one, I say. You keep animals and sell the wool. You sell cloth. You suit yourselves. Dangerous women, as we have heard. You will answer for it." He peered into her basket. "Have you poisoned Master Overton now? And you come to finish your work?"

Catherine stiffened while he removed the cloth. "I have poisoned no one. Stand aside so that I may see him."

"What will you do with these stuffs?" the man said, picking through her supplies. "Kill him in his bed? Or do you mean to climb under the sheets with him?" His companions snickered and knocked their cups together.

"I study physic and I was sent for by Simon Stubbe," said Catherine, yanking the basket back. "I will prescribe a remedy if I am allowed to see whether the man is still living." She stretched as tall as she could. "Perhaps one of you could go in my stead and bring me the signs. Perhaps you may carry them on your person to me. I will be happy to lance your boils for you."

The soldier's eyes brightened with fear and he lowered his arm. Then he settled back into his boots and leaned forward. "Hmph. A girl practicing physic. What will you want next, woman priests?" He side-stepped just enough to let her go by and she held her skirts away from the prominent codpiece.

William Overton lay in a small room, so still that at first view Catherine believed him dead. When she put a palm on his forehead, she felt too much heat and he grunted, thrashing from side to side. His eyes did not open. It was either the sweat or the small pox, and she would not know which until the disease revealed itself in the skin. Catherine smoothed back his hair and said, "William. Open your eyes so that I may look at them. You are in need of physic, and I must decide the best course of action." The man opened them halfway but could not train his gaze upon her face. His eyes swam, the whites gone yellow. Purple moons hung under them, and his cheeks were pale and slick.

She heard boots clambering up the stairs, and John Bridle skidded into the room. "How does he?"

Catherine shook her head. "Not dying. Not yet. Fever. His eyes are bad. I must cool him." She pulled out her urine flask and handed it to the priest. "Get his water. I will check it for clouds."

The priest touched William's forehead and frowned. "The soldiers spared your garth?"

"Yes, so far. Thanks to William." She bent and whispered to the sick man, "I will

70

fetch you a draught," then she turned to John Bridle and Simon Stubbe, who was standing in the doorway again, terror drawing his features tight.

"How does Master William?" the innkeeper asked plaintively.

"I will have to run back for something to draw off the heat," she said, leading him downstairs. The soldiers were all on their feet now, and they crowded around her.

"What does he suffer from?" asked the tall one.

"The disease is still unclear," said Catherine. "Either the sweat or the pox is my judgment. We shall know soon enough."

"What sort of sorceress are you that you touch disease without fear? Have you spells to protect you?"

"Someone must tend him, and if I don't, who will? Will you?"

The soldier stood silent, and John Bridle soon came downstairs, waving the flask before him. A dark yellow puddle sloshed in the bottom, too little for a conclusion. Catherine and the priest looked at each other. John Bridle shook his head.

"Come, we will talk on the road." Catherine turned to the innkeeper. "Simon, please, will you walk with us?"

"Will he die on me, then, mistress?" asked Simon as they hastened back down the road. "Do you want I should send for the brother, then? The brother could have him back at home, where a sick man belongs. I have no place for fevers here, mistress, I can tell you." He was worrying his cap into a small mess.

"He must not be moved, but I have no doubt that Robert Overton will provide for his expenses. Surely you would not put a man in a sweat onto a cart and send him down the road alone?"

Simon deliberated this. "Why no, mistress, I would not do no such thing for the world. That would be to send him to his grave, then, I am supposing. No, such a thing would not do for my sort."

"Very well. He will stay out of the air and in his bed until such time as he can rise on his own."

Simon ran back down the road, and Catherine said to the priest, "We need to find Thomas Aden. Ann and I have spoken to Maud. On my honor, the altarpiece is not in her croft."

"And I have searched every inch of Nicholas's cottage," said John Bridle. "If Maud has it, she has buried it among the trees. Myself, I suspect Thomas Aden in this. Here, I brought you this from Nicholas's bed for the body." He pulled a sheet from his satchel. "We will need to dig him a grave today." He looked at the sky, which was already spreading clouds over the sun again. "Christ, no one will come out for a funeral. I will say a few words and have done. Will this rain never cease?"

"You cannot think Thomas Aden has done this, Father." Catherine stopped at the door. "He wouldn't pinch a mouse's nose."

"Maud knows more of poison, to be sure."

"And she knows Nicholas went over to the king."

The priest chuffed. "Maud couldn't care less who leads the church. That woman would spit on the toes of Jesus himself. She hates him because he is your sexton and you have surpassed her in physic. That's the long and the short of Maud Peters."

"We must get William Overton on his feet. He's the only chance we have just now," Catherine said, and the priest nodded his agreement.

But William did not get to his feet that day and the other guests suddenly saw fit to decamp. When Catherine returned with the jug of lettuce water, the soldiers were already on their horses and Simon Stubbe was hanging onto the bridle of the nearest. "You owe me a reckoning! Pox or no, you have slept in my beds and ate my meat and drank all my ale."

The tall soldier threw him a small bag of coins and eyed Catherine. "That should settle you, my man. And you, pretty little sister. You get the other women in a mind to answer our charges when we return. We will require you to accept the new succession. You will need to sign to it. It would be a shame to see that head roll in the dirt." He bent closer to her. "We know you have hidden your real wealth, lady, and we will take that church down to the earth if we have to. And we will take you down with it. You and all your potions. We will return and you had better make yourselves ready." Then he slapped the horse's neck with the reins.

Catherine breathed more easily to see them riding away on the road toward London, but William Overton did not rise the next day, either, or the next. The fever held him down, a strong demon working on him, and he struggled against it, refusing the lettuce juice and squirming under the cool cloths. Catherine tried a tea of holly leaves, Father John and Simon holding his shoulders while she got a spoon between his teeth, and when the smallpox blisters erupted on his face and the backs of his hands, they poured posset ale down his throat. Catherine prepared a wash of fragrant basil for the men to use in cleaning William's body, a green perfume to drown the yeasty stink of disease. Then she gave them a poultice of chickweed for the boils themselves. "Rub him all over with it," she instructed. "Do it gently."

"We will be making another grave by week's end," said Father John downstairs at dinner. It was the first day in a fortnight without rain. "There is no one else, Simon. We had better get to it. We can put him next to Nicholas."

"Someone should send word to Robert Overton," said Catherine. "He might want him at home."

They walked back to the church, the men veering off to the yard and Catherine heading to her infirmary. The other three women gathered at the door while she went through her stores. "There's nothing more here that will help him," she told them. "A bath of boiled tortoises might help, but I haven't enough of them. Perhaps you could pray." But they listened silently to the sound of the spade working again in the back, and Catherine finally pulled a sheet off a shelf. "We can at least make a winding cloth for this one before he goes."

"You can do this without me," said Christina, turning to go. "I will say a word for his soul."

Simon Stubbe rode to Overton House in the morning, and he returned the next day with Robert beside him. John Bridle had stayed the night in the inn, and Catherine was sitting by William's bedside, mopping his face and listening to the laboured breath wheeze from him, when she heard the horses on the road. Simon Stubbe was already on his feet, taking a bag of money from Robert, by the time she ran downstairs. Robert did not dismount. "Have you found this Thomas Aden?"

"Not yet," said Catherine coldly. The man was stone. "We are taken up with your brother."

Robert glanced up at the window. "How close is he to death?"

Catherine's muscles bunched and recoiled, as though she might strike out at him against her will. "Not so close that he has stopped breathing. You needn't take my word for it. You may go see for yourself if you will."

Robert Overton stared down the road. "Two of our men died of it in Nottingham. Our clerk and one of our Court of Augmentations officers."

Catherine counted the days. They must have all been infected in the same place as they rode north. It could have been anywhere. She mused, "William's constitution is stronger, perhaps."

Robert pulled a nosegay of bluebells and buttercups from his pocket and pushed it to his nose. "Take me up." He swung down and followed Catherine to the doorway of William's room. "What say you, brother?" he called across the room. "Will you rise and come to a masque this evening?"

William did not reply, and Catherine said, "I have given him a strong draught."

Robert fixed his squint on her. "Of what?"

"Henbane seeds in wine. It forces sleep. Rest will help him heal." William flopped in the bed, deeply dreaming.

"Not dead, then." Robert was already backing away.

"As I said." Catherine stepped quickly into the room and adjusted the bedclothes to show Robert a model of courage, but he would not enter. "They must have found the disease somewhere along the journey," she said over her shoulder. "If he had been allowed to stay in London, he might still be in full health."

"It is as it is." Robert clattered down the stairs, and Catherine followed. "This carpenter. He will need to be sought. And what of the dead man's sister?"

"I have spoken to her," said Catherine. "Ann was with me. I searched her room but there was no altarpiece."

"I hear she is filled with bile."

"She suffers from temper but she accomplishes little. All thunder, no rain."

"A forest creature who knows the forest." Robert peered in the direction of the sheepfold. "It could be anywhere by this time." He tossed the sprig aside and swung into his saddle. "Find me that carpenter."

"As soon as your brother is out of danger."

Robert Overton wheeled his horse around and rode off without answering.

By evening, Catherine had harvested what she could from her garth and sat for supper with the others in the refectory. "Will he recover?" asked Christina.

Catherine drank. "The signs are bad."

"How many days have we before the soldiers return?" Veronica asked.

"Two of them have died already, Robert says. Their clerk and an Augmentations man. They will stay away until the disease clears off. I think Robert will, too," said Catherine.

Christina's eyes widened at this. "Perhaps we can send word that the pox has taken over the village and they will forget about us in time. Time enough for the king to come to his senses. We will have a chance to send word to the queen."

Veronica sputtered wine across her plate. "Christina Havens, I have heard you predict many an unlikely turn of events, but this is the wildest yet. You think Robert Overton will forget that the land has been promised to him?"

"He seems to have forgotten his brother already." Christina poured Veronica another cup and pushed it toward her with one finger.

"Brothers cost money. Land increases money," said Veronica. "He will not forget.

And the queen? If you mean the old queen, she is already forgot." She had her needlework in her lap, and she took it up. "Read to me a little, Christina, won't you? From *The Book of the Duchess*."

The light was still strong, and Christina loved the sound of her own voice reading. She fetched the book. Ann got her embroidery and sat with Veronica, handing a pillowcase to Catherine with a smirk. Catherine couldn't sew straight, but Christina kept insisting that she try. Catherine bent over the work with a sigh, but before Christina could begin, she looked up again. "Perhaps I treat the disease incorrectly. Who else knows aught of physic?"

"You proceed correctly," said the prioress, her finger on the page, "but Elizabeth Aden has some skill with herbs if you need more eyes."

"She must not be allowed near William. She is too heavy with the child." Catherine jabbed her frustration at the cloth. She had never been a patient seamstress in the best of circumstances.

"Too heavy with suspicion as well," said Ann.

"Maud Peters might assist," said Christina, "if you can find her again. The request might mollify her." She regarded the book again. "Though she has probably high-tailed it into the woods by now."

"You cannot mean to send her to treat William Overton," said Veronica. "That woman is mad as a cat with its tail afire."

"She midwifes to the poorer sort," said Christina, "and you see how they multiply. She must know what she does some of the time." She turned a page and examined the illustration.

"That woman knows no more of physic than this," Veronica said, holding up her small finger. "My old grandmother knew more of the gifts of herbs than Maud will know if she lives to be a hundred." She tapped the side of her head. "If I had an ailment, I would have you as my physician, Catherine, or Christina. But that woman? I wouldn't let her touch my wimple to unwrinkle it."

"What if William dies and they lay it at my hands?" asked Catherine. "They called me a sorceress to my face. They will not hesitate to say it in a court."

Christina snapped the book shut and stood. "I would see to him, but you know everything I know."

"You could be taken as well as I," said Catherine. "No, Mother, you cannot put yourself in such danger."

"We are in no danger, Daughter, I tell you. The queen will send her word for us."

Catherine's thread knotted and, when she yanked at the needle, broke, snapping backward into a small dark tangle. She tried to dig out the ruined work with her nails, but it was stubborn and would not come loose. "Damn the stuff," she blurted. She dropped the pile on the floor and sank her chin onto her fists. "If William does not heal, we will be the next ones dead."

CHAPTER TWELVE

William Overton was not healing. Simon Stubbe also went down with the pox, but it seemed to sit more lightly on him, and within two weeks he was mending and lay sleeping quietly in an adjoining room. The tapster and his son fell next, and they both died within days, at the height of their first fevers. The tapster's wife threw old apples at the windows of the Hare and Hound, screaming that the Overtons had brought plague to Mount Grace. The woman went up and down the high road shouting that everyone was doomed unless they turned him out and kept their convent safe from the king.

"He cannot go on like this forever," said Catherine one evening. They were at the table, emptying their third bottle of Spanish wine. "He will have to rise or die."

Christina laughed. "You look as though you don't care which one it is."

"I am tired."

"It seems the people of Mount Grace will protect us," Christina said, a lilt of triumph lifting her voice. "You see, Daughters. God is on our side. Strap William to his horse and send him down the road to Overton House. Be done with him. It is no more than his brother will do to us."

Exhaustion let Catherine's tongue loose. "I will not. He is my charge and I will care for him. And Father John will not allow it. He has bought us some time, Mother, and we need to find that altarpiece."

Christina was milder than usual in her confidence. "I know, I know, Daughter, he has been somewhat of a friend to us. But when that altarpiece is found, we will be the ones who keep it." The prioress rose. "And whatever he has been to us, you might do well to let that Overton go to his maker. He has taken too much of your time."

But he stayed among the living, and Catherine left him sleeping alone for longer and longer stretches. She took one empty afternoon and searched Elizabeth's cottage while her friend sat stony-faced and silent. There was no letter from Thomas and no altarpiece. Maud Peters disappeared from her croft with the dog. Catherine and Ann went through her room again but found nothing beyond old herbs and old smells. Catherine sat at her books in John Bridle's house but could find no other cures. It rained every day, a low-browed, cold shower, and the world seemed to have drawn to a halt. The soldiers would return, they would be turned out, and William would not be able to intervene for them. They would likely be charged with the murder and theft and black magic. If William died, she would likely be called to account for that, too. Catherine fell asleep every afternoon over yet another book, her head on her arms.

It was clear by the end of May that William Overton would need to be bled, but neither nuns nor priests were permitted to perform acts involving blood. The priest walked back and forth in his library, while Catherine sat patiently on a stool, fingering the little surgical knife in her pocket. "I can do it, Father, if you will give me your consent." She did not tell him that she had already learned to use her fingertips to probe open wounds for wood slivers or metal, that she knew what a cracked bone felt like through living skin, that she had already replaced the dislocated shoulder of a mower and braced the broken finger of the blacksmith. "Or let someone in the village who works with animals to do the bleeding, and I will direct him as he works."

"Animals? Catherine, you stun me. Do you presume to equate the human form, created in the image of God, with the material body of a beast? We must not admit a hand that has spilled only the blood of swine and old cows to defile the divine shape of a human man. The skin holds in the soul as it ripens toward perfection, Catherine. Only the most skilled of physicians must pierce it."

Catherine's memory scrolled through the many times she had plunged a blade into the head of a swelling cyst and wiped the pus until the spot was pink and clean, had twisted a loose tooth out of a reeking jaw and let the blood run until the dark matter had worked itself out. She had peered under flaps of loose skin for bits of glass and bone and wood chips and had never believed that the soul was lurking nearby, waiting to make its escape as though it were a rabbit kept locked in a cage while its captor tried to tame it. But she said nothing. John Bridle was the priest, after all.

At last he decided. "There is no help for it, Catherine. The blood must be let, and I am the only one with the knowledge of the body to do it in all of Mount

Grace. You may assist me. May God forgive me for my transgression." And with that, he went to his kitchen and chose a knife and Catherine, wondering on what evidence he had based his conclusion, let hers fall in her pocket. He opened his almanac and considered the position of the stars. When he was satisfied, he slapped the book shut. "Come, Catherine, we must not let the man lie in the grip of the disease any longer."

William was awake but delirious when they entered his room. "I'm cold, cold, someone take these blankets from about my neck. I can't breathe, please. Anyone?" He picked at the covers, but his hands were weak, and he could do little more than lift the edges and drop them again. He called for his dead mother. The pox covered his face, and the windows were curtained and shuttered to keep the deadly air and light from his devastated body. Catherine pulled the door shut and wadded a sheet under the crack. Then she opened the shutters and folded back the covers, washed William's exposed soles, wiped him down from ankles to toes, and held the basin out, indicating that she was ready. Father John took a deep breath, murmured a prayer, and sliced into the soft arch, taking care not to damage the heels. The blood spurted out of the slit.

"Ah, that's good," said John Bridle. "You see? A robust soul, to be expected from an Overton. Good blood, drives out infection. He will fight this disorder, wrestle it down." He then cut the other foot, more assuredly, and the blood arced in a similar way.

Catherine swirled the wide bowl. The blood was bright, signifying health, but the man in the bed was flaccid and pale as any sickly child. Perhaps this meant that a turn in the illness had already taken place deep in the body. But then she looked at the gashes in his feet and doubted this method of treatment.

The next day, the lesions had sheeted William's face and throat, his legs and arms, and he looked like a grotesque, a sickening distortion of a human being. His fever rose again, and he began to cough, a shuddering hack that left him spent, panting and flat.

The day after that, Catherine found lice crawling across his scalp and she shaved off his hair and ordered it burned. She tried to wash the blistered skin, but it felt like cobblestones under her hands. Then, worse, it began to lift under her ministrations like a thin blanket, loosening from the muscles beneath.

Catherine dropped her cloth and ran from the room, hitting Richard Mundell full with her body as she raced from the inn.

"My God, Catherine, has he passed?"

"No, no. It's too hideous. It is like the torment of Hell. Richard, I will give up physic." She was almost weeping.

"Not just yet, you won't. I've come to find you. Elizabeth is in labour."

"Oh Lord, no." Catherine ran, wiping her hands on her apron, and Richard followed more slowly down the road. She could hear Elizabeth's screams before she was through the gate, and she hurried to the woman's side, feeling her belly as she knelt. Elizabeth's coif had slid off, and her masses of copper hair tumbled over the pillow. "Go get Ann," Catherine said to Richard when he showed himself at the door. "Run. I need another pair of hands."

"I have made my shroud," whispered Elizabeth, pulling Catherine close. "It is in the kitchen, on the shelf above the bowls. I will not die and leave my father with nothing for my winding sheet."

"Stop that talk." Catherine passed her hand over the great mound of the child and her heart went cold. "I am here to see you through it."

Elizabeth put her own hand over Catherine's. "I've been unkind to you, Catherine. I've been selfish."

"It is nothing," Catherine said, but Elizabeth did not hear. She gripped Catherine's fingers and pitched forward, a cry heaving from her as her body tightened. Catherine caught her as she fell forward and guided her into the birthing stool in the corner.

"Where is Thomas?" Elizabeth cried out. Her face shone, and Catherine wiped the tears away.

"Hold here. Tight." Catherine fastened the other woman's hand onto the handles of the stool. Thomas had made it solid, and Catherine felt a small lurch of gratitude. She untied all of the knots in the house and closed the windows and doors against any noxious air.

Ann knocked and came in, rolling up her sleeves. She had left her wimple behind, and her hair shone from under her coif like a nimbus around her big head. "Now, what have we?"

Richard was behind Ann, peering over her shoulder.

"Richard, you go away from here," said Catherine, pulling the garments from Elizabeth. "Take a pot of ale. Drink it. We will call if we need you." She stripped Elizabeth and oiled her legs and groin. "Will you knead her belly? Push it down?" she asked Ann. But there was nothing yet to bring out. They raised Elizabeth to her feet, each catching her under an arm to guide her around the room. Catherine tore off her headpiece to move more easily, and they walked her all the afternoon and into the night, taking turns sleeping.

By morning, the infant had shifted position, and Catherine was able to slip a hand inside her friend and feel the nub of the head pushing there. But it would not move. The child was large. Very large.

Catherine's breath stopped when she realized how wide the head was. All she could do was wait for the child to descend and try to draw it out without tearing the mother apart. Her fingers shook as she wiped the sweat from her eyes and oiled Elizabeth as far inside as she could reach. There was little yet to see, and she worked mostly by feel. "We must move her to the bed. I need the light."

Ann lifted the struggling woman, her hands under her armpits, and Elizabeth screamed in pain. They flopped together onto the mattress, and Ann held her shoulders to the meager pillow.

Catherine coaxed and kneaded and tried to ease the head into the birth channel. Ann went for bread and wine when the sun got high, and they ate a miserable meal with Elizabeth moaning from her bed. The rains blew out the sun, and Catherine worked until she could no longer see, Ann holding Elizabeth's head and wiping her brow. Just before the sky went full dark again, Catherine withdrew her hand, wiped it on her tunic, and opened the *Passion of Saint Margaret.* She read all the way to *S. Margaret praying and chanting in this manner, the dragon opened its mouth above the saint's head and stretching out its tongue as far as S. Margaret's heel it swallowed her. But once the sign of the cross had been made that fearful dragon split open in the middle and she came forth from its womb unharmed and without any pain.* Elizabeth lay without motion or sound, and Catherine added a prayer to the saint, *"S. Margaret, who could not be held in the monster's belly but escaped perfect and whole, perfect daughter of God, help me deliver this child unbroken and sound. Bring this child into the world as you brought yourself back to life and thwarted the demons that surrounded you."* She would be the death of this woman and her child, she thought. She would give up physic. The room was so dark she could no longer see Ann, bent over Elizabeth.

Catherine must have dozed on the floor, her head against the foot of the bed, because when she looked again, a blade of moonlight cut between the shutters across the bed. And the head had moved. Ann was fast asleep over the pillows, and Elizabeth was resting on her breast, groaning softly. Yes, it had moved. Catherine stretched her fingers again into her friend. "Ann, wake up." The other woman bolted upright, pushing Elizabeth forward.

"Get her onto the stool."

Ann lugged Elizabeth up. Catherine could already see the little chin. "Here it comes. Get her down. Quickly."

Ann eased Elizabeth forward so that her feet touched the satiny packed earth of the floor. Catherine was kneeling between her thighs. "You must push this child now, Elizabeth. It wants to be born." She could tug the jawbone, gently, gently, then she could get her hand around the head, and when she gave a firm pull, the baby slid free into her hands and glistened in the low light. It was a perfect girl, and Catherine cried out, "She is here. She is whole."

The afterbirth came without effort, and Catherine stanched Elizabeth with a poultice of lady's mantle and shepherd's purse. The mother fell backward, spent, and after Catherine cut the cord, she wiped and swaddled the newborn while Ann helped Elizabeth back into bed, tucking some clean rags under her buttocks to catch the blood. The child had begun to wail, and she carried it back to place next to Elizabeth's breast.

It was past midnight, and Catherine fetched Richard down from the green, where he sat alone whittling pins under the moon. He came in on tiptoes, and when he looked down at his granddaughter, bright red with a pointed head, he laughed. "Well, I am Rich in fortune as well as Rich in name. What shall we name her, my girls? Shall we wait until her mother awakens?"

But Elizabeth's eyes were open. "We will call her Beatrice in hope of joy." She grabbed Catherine's hand. "You will find Thomas at his cousin Barnaby's in Huntingdon, if you will seek him. Barnaby keeps the brewery there."

Elizabeth Aden slept quietly then, and at break of day Catherine trudged back to the convent. She washed herself head to toe in her infirmary washbasin and peeled the sweaty woolens from her body, then fell onto a pallet on the stone floor.

She was inside a dream when Ann shook her shoulder. "Who is it now?" she said, sitting up.

"A serving boy has come from Overton House. Three of their household lie ill and are not expected to live. They wonder that William hangs on to life."

"I wonder at it, too," Catherine said wearily. "Tell him to have all the house drink ale infused with rosemary and orange peel." She rubbed her eyes and heaved herself up. "I will get the herbs for him."

The boy was standing in the porch, his back to the wall. He turned big eyes on Catherine when she came through the door. He was trembling, and Catherine looked him up and down. "Are you feeling a sweat?"

"Feel nothing but a damn ache in my bones. It's the rain. You ride that road from Overton House and see what you feel like. Gimme the physic and lemme go."

Catherine handed over the package and gave him instructions. His pony was at the gate, and the boy was gone in a minute.

The sheep bleated from the fold, and Catherine watched Ann turn them out to pasture. The animals ran, their long wool dragging in the grass. "Who will shear them with Thomas and Nicholas gone?" she called.

Ann met her halfway. "Who will buy our wool now anyway?"

The Mount Grace nuns had always saved their urine for wool-dealers in the village, who bought whatever was not used for bleaching. It was a selling point in the London markets, to declare that the colors of the wool from Mount Grace had been uniquely and miraculously fixed in the water of nuns. Robert Overton had bought Mount Grace wool especially for that.

"Now our urine will be like all other women's and Robert will have to find a way to maintain that reformed water dyes as fast as men's does," Catherine said. The sun glared down on them, cold and bright, drilling through the young leaves.

Ann spread her arms and put her face up to the light. "Pray that we have fine weather. I think if I do not feel the sun on my skin for a whole day, I will fall into a palsy. And now I suppose you must go attend to Master Nobility."

"Yes, I suppose."

Simon Stubbe was up, sitting by the fire downstairs with John Bridle, who shook his head at the mention of William. His room was cold, the man seemingly insensible of her presence, so she opened the shutters. When she laid her hand on the glass, it left a specter of itself. Catherine sat on the bedside, and put her cool palm to his forehead. She pressed hard, feeling for the life. "If these hands can drag that child into the world, why can they not draw you back from the brink? Why will you not heal? Open your eyes, damn it, and be well."

Suddenly, William opened his eyes. He raised a weak hand to her face. Then the fingers dropped and he lay unmoving. His face was rutted and rough, like an old map, and he cast one foot out from the blanket as though his back were tormenting him. But his bones were still straight and good. His hand came up to her cheek again, as if to feel the grain of her skin. "Beautiful Catherine," he said, and something lifted itself inside her belly at the sound of his voice. She thought it felt like pride, and she forced it down again. "No one has been here, and I have lain awake for hours. I knew you would be the first to come. You look like an angel to me."

"The same mortal woman as ever," said Catherine, wrapping her hands around his. "A bit older but no wiser."

He smiled and said he would like to sit up, and in the new light she could see that the sores had shriveled and scabbed, like a sin withdrawing and leaving a memory of its darkness. "Do I want a glass?" he said.

William's face and neck were scarred in dozens of bluish pits, his nose and lips mottled. "Not yet," said Catherine. "I am glad to see you improved, because I need you to accompany me on a journey."

He laughed, but the noise went quickly to a cough. "I may not be able to ride for a minute or two yet."

A warmth rose in her face. "I meant when you are well. Forgive me, it has been an anxious time. Do you recall? When you fell ill—our altarpiece has gone missing and the sexton was dead in the road. The husband of my friend Elizabeth has been named in the murder and she has just given birth." She was rambling, a weakness thought common to women, and she stopped, ashamed of herself.

"You have left the convent, then?" He tried to stand, leaning on Catherine's arm, but dropped back in fatigue.

"No. I stay with Christina, Veronica, and Ann. Your men have fled."

"Robert's men. Not mine." William put his head back and closed his eyes. "I suppose they were afraid of the sickness."

"They took to the road the morning you fell into your fever."

He opened his eyes. "A small blessing," he said, and Catherine laughed a little.

But then she went sober. "Two of them have died along their way. Your brother has brought us the news."

"I am sorry to hear of any man's death." William struggled to stand again and Catherine offered her hands. "No, let me do it. I need to do it."

"I will find you a stick." She called downstairs and John Bridle came running.

"This is a miracle," the priest said, propping the stick under William's hand. "We have performed a wonder, Catherine."

William wobbled to his feet. He was upright. Then he sat again heavily. "And you have not found the altarpiece?"

Catherine, standing beside him, shook her head.

"Nor brought back the carpenter for trial?"

Catherine glanced at John Bridle. She would have to trust them both. "He has a cousin in Huntingdon. We must go to seek him there."

William forced himself up again, hobbled to the window, and studied his distorted reflection. His hands traveled the length of his face, from temple to throat. Then his palms came together in a brief motion, like prayer, and began their pilgrimage down his skin again. "I am saved," he said finally. "And it is your doing, Catherine."

She started to deny it, but he stopped her with his upraised hand. "I will go," he said sitting on the bed wearily. "As soon as I can bear it. If you will have me as your companion."

CHAPTER THIRTEEN

William's eyes were still piercingly black, but as he recovered, they began to wander, as though he were always searching for something. The rains would not relent, and he often stood alone in the nave of the church, staring out one window, then sliding along to another. He wore a beard, but it grew in patches now, and he kept it trimmed short. He had always lacked the facility of easy talk in company. The prioress kept her distance, sitting with him at table in the refectory when he came to visit but mostly ignoring him. Once in a while, she favored him with a reminder to keep her wine goblet filled.

"William is still weak, Mother," Catherine said one evening. "You must not treat him so hard. He has helped us. He means to assist us more."

"He had better get stronger," Christina said. "He has a rougher task ahead of him than pouring drink."

Now John Bridle came to meals with them, too, and reminded them that the wool should be sold before they went. He hired Richard to do the shearing, and the old man complained loudly about the stink of wet animals until William went out to help as he could. The priest sent for Robert Overton's manager, who sent a boy with pack animals instead of making the journey himself. The boy kept his glove over his nose and mouth and would not touch the priest's hand.

Simon Stubbe had no disease in him anymore, but no custom at the inn either, and since he was friendly with the Adens and owned a small stable of horses, he offered to go as William's manservant. Ann could act as Catherine's maid. It was decided that Catherine and William would present themselves on the way as cousins seeking a kinsman to deliver an inheritance.

Elizabeth made over two of her plain wool skirts to fit the women and found hoods and sleeves enough. Leather gloves for riding. "You must keep those rings of yours covered," she warned, "if you must wear them."

Catherine balanced on a stool as Elizabeth took in the waistline of a skirt. "Have you sent Thomas word that we are coming?"

"No." Elizabeth pulled the fabric tight and pinned it. "I want you to see him for the innocent he is. Should I send warning, it will go badly with him if he comes to trial. He could bolt, as well, and then what would you think of him?"

A clear morning early in July finally allowed their departure. Christina called Catherine into her chamber. "When you find Thomas Aden, you must tell him that you went to find him with my permission. Can you remember to say that? Say that I know where you have gone."

"Do you think he will confess if I do?"

"Thomas Aden's mind is a mystery to me," said Christina. "Just remember what I have told you."

"It is easy enough. Perhaps it will persuade him to tell the truth."

"Perhaps." She patted Catherine's chest. "You have your locket?"

"Always." Catherine withdrew the silver necklace from her shift.

"You must show her Grace. Remind her that it was her gift to you." Christina opened the case. "The likenesses are still fresh."

Catherine took the locket from Christina's hand and gazed at the miniatures of the queen and her daughter Mary. "I have scarcely opened it in all these years for fear of ruining the images."

"Very good. Now come here and study this." The prioress took up a candle and went to her cupboard. She brought out a map, unrolled it on the floor, and knelt. "The queen is at Kimbolton. Here. Look here. It is not far. You may ride it in less than a day."

Catherine hesitated, then got on her knees beside Christina. "They say she is much alone of late."

"She will receive you. I am sure of it in my heart. Remind her that you are a Havens. She will recall your name, even after these many years. Your face. She is still the queen, and when the king tires of his whore, she will return to court. Now. Have you committed the way to memory?"

"Yes, Mother," said Catherine, and they stood.

Christina took Catherine by both shoulders. The two women were almost the same height. "She will intercede for us. You must speak to her. Face to face. Give her this." Christina brought out a letter, sealed with a great smear of wax. "Recall to her mind who you are."

Catherine pocketed the missive. "William will not approve of this. It goes against his brother and the king. He will think I have deceived him for my own purposes."

Christina rolled the map and stuffed it back into her cupboard. "Then travel on without him. Simon favors the old ways. He'll go with you. Beg of her some sign that we are to remain at Mount Grace. It is my home. It belongs to me. It has always belonged to me. It will belong to you one day and everything in it."

Catherine felt the fine vellum with her fingertips and finally she nodded. "I will do what I can."

Simon had ponies for the women and his own cob for himself. William's horse was getting fat in the stable, but he chomped at the bit, ready for exercise. Catherine had gathered some of her herbs in a bag, and Christina walked her out, where the others waited, Ann looking askance at her pony. The prioress raised her voice. "You must look in Thomas Aden's eyes when you tell him what is suspected. If he cannot meet your gaze, you may be sure he has secreted our Mother. Or sold Her. You may tell him we have buried Nicholas Hale with our own hands. Watch his eyes at that news." She nodded as though the matter were already settled.

John Bridle was looking at the sky. It promised to be the first fine day in a week, but the dawn was barely showing yet. "You had better ride while God favors you."

Veronica stood by until they were ready. "I have something for you to deliver on your travels, if you can," she said, holding out a letter to Catherine. "It is addressed to my niece in Lynn. Will you see that it goes in that direction?" She pulled Catherine in for a fierce hug. "I don't know whether she still bides there. I can't say whether she still lives. But take the message if you will."

Catherine slid it in with Christina's. "I will do everything in my power."

"Well, coz," said William, tying the bag onto the back of her saddle. "The road beckons." He handed Catherine onto the pony and swung onto his own horse with a slight grimace.

"You keep a watch on that fellow," said Simon Stubbe to Ann, taking up his reins. "He likes to nip."

The road was harder on William than the others, but he made no complaint as they rode south. The clouds rolled in by mid-morning and rain spat down now and then, for one hour pouring viciously as they waited in an empty barn. Ann fought with her steed, who preferred to graze than walk, and Simon finally took one of her reins and yanked the beast along while Ann cursed.

William and Catherine rode in front, and as they came through a showery canopy of trees, he slowed and watched the water drops through the shuffling leaves. "What have you decided to do when this business is ended?"

"I have decided nothing." Catherine glanced at him without turning her head. The gabled hood felt soft and she pushed it back a little to see more widely. "Mother Christina and Veronica are determined not to take the oath. They have cared for me all my life. I have no other family. I was a foundling, do you know that?"

"I see how it stands now," said William. "I think I had heard at one time of your condition, but it had faded from my mind." He put his palm against his cheek, which still showed dull spots. "Your faith has healed me."

"It has not. It was my knowledge of certain cures and the strength of your own body, fighting the infection. If faith had aught to do with it, the faith was yours. But speak of it no more. I will not be allowed to continue in my calling if this new order of things persists."

"But you sat with me. Simon told me, you came day and night with no thought of your own strength."

"I study physic. It is my calling. It has been. I tell you, speak of it no more."

"A calling. For a woman. Luther says women should be called to bear children and look after their husbands."

Catherine laughed bitterly. "I expect that serves him right nicely. It is a sentence that does not sit well in my books. You are turned Lutheran then?"

"No, not I. The king will take the head off a Lutheran as fast as he will a priest." William studied her and grinned wickedly. "Will you not take a husband then?"

"A husband of clay? I had not thought to. It would mean putting my neck to a yoke I am not trained for." She touched the strange headgear. "Though I like the clothes well enough."

"They are just words, Catherine," he said, suddenly serious. "The succession, I mean. Men swear all sorts of things to keep their heads on their shoulders."

"If words mean nothing, then why be required to speak them at all?"

"The king requires it."

"I speak the words that I require, not the king."

"Not the Pope in Rome?"

"We are a long way from Rome, William, and I know of the corruptions Luther speaks against. I have heard from John Bridle and Mother Christina of the reasons for reform. But we are a long way from London, as well. We have done as we thought best at Mount Grace and have been our own mistresses in our daily affairs. You have seen what most women's lives consist of—mending and washing and wiping up dirty children. I do these things, as well, but I also read and write and tend my garden and study what grows in it. Can you tell me I will better invest my talents as a wife? Can you tell me Luther would leave me be to do my studies and tend illnesses such as yours? Would the king let me live so? No, I will be hounded and hanged for a witch if I walk the path God has led me down. It is not to be borne."

He was silent at that, and they rode along, side by side, listening to distant thunder and, closer, Ann consigning her pony's soul to eternal flames.

The first long day brought them as far as Doncaster, and Simon Stubbe was able to secure them two rooms. Catherine and Ann said they would rest and shake the mud from their clothes, and William said he would walk the high street. Catherine, removing the hood carefully, watched him from their window, making his slow way. Then she pulled off her skirt and sleeves and flopped onto the bed in her shift and cap, throwing her arm over her eyes. "You will be the death of that pony."

Ann blew through her nose. "I would throttle him with my bare hands if I had another." She undressed and lay next to Catherine. "I can still feel his spine, the damn skinny thing." She rubbed the insides of her thighs and Catherine giggled. "Easy for you to make mirth. You've got a nice plump one and a handsome man riding beside you. I have a bedeviled stick to ride and a twitching jester to drag it down the road."

They fell asleep laughing, and it was full dark when they woke. The scent of meat was on the air, and they pulled on their skirts, Ann tying Catherine up and showing her again how to arrange the hood. William and Simon were already at table, and they poured wine when the women appeared. "I thought you would sleep until dawn," said William.

"I could have, but my stomach says different," said Ann. She put her hand on it and they all heard the grumbling. "Says it loudly. Here, hand me some bread." She pulled her spoon from her pocket and wiped it clean.

William withdrew a handful of small packages from a bag while they ate. "The shops here are grand," he said, pushing them across. "If you will be fine ladies, you will need to learn to browse." He had brought them a packet of colorful buttons and two fans, some beeswax candles, and soap scented with lavender.

"No one has ever accused me of being fine," said Ann, putting her nose to the soap.

For Catherine he had another, larger package. Quills and a pile of loose sheets of creamy rag paper, wrapped in soft washed linen. A twist of twine and two covers of leather so soft they felt like fabric. She lifted one of the snowy blank pages and sniffed it.

"It is for recording your receipts," he said without looking up from his meat.

Simon Stubbe went to the door. "There's a storm blowing in again. The moon hides her face already."

The women went to their room and undressed while the thunder boomed far off like a distant war. Ann soon fell asleep, but Catherine was alert. Lightning kindled the walls and floor, and she sat up, broad awake, watching the twisting light and thinking of the court. She fetched the new paper and held it in her lap, letting her palm drift over the silky nap of the leather's surface while she remembered. Greenwich, the grand room of the queen. How frightened she had been. How hopeful. And now William. She could see him, at court, bowing to the king. Standing with his hat doffed as Henry drove by with the Boleyn woman at his side. Perhaps William kept a wife somewhere in the south and no one had told her. "Oh," she said out loud, and the sound echoed like a hawk's call. Catherine laid the writing materials aside and went to the door to listen for footsteps. The thunder sounded again, and when she turned, Ann stood there, big as a ghost, and she let out a short high shriek.

Ann whispered, "I thought I heard you rise."

"Ann, you scared the life out of me." Catherine put her hands on her knees. "I have made use of the chamber pot already, thank God."

Ann laughed softly. "Why are you not sleeping?"

Catherine straightened up and shoved a finger under her coif to scratch her head. "I am wakeful as any watchman."

"What ails you?"

"William's conversation has me thinking about that time Mother and Father John took me to the queen. Your man was still living then, was he not?"

"I recall when you went. Everyone so hopeful for your prospects."

"It's all nothing now. I have known it for a long time. But my mind runs over our words again and again. My heart goes like a mouse in a cage when I talk to him. I cannot put a name to my feelings."

"Ah, Catherine. God has made you a woman." She put her hand on Catherine's shoulder and smiled. "It's no great sin."

"What do you mean to say?" said Catherine, but Ann just smiled and shook her head.

They stood by the window for a while, but there was nothing to see but the darkness. "Do you know where you will go?" Ann asked.

"No. William asked me the same question as we rode along today. Mother will refuse to the last. You know she will. Veronica as well. And I will not leave them to answer charges by themselves."

"And what will become of you then?"

"There is nowhere for my skills. We will be in danger if we lift our hands. Who can say?" She sighed. "Maybe the king will come to his senses and reconcile with Rome after all."

"You sound like Christina," said Ann, a little admonishing.

Catherine did not want to say, surely the king will die. "Have you thought of buying back your old cow lot? You've become a good baker. Maybe you could buy a shop."

"With what? Our pensions?" Ann snorted out a laugh. "I will never see any money from the king. I think it is a lie. No, there is nothing for me. Nowhere. You were the only person in Mount Grace who cared for me in my grief, and I owe you my life for that." Ann tossed her head. "And even if there were a man who wanted a big old widow with no money for his bed, I would not trust another with a penny."

"It was hard, what he did."

Ann examined her fingernails. Her handsome husband had spent every evening of their short married life playing at cards in the Hare and Hound and drinking expensive wine. When he staggered into the high road one evening and was run down by a farmer bringing his oxen home, no one mourned much. "He wasn't the first man to lose his money at gaming. Nor the first to conceal it from his wife. Nor the only one to die and leave his woman in debt. I just want to be at peace. But I suppose that is not to be, neither. At least you could find someone to marry."

Something outside screeched like a girl, and Catherine jumped.

"A coney," said Ann. "Some fortunate owl has gotten its supper."

"They sound like people."

"Too much so."

"Ann. I have been thinking about William Overton." Ann squeezed up her mouth to keep the smile down and Catherine saw it. "What are you thinking?"

Ann said, "You like him. You see? You could get you a husband."

Catherine rubbed her eyebrows. "I wander around in my head until I am lost."

Ann put her hand on Catherine's shoulder. "We are all lost now. He seems a good enough man. For a man. Get a child out of it if you get nothing else."

"Do you believe Robert will let those men harm us?"

"If they find evidence of our corruption? If we refuse the new succession? If we will not bow to him as the head of the English church? Yes, indeed. He will turn his back and pretend that he never saw us alive in the world."

That sobered Catherine. "How could I marry a man whose brother would put us to the sword?"

"Come on, we can't have talk like this on empty stomachs." Ann creaked the door open an inch, and they sneaked down to the kitchen and found a bottle of wine in the pantry. They took that and a loaf and went back to their room.

Catherine drank. "Do you ever think about hiring yourself out? You can milk. You can stack hay. You did more of that than your husband ever did."

"For wages enough to starve me. And for how long will a woman alone be allowed to do such work? A woman of my age?" Ann put on a look like a black wolf. "You are beautiful, Catherine. And you can read and write. That would be useful to a landowner. And you are strong, stronger than you realize."

"Mother calls me a green girl. And an unmanageable one."

"You are no girl. You are fully a woman. And I am already an old one."

"The Marys are older than you. You are no more than five years beyond me."

"It was a busy five years." Ann drank again and bit off a chunk of bread.

Catherine took the crust and broke it. She ate half and gave half to Ann. "They are all villains. I will not take their oath."

"Nor will I. Nor would it do me good if I did."

"So where will we go?"

Ann just shook her head. "I can make no map of it in my head right now, Catherine." She stood and stretched. "We should sleep if we can."

Catherine nodded. "You go on. I will watch a while yet and try to settle my mind."

Ann patted Catherine's shoulder again. "Stop thinking on William. If you want him, you should have him. Have him while you're young. But have him on your own terms. We can be in no worse conditions, as far as I can see. You will not serve your calling at all if you plague yourself to death over him."

CHAPTER FOURTEEN

The next morning, it was raining hard, and they stayed. Catherine slumped at the open door, watching the sky flicker and crack. The cold, wet summer seemed a judgment on England. William sat by the fire, reading out of Chaucer to Ann and Simon, and she finally joined them.

"You think you can wish the rain away?" said Ann. She had taken some needlework from her bag and bit off a thread with her teeth. "You must be patient, Catherine." She grinned. "Physician, heal thyself."

William read the *Knight's Tale*, and Catherine closed her eyes, imagining herself as one of the pilgrims. She was falling asleep at the melody of his voice when he stopped reading and closed the book. "This next is unfit for the ears of young women."

Ann pricked him in the fat of his hand with her needle. "I am not so young."

He jumped in mock terror and cried out that he was being attacked at his own fireside. Ann laughed, and he yawned, his knuckles against his teeth, and said the light was too poor anyway. "The Lady Catherine will entertain me," he said, offering his arm to her. She took it with her fingertips, and they walked through to the back porch, where they watched the garden bubble and pool.

Catherine's thoughts blackened. God had sent obstinate rains like a plague and they would suffer a bad harvest again. The poor would starve and the rich would get richer on the higher prices. And the soldiers would prosper. If Henry was God's new prophet on the face of this earth, thought Catherine, then the tales of his cold killing madness were fitting enough.

"Tell me your thoughts," said William.

"Ah, I am full of bile to no good use. There, that's what I need." Catherine pointed to some young lettuces that were drowning in the downpour. "Salad greens are excellent purgatives, but, like our souls, difficult to keep from worms. I must check mine every day, leaf by leaf."

"The leaves of your plants or of your soul?" He was smiling, and her face began to burn.

"I am a fool." She turned away.

"No, Catherine. I tease you too hard. Come, your skill is unmatched." William pulled her back by the arm. He bent to look closely at a plant that had overgrown the neat rows and was sending tendrils up between the boards at their feet. "Tell me, what is this one?"

"Mint," she said, squatting to rub the leaves between her fingers. "Good for the digestion."

He had reached for the same stem and he brushed her hand. "I have never turned my mind to physic," he explained, bending closer. They were both getting wet, but she put her hand near his face and the scent of mint from her skin made him smile. He straightened suddenly. "And what do you think of John Skelton?"

Catherine had read the poet but could not remember the words afterward, and she felt her face blushing again. "I find him difficult, though the parrots and sparrows please me. Chaucer's stories are better. Skelton leaves me feeling jangled like a rung bell."

"When I read him, my tongue feels as though it has been tied to a team of horses." William hung the offended part from his mouth and made a jester's face.

Catherine burst out in giggles she could not control. "I cannot understand his conceit much of the time," she admitted.

William nodded. "He writes a cloaked satire, but the cloak is cut too short and I wonder that he keeps his head. He was Henry's tutor when the king was a boy, you know."

"I did not."

"Not so doting in the king's memory that he may not fall from favor. As far as you are from the court and Cardinal Wolsey, you are innocent of the vices he seeks to correct."

"I am not so naïve as all that," Catherine said archly. "I have been at the court myself."

His eyebrows jumped. "You go to court?"

"I said I have been. You will think I mean to boast, but I have been there. It was many years ago. Mother took me to show the queen my script and my illuminations. She thought I would be called into the queen's service. I was but a girl. I remember it, though. We took a barge from Greenwich to Syon Abbey.

There were heads on long spikes on the London Bridge. I could smell their flesh as it rotted."

"You were never sent for?"

Catherine shook her head. "But I can read, William, and I can think. I am not altogether the innocent you imagine. Besides, innocence is selling lower on the markets these days. And truth will get a person's head chopped off. So will knowledge."

He looked at her a long moment. "Someone will seek us if we do not go in."

The afternoon continued soggy and dark, and the women went up early to bed. Ann was snoring within minutes of heaving off her skirt and bodice and sleeves, but Catherine lay wide awake again, trying to will herself into sleep. The rain had faded to mist, but the bed was strange to her bones, and she flipped onto her left side, then shifted to her right. An owl whinnied nearby, and some small animal scratched in the dirt outside. Once as a girl, running back at dusk to the convent for prayer, Catherine had seen a badger's nose poking from a hedge, like a conjuration of her failings, showing its teeth at her. She wondered now if the soft body sliding along the wall was another such creature, journeying only through the nights. She wished the moon were great-bellied and bright, so that she could see out, but it was just a slip of a maid and would act as no lantern to her.

Catherine stepped into her shoes, pulled on her skirt, and, wrapping her shoulders, slipped out. The big front room was empty and almost black, and she let her eyes adjust to the gloom before she tiptoed in. She went to the closest of the south windows and cupped her hand to her forehead, trying to see, but it was too dark. She went to the door and pressed her ear to the crack. She could hear a whirring of small wings and water rushing down the road outside. She turned and saw a figure in the doorway across the room. Her heart twisted and she almost screamed, but when he lifted the taper she saw it was William.

"What are you doing up?" he whispered. "The rain has ended."

"I cannot tame my mind."

"Come sit with me." William put the candle on the table and poked at the embers. A small flame curled upward, and he laid a few sticks on it.

She curled into a chair nearby and pulled her feet under her skirt. "I wonder that you can ride so well and so long. Do the scars not itch you none?"

He watched the fire lick the new wood. "I feel them deep in my skin. Sometimes it is like vermin. I am almost accustomed to it."

"I used up my store of chickweed when you were in the bed, but I will search for some cyclamen root to mash you an unguent. It will make the redness vanish and bring the new skin out."

He looked up at her. "You are the only one who does not draw away from my appearance. Is that how you continue with your work? Do you not see the disease? Only the man?"

"I see a man, indeed, and I see the scars as well as any." He put his palm to his wrecked cheek as she spoke without knowing he did it. "These are the marks of a mortal body. I still see a whole man, for all that. They are the signs of a battle won. You feel them more strongly than others see them."

"You have a mind as well as a lovely face. I have never known a woman like you."

Their eyes met, and Catherine felt a twist deep in her. "I think I can sleep now, William." She put her hand on his face and he gripped her wrist. She pulled back. "I will see you on the morrow." He let her go, saying he would watch a while longer, but as she lay in the bed next to Ann, Catherine felt the movement inside her again, hard. She listened to the house, but it was still and silent. She arched her back slightly, in the grip of something. Not of pain, she thought. It was not pain. It was pleasure. But desire was forbidden. All desire, of goods, of place, of praise, but mostly of the body, of the secret recesses of the body that Mother Christina had taught her years ago to avoid with the eyes, with the mind, with the fingers. Forbidden. Yet Catherine could feel the pull of it, moving within her, and she forced herself to think on wounds and abscesses and childbirth until she descended into a fitful sleep.

They rode on the next day, and Catherine kept her hood pulled close to conceal the sudden retreats and resurgences of blood in her cheeks. The color burned in her face, even when the wind and gusts of rain blew full upon her.

"You are meditative this morning," said William, idling his horse closer to hers.

"I am thinking about your illness. Do your soles give you pain in the stirrups?"

"Your Father John gave them quite a hacking, and they hurt me on the hard ground. But they will do in the saddle."

"I will study on something to ease the discomfort."

"It was you who preserved my life. Robert has wanted me to take up the life of a soldier, and at least John Bridle has saved me from that." He was smiling.

"Father John has books that said you needed to be bled. They recommended the feet."

"So it was not your decision?"

Catherine pursed her mouth at the memory. "I have seldom seen a speedy recovery after bleeding. It is likely my lack of experience, but it is not a remedy I favor."

"It was you who saved me," he repeated.

They were passing through an open space, full of wildflowers, and Catherine raised her hand to one. "Do you see that? Belladonna. It prevents miscarriage when taken in small doses. In larger quantities, it poisons the blood."

"I have heard of its venomous qualities. I did not think it a cure for anything."

"All things in the earth have their good angels and bad," she said. "My task is to sort them and use them according to their better properties."

"Shall we stop and gather some for your stores?"

"No, I can find that near home. But I do spot something we can use." She stopped her pony and Ann bumped her from behind. "Hold him for me," she said, tossing the reins to William. She picked her way through the nettles, plucking stickers from her skirts, until she came to the small stand of pink flowers. She pulled leaves enough and wrapped them in a linen cloth from her pocket.

"What is it?" Ann said when she returned.

"A kind of geranium. The leaves are good for the skin." Catherine remounted and they went on. "Also called Herb Robert," she said to William.

"By the wounds of Christ," he blurted, "I thought you would fetch something to make me well, not mar me forever."

She laughed and took her reins from him. They rode on.

Nightfall found them in Grantham, and the innkeeper's wife tutted over the women, how weary they must be from the road, how sloppy the way. She had a greenhouse, and Catherine sorted through her stores for the cyclamen root. "Have you rosewater?" she asked, and the woman brought out the bottle.

"Your complexion is perfect," she said, handing it over while Catherine pounded the root. "You have no need of cosmetics."

"It is for physic. My . . . my cousin suffers from smallpox scars."

The woman watched Catherine work. "I have not heard of this use. I will see what else I have in my cellar. You rest now and I will make the infusion."

The innkeeper's wife brought them wine in their room, and Catherine and Ann drank it at the little table by their bed. "God, how I need some refreshment," said Catherine, dragging off the hood and tossing it aside. "I am almost sick with the beat of that pony under me." She drank off a draught. "Mine is better than yours, though, Ann. You have got Beezebub himself under you."

"Ach, he's coming around. Put a bridle on the devil and I can tame him in enough time." Ann peered into the jug. It was almost empty. Catherine lay back on the bed, laughing to herself, and Ann said, "Are you well, Catherine? Sit up here and let me see your eyes." Ann pushed the jug aside and leaned closer to her friend. "They are bright, as always. Very bright this evening. You would do well to get some food in you." She poured the last of the wine, a private smile working the corners of her mouth.

"What do you mean?" asked Catherine, putting her palms flat on her cheeks. "I am as always. What are you smiling about? You are a grinning ape these days."

"You were laughing just now. I am only following your lead." Ann narrowed her eyes at Catherine. "Some small joke William has played on you?"

"William rides well, and I am glad to see him in full health, that's all."

"From your excellent ministrations, I have no doubt." Ann drank, though the cup was empty. The jug seemed suddenly to absorb her complete attention.

"I practice while I may. The time for using my talents runs short."

"You may have talents yet to explore, my dear friend." She placed one hand on her waist and stretched her back. "Oh, Catherine, you're young. Like a green tree in a forest of puckered old oaks. You'll see. The body wants its own way. I think I am getting my courses on me." Ann had never given her monthlies more than a grunt and a sigh. "Why does the body not give up this nonsense, eh? I will have no child now. Have we rags upon us?"

"I have a pile in my bag," said Catherine. "Elizabeth is ten years your senior and she has a babe. And after all those years of barrenness. She was my age when they married."

"And you saw for yourself what a time she had of it. She should be on her knees thanking God you were there." Ann took a handful of clouts, folded them, and laid them by the washbasin. "Curse the damn curse." Then she chuckled, nudging Catherine. "But they say a body that doesn't spring a leak now and then is a body that's going to burst itself one day."

When the innkeeper called them for their supper, Ann slapped Catherine on the back and said she needed sustenance. They washed their spoons in the basin and headed down. Simon and William had again beaten them to table, and the wine was good. Catherine drank, her spirits waxing brilliant and bold, and argued with William about the relative uses of contemplation and worldly action. William took the position that work kept the hands busy, exhausting the bestial elements of the body and cleansing the mind for contemplation. Catherine countered that contemplation ordered and soothed the soul so that actions were not distended by wayward thoughts and intentions. Simon was silent, his eyes darting from one face to the other. Ann leapt in on the side of good acts as the true model of Christ. The wine heated their voices and Catherine raised her finger in Ann's direction. "We must aim for a golden mean. Answer me this. Is not the community of men the testing ground of our hands' industry? And is that not why we enter the village to do service?"

"Exactly my point," said William, triumphant.

"But do we not then retire to our minds of an evening and give ourselves wholly over to thought and study? And if we did not, how could we know whither to direct our feet when we step from the convent?"

"All right, I give you your middle ground," said Ann, thrusting her hand into the air between them. "We will serve those in need with our minds and our bodies equally." She moved the hand to pet Catherine's hair. "I think you are best prepared for this," she smirked, and Catherine's tongue froze in her mouth. The blush flamed mercilessly in her cheeks, and, mortified at her loose tongue, Catherine said "Yes."

She knew William's eyes were on her but she dared not look at him. She stuffed a wad of bread in her mouth and chewed. "You see?" said Ann. "She proves her own point. Intellectual debate makes her eat like a haymaker." They cleaned their trenchers without more talk and the innkeeper's wife brought out the cyclamen unguent.

"This is for you, William," said Catherine. "You must rub this into your skin and let it dry there."

He took it, smiling. "I dare not say no to you. And this will make me fresh and handsome?"

Catherine ducked her head. "It will be good for the scarring."

As they prepared for bed, Ann said, "You were on fire tonight. All this rain must be cleaning your wits."

"I am turned jester despite myself," said Catherine, washing her face.

"You are no jester, and you were born for no cloister, neither." Ann kissed her friend on the cheek, flopped onto her back, and promptly fell asleep.

Catherine closed her eyes, but instead of sleep William's face came down upon her, and in her mind he leaned closer, closer, until his lips touched hers. She twitched and opened her eyes, her mouth still feeling the vaporous touch, a trickle of sweat running between her breasts. Ann was deep in dream, and Catherine gently pulled off one of the blankets and lay on the cold floor. She tried to pray, but the regular night sounds of the house intruded, and in the dark William's face again lowered over her own. Her left hand moved stealthily under the cover, over her own body, brushing her nipples and flattening her palms over her stomach, sliding two fingers between her legs to explore the dark place that was banned from her thought.

Ann murmured in her sleep, and Catherine saw the face of Christina, as she was when Catherine's first courses had come. She had run to the prioress, the slick between her legs, horrified that she had been visited with some unspeakable disease. Mother Christina had dragged her to the wash house, saying the sin of Eve had wormed its way through from her soul to her body's most secret opening and would spill there with every moon as a sign of her uncleanness. "It is dirty, most dirty, most sinful," Christina had said, scrubbing Catherine's belly and thighs with a rough cloth until she was red and raw. Catherine rolled to her side and cried quietly, the blanket pressed to her mouth, but when she lay again on her back, gulping the air, hoping that Ann could not hear, she wondered again what a man's body would feel like, pressuring her own down, then open.

In the morning, she wakened from a restless, heated half-sleep, drowsy and heavy-lidded and feeling thick in the belly. "What are you doing down there?" said Ann, rolling over to find her.

"I was hot." Catherine sat up and scratched her itchy scalp. Her hair must be growing.

"I expect you were. Come, the sun is already high and the men will be raging."

Catherine picked at her breakfast, and Ann had already packed their things when a traveller came in, dusting his coat with his hands. The innkeeper and his wife were standing over Catherine telling her to eat more before their journey. William was paying the reckoning, Simon lingering beside him, and the traveller said, "Simon Stubbe, as I live and breathe."

Simon stuttered a few unintelligible notes. "No sir, I am this gentlemen's man," he finally said.

The traveller looked from Simon to William and back again. "You are not no servant. You are Simon Stubbe, the innkeeper at Mount Grace. You keep the Hare and Hound. I know you of old, man, I have stayed under your roof." He examined William more closely. "Are you a gentleman by the name of Overton?"

"My name is Fitzstephens, if it concerns you."

"There is commotion at Mount Grace, I can tell you." He stared again at Simon. "There is a warrant out for a William Overton, of a description much like this Mr. *Fitzstephens*." He jabbed a thumb toward William. "His brother is swearing that he has stolen his property and has gone over to Rome. They say he has fallen under the spell of a witch-nun." He put his hands out. "But I see I have the wrong men. You are a gentleman's servant and you are Mr. Fitzstephens." He leered at Catherine. "And you must be the gentleman's sister, am I right?"

Ann came down with their bags, and Catherine jumped up. "Give me those," she said, running from the building. They were already on their horses when the man came to the door and called out, "Safe journeys now, Master *Fitzstephens*. Careful of highwaymen along the way."

CHAPTER FIFTEEN

Catherine's heart was banging so hard she could feel it in her ears, and they galloped until Grantham town was a dark dot behind them. Her pony began to pant and wheeze, and they all slowed to a canter.

Simon rode up between William and Catherine. "What do we do, sir? That innkeeper heard it all."

"And his wife as well," said William. He pulled his horse up short and let the animal breathe. "Robert swear out a warrant on me? It's not to be believed. I will be found. I must. I will not be taken for a coward."

"But we have to speak with Thomas first," said Catherine, pulling on his arm. "We can't turn back now. He may have the information you need."

"We are within the day's ride," said Simon Stubbe noncommittally.

William looked down the road, first one way, then the other. He frowned, but then he looked at Catherine. "Very well. For now, we ride toward Thomas. For now."

They hastened on, watching over their shoulders for approaching soldiers, but they met no one except tinkers and peddlers and one old woman, who did not raise her eyes from her broken shoes as they passed. The dinner hour came and went, and Ann fished apples from her bag and passed them around without stopping her pony. The sky held back its showers and let them ride on, the two men behind the women.

Ann sidled up close to Catherine. "If they arrest us, it will go hard with Christina and Veronica. They will be charged with aiding us in escape."

"I will deny it. They may rack me if they like, but I will not speak against Mother Christina or Veronica."

"Brave words. Let's pray we have no need to try them." They rode along, Ann glancing at Catherine now and then.

After a mile or so, Catherine laughed, a bit feebly. "You seem to study me. Do you mean to turn cunning woman and outdo me?"

"I do see a malady brewing in you." Ann threw a look over her shoulder and lowered her voice. "But perhaps I speak out of turn."

Catherine eyed the other woman. "Is my condition so clear?"

"You are in a consumption, as I am sitting here beside you," murmured Ann. "You would do well to save yourself, whether you succumb to it or no. Especially in this state of events. You must make yourself immune to any charge of unchastity however you conduct yourself."

"And how is one to do that? I'm unsure even what I am these days."

"You have wit. You have skills. Use them."

"I have always had Mother to keep me safe."

Ann nodded. "The times change. Those days have come to their end."

It was nearing suppertime when they rode into Huntingdon. William directed his horse into a side lane, and the others followed. "We must find Barnaby Aden or part company for the night. Simon, you are the least wanted among us and could ask at the inn where the brewery is. Can you manage it?"

"Of course," said Simon. "Wait here." He leapt from his saddle, slapping the grime from his hat, and entered the door of a shambles. He returned, beaming, before Catherine could count a hundred. "Butcher says there is a Barnaby Aden here, for sure. And he keeps the brewery." Simon pointed down the road. "About a mile on that way. Butcher says he's got some family staying with him, too."

William was in the high road already, and Simon retook his saddle. "Can it possibly be this easy?" Catherine asked no one in particular.

"Knock on wood," said Ann, rapping a nearby doorframe. "Don't blight us just as we arrive, Catherine." She turned to Simon. "You didn't happen to see our altarpiece on the wall of the inn with a sale sign upon it?"

The innkeeper laughed. "No, mistress, I didn't."

The day was fast waning, and they rode straight to the Aden brewery. "If he sees us from a distance, he will be gone faster than you can say John-a-priest," said William as they approached. "Ride up near the hedges."

"We look like a couple of field wenches," said Ann, pushing back her filthy hood. "He may not recognize us." She knocked some of the dirt from Catherine's skirt as they passed through the gate.

The brewery was small, and the owner was at the door by the time they were all on their feet, his wife behind him, on her toes to watch the visitors approach. "Are you Barnaby Aden?" said William.

"That I am, in all my flesh," he said warily, flexing his arms. He had rolled up his shirt sleeves, and in the white linen, he looked brown as a nut, his wavy hair the same color as his sun-scorched arms and hands. He smiled, showing a faceful of teeth tending to the same hue. "And who is asking?"

"William Overton. I seek your cousin, Thomas. These ladies and I have travelled from Mount Grace to speak with him."

The woman fled into the house. "Have you got a warrant to take him?" said the brewer. He was not smiling now.

William shook his head. "I'll do no such taking. The women know him. This lady has delivered Thomas's first child into the world."

Catherine nudged her pony forward. "We only want a word with him. I bring greetings from Elizabeth. She has borne him a daughter." Catherine opened her palms as though to offer the baby.

"I am here," came a voice from inside. "Let them in, Barnaby."

The brewer stepped back. "You sure?"

Thomas Aden opened the door farther and his eyes widened at them. "Catherine Havens and Ann Smith, as sure as rain in May. Look at the pair of you! Have you left the convent, then?"

"No, Thomas," said Catherine, jumping to the ground. She went to him and he held her like a sister. "Elizabeth sends you her love."

He looked them over. "She seems to have sent a pair of her old skirts as well. But you have not ridden here in her clothes to bring me that message."

"Our altarpiece is missing and Nicholas Hale has been murdered in the road. The word has been on you for both crimes."

"Come inside, quickly," said the brewer. "This is not a conversation for the air to carry." He ushered them through the door and bolted it behind them.

They sat at a large wooden table and Thomas worried the grain with his thumb while Barnaby's son set out ale and bread. The evening turned cool and they sat as though they were simple companions, the wind blowing gently through the window. Barnaby called for claret for the women, and he poured it, bloody in the slant light, into pewter goblets.

"England is become a sewer over this reform business," Barnaby said, handing a goblet to Ann. "The king is in the right this far: men of God must not concern themselves with the price of wool or the size of the harvests. They must keep their eyes on the condition of men's souls, not the bellies of townspeople. And they must not sell indulgences to smooth the consciences of the rich, neither." He looked up quickly at Catherine and Ann. "I do not speak of your order in particular, you understand, but in general terms." Barnaby stirred up the fire in the hearth and poked at the flames angrily. "I cannot bring myself to go over to Henry's side, though. And now his men charge my cousin with theft. With murder. There is no fairness in it and they cannot expect to win my love with it."

The visitors sat at the table and drank. "Surely we are enjoined to care for the poor and the hungry, Barnaby?" said Catherine. "How will we do it if the house is dissolved?"

"You cannot, that much is clear. I cannot speak to the plight of the women. But there are priests taking up arms to keep themselves in their luxury. Religious taking up arms. Monks, who are sworn to poverty and charity, buckling swords on their sides. I cannot hear of it without my blood boils. And yet, there is the king, speaking of reform and godliness and at the same time putting his lawful wife away for a piece he's had the sister of. I can't see my way clear of that neither."

"My cousin speaks truth," said Thomas. "You see why I shelter me under his roof."

"The king was named Defender of the Faith," said Catherine. "He is the pope's own king. Our prioress is convinced he will not sustain this break. And we are his people. She says he will not pursue this persecution of us."

Barnaby returned to the table and sat with a thump. "Then she is as mad as the man in the moon. The king has already signed the orders that will turn you out, all of you, and he has made that Cromwell his general in the war against all the religious houses. He does it through the likes of these," he flung a hand toward William, "but Henry VIII's fist is the hand in the puppet, you mark me."

William stiffened. "I was myself raised to be a priest. My family was ready to give me over into it. I was educated for the church. But then our father died and the reforms came. I ride at my brother's command. I have subscribed to the oath of succession because I have been required to do it. I have raised no arms against no one."

Catherine laid her hand on William's arm and he relaxed. "We are so small, Barnaby. So remote. And we are women."

"So was Elizabeth Barton," said Barnaby. "She was a nun as devout as you and they hung her. Stuck her head on a pole like any common murderer. Think about it. That's been over a year ago now. You think the flames of the king's zeal have weakened? Let me assure you, they have not."

"And your prioress is no better than she ought to be," added Thomas bitterly. "I have seen enough of her."

His anger surprised Catherine. "But Mother sends you greeting. She wants me to tell you that she approves of our coming."

Thomas pushed back his chair and strode to the window. "I expect she does. I say again, I have had no part of your altarpiece. Search the building if you want. Search me." He spread his arms wide. "I have no money. Go look at the church. No one here would purchase such a thing. And as for Nicholas Hale, he was at his table drinking ale, fat as a pup, the last I saw of him." His hands were trembling and he crossed his arms. "How did he die?"

"Badly," said William. There was still an edge on his voice.

"Poison," said Catherine. "He died with a vomit and a sweat. I would swear to a draught of monskhood or some such. Or so it appeared to me."

"You think I know aught of such things? You think I have time to brew up potions of an evening?" He pointed at Catherine. "You know more of deadly plants than I do. You and yours. I am no gardener nor no cook. God's blood, his own sister knows more how to kill the man than I do. And Maud would do it, too, if she got the chance." He balled up his fists but did not unwrap his arms. "I will not come back to Mount Grace to be strung up for a killer."

"You will stand fair trial," said William. "I will see to it."

"There are no fair trials anymore," Barnaby said. "You have heard the news from London?"

"What news?" said Catherine.

"John Fisher and Thomas More are beheaded."

"It's not so," said William, starting backward. "Thomas More? The king would not stand for it."

"He stood for it and then sat upon his fat arse upon his fat throne for it," said Barnaby. "And on the same day More lost his head, three Lutherans were burnt. So don't think the words of your reformers on the continent will save you, neither. Our king burns to the right and the left."

"What is the king's position?" said William. "Where is the logic in this?"

Barnaby laughed. "You think the king chops logic? The same day he killed the Lutherans, he had three priests of the true order hanged, drawn and quartered. The same day, man." Barnaby poked the tabletop. "Your king murders Roman and reformer alike."

"Are the nuns at Syon still in their house?" said Catherine.

"Richard Reynolds has been on the block, as well. The house is dissolved."

Catherine's heart sizzled at it. "This king is a butcher," she said to William.

"It is not his doing alone," said William, but he stumbled on the words. "He is . . . he is not—there must be advisors and counselors who steer these courses. Cromwell. The Boleyn woman."

"She leads him on, no question," said Barnaby. "They say he runs along after her with his tongue out. But when it comes to executions, nobody calls Henry VIII cunt-struck." He bit his lip. "Forgive me, ladies. But you know what I mean." He directed his words to William. "No sir, it's not just the Boleyns. Nor them Howards neither. This is the king's doing."

"I have no defense for the king's acts," said William, hesitating, "but the pope is no better. You disapprove the selling of indulgences? I hear the pope signs them by the hundreds without knowing their destinations. Mount Grace may be small, but there are monasteries richer and dirtier than Henry will ever be. There is no going back to the old ways."

Catherine glanced over at Ann, who lifted her shoulders. "What he says is the truth, Catherine. We have known it already."

Catherine shook her head. "It is too much change. It is too fast." She dropped her voice. "But the charges are real enough." She was almost mumbling. "We have been delivered a scourge in this king and there is no getting from under him."

"There is reform outside England, Catherine," said William. "Henry does not own everyone who thinks the church is corrupted."

"I will not go back," said Thomas, as though he had not been listening to their argument. "However they accuse me in Mount Grace."

Catherine looked up, shaking her head. "There is more. We have heard that a warrant has been sworn out upon us."

"Because of me?" asked Thomas.

"Not precisely," said William. "Because we are not in Mount Grace. We have only the bones of the story, but we are marked for traitors and thieves. We cannot stay at the inn. Not together."

Thomas and Barnaby exchanged a look, and Barnaby said, "You will stay here. We will conceal you."

"Who knows you've come?" said Thomas.

"Elizabeth," said Catherine. "Mother, Veronica, Father John." She counted them off on her fingers. "Richard Mundell. Some few must have seen us depart. They may have spoken against us without knowing our destination."

"How does my Elizabeth?"

"She misses a husband for her bed," said Catherine.

"Her father is with her. She will have to play Penelope for a while."

Catherine laughed a little. "Elizabeth is a flesh and blood woman, Thomas, not a figure from a story. But she will bear up a few days longer, I suppose."

Thomas ruffled his hair. "You tell her for me. I am no murderer. You tell her."

"You tell her with your own mouth. Come back with us, Thomas, and clear your name. If there is no altarpiece, there can be no crime. You have a daughter, you know."

His face softened. "What have they named her?"

"Beatrice. After your mother."

"Then she is already happy, and is as well as she can be with Elizabeth. The child does not need a father with a price on his head. You will send them my love."

Barnaby disappeared for a few moments and returned with a small pouch. "Take them this. Not what Thomas might have gotten for an altarpiece, but it will buy some household goods." He passed it to Catherine.

William asked, "Barnaby, would you bear witness in court that Thomas arrived here without that altarpiece?"

"I will swear to it on any Bible," he said.

"May we see the cart you brought?"

"I brought no cart," said Thomas. "Who has said that I did?"

"It was . . ." William began. "I cannot remember. It seemed that everyone agreed you had taken a cart. I was ill."

"It was Robert," said Ann. "He could not have known how you left Mount Grace."

"Robert carries a household with him wherever he goes," said William. "He thinks everyone else does the same."

"Thomas arrived on horseback," said Barnaby. "On one horse."

"That will not answer for the sexton's death," said Ann.

"No. We will have to see further into a solution," said William.

Catherine rose. "We never meant to torment you further, Thomas."

He chewed his lip and studied her. "I cannot persuade me to go back to Mount Grace. Tell your Mother Christina that I will not hang for Nicholas Hale. Or for that altarpiece. Tell her that for me. Whatever I have to say, I will not hang."

CHAPTER SIXTEEN

William was pale with worry, and the scars showed themselves, like blue constellations, across his face and neck. He wandered to the front windows and fingered the curtain aside three or four times before it was full night. He had worn a high collar since his sickness, and Catherine could not see his expression.

They doused the lights and Barnaby put the dogs in the yard before bolting the doors and shutters. They went to their chambers, and Catherine felt Ann's eyes on her as she undressed for bed. A sliver of moonlight cut into the room, and Ann put her arms around Catherine's waist, bunching her shift. "Do you see how you wither? You must take in more food."

"I eat like a cow," said Catherine.

"You are being eaten from within then. Who will trust a physician who looks like a skeleton herself? You put me in mind of Death in the plays. You will have to carry a scythe to your patients instead of a crucifix."

Catherine gazed into her friend's brown eyes for a long time but could not say it. Ann stroked her hair. "You are a young woman. We women are always surrounded by temptations and perils. Please take care." Catherine meant to put on a look of shock, but Ann stopped her. "I make no pretenses to innocence, Catherine. I know what I see. A woman, born in a woman's body and suffered to be here still." She hugged Catherine tight. "Now, I will get me to bed, where I will sleep the sleep of the dead. You will see, nothing will wake me."

Catherine watched a while through the crack between the shutters. Ann's breathing grew deep and regular, and Catherine drifted to the door, placing her hand on the latch, then dropping it to her side. She paced the room, scuffing her toes against the boards, and finally slipped on her skirt and went downstairs, feeling her way in the dark toward the big front room. All was silent, and she moved from window to window, bumping into chairs and tables on her progress. When she heard the steps behind her, coming from the back of the house, she knew who it was. He was leaning on the stick he sometimes used of an evening, and she backed against the wall, her throat blocked by some impediment she could neither raise nor swallow. It seemed to be lodged in her chest, and she placed a hand against her ribs to steady her breathing. Her hands were shaking as she adjusted her shift, then her skirt, and pushed herself straight. He had not moved, and she edged her way toward the stairs.

"Catherine, do not run from me, I beg you," he said quietly. He stepped in front of her, his hand out.

"The others will wake," she answered, but her mouth was dry with the effort of speech. He was close to her and as he moved closer, Catherine flattened herself against the wall again. She choked on the breath swelling in her chest, she could not think to push him away, and then his mouth was on hers. Her body loosened beneath her and the warmth in her belly grew hot. His lips pressed down on her, hard, and he flattened his length against hers. Even through the thick cloth she could feel the hardness of him and the muscles in her thighs trembled. She was sure she would fall.

But William held her up, his arms around her, under her, lifting the skirt and searching under the folds for her skin. The blood rushed in her ears, loud so that she thought a storm had come, and her arms went too slack for any use. She could not think what to do but lie back against the wall and feel his hands working under her garments, up her thighs and finally cupping the soft flesh between her legs. There he hesitated and drew back to look into her eyes.

"You must not," Catherine said, but it was a halfhearted whisper and when he said no, he must not, and dropped his hands, she continued to lean back, her toes digging into the floor to stretch up to his height. "I must not," she said, straightening her shift. He stepped away and watched her. She peered through the slats of the shutters. "There is no rain," she murmured, startled.

"I will go to my bed," he said, and left her there alone.

Catherine hurried back upstairs. She stood vigil a while, and through the dark hours listened for horses, but nothing came. Ann tossed and talked in her sleep, but Catherine could not make out the words. She undressed and lay on her back and closed her eyes, but as she drifted toward dream, she heard a soft babbling, like the voices of distant devils trying to get loose from some confine, and she woke with a start and sat up. It was just the yapping of dogs in the far fields, and she imagined them chasing a vixen or a doe. In the early hours before dawn, she slept, but when she woke her cheek was on the cold polished floorboards, and she remembered a dream of William's body, naked over hers, and she was damp with the dull flame that simmered inside her.

Ann was already up, splashing water on her face, and she came around the bed and smiled. "You were fighting a nightmare," she said. "You tumbled out of the bed like Boudica going to battle." She offered her hand and hauled Catherine to her feet. "Some wars are destined to be lost, you know."

The Adens were at table with William and Simon when Catherine followed Ann down, rubbing her eyes. A boy was at the front door, stroking the slick head of a hound. "Have you been at the watch all night?" said Thomas.

"I have not slept well," said Catherine. She drank a cup of small ale, and Ann slapped her back.

"She has been vigilant as a sentinel, diligent and unblinking. And you see what it has cost her." Catherine was rubbing her face again. "Your eyes are dull as shriveled ponds, Catherine. You need a real draught." Ann poured her a cup of stronger stuff and broke off a chunk of bread, but instead of handing it to Catherine, she ate it herself. "I think you need something heartier to break your fast."

Catherine knew her face was red, and, mortified, she drank off the ale.

"I will fetch a bite to fortify her," said Barnaby, and he called into the kitchen for some beef. A girl brought a platter of cold meat but Catherine's stomach flipped and rolled at the sight of it.

"You must all eat," said Barnaby. "You have a long way riding back."

"Will you go with us?" Catherine said to Thomas, but before he could answer, the boy at the door announced, "There's men on the road."

"Take the horses and ride up into them trees," said Barnaby, pointing over the back field. "That woods is deep and a man cannot be found there."

Catherine fumbled in her pocket and brought out Veronica's letter. "You must see that this gets to Lynn. I have made a promise."

Barnaby took the letter, glanced at the inscription, and nodded. "Go now. Get on out of here."

The saddles had already been laid on the animals, and they dashed across the field. Thomas knew the way, leading them to a small open patch and whirling around. "We can see it all from here," he said, swinging himself down and leading his horse to a large oak. "Tie them up over here."

Catherine's mind was ragged and dazed, but she got her pony fastened to a solid trunk and crept back to the edge of the wood. Below them, three men had entered the front gate and were taking off their caps. Barnaby stood among them, shaking hands and nodding. He led them inside and all was quiet.

"They will know already that you have been there," said William. "People in the town have seen you."

"You are sure there is no warrant for me?" said Thomas.

"I have not heard of one," said William. "It was only ever my task to seek you. The warrant is for me."

"They may think you conspire," said Ann. They waited in silence and when no one showed, she finally said, "What on God's earth are they doing?"

"Searching," said Catherine. William moved to her side and they stood together, his hip against hers. He put his arm over her to lean on the tree, and she could feel the heat of him across her shoulders. She blinked and swayed, her knees shaking. "When will they come out back?"

"Soon enough," said William.

And there they were, in the poultry yard heading for the barn. Barnaby was in front, walking along loose-limbed and shrugging, his hands out and lifted into the air, broadly acting the part of pure blamelessness. He motioned one way and another, inviting the men to look anywhere they wanted. Two of the strangers were in close conference, and William said, "Those are like to be the constable and the head of the watch." He slid behind another tree.

"One of them's the sheriff. Keep yourselves concealed," said Thomas. "They will have their best view from the back door of the barn."

The three men came to the edge of the field and surveyed the wilderness above, their hands shading their faces from the early sun, and the fugitives stood still as hunted deer. "The light protects us," whispered Thomas, "and this woods is well-known to be dangerous for vipers."

Ann twisted her skirt up to her shins. "You might have told us that before."

"Be still," said Thomas.

"There is no viper in England that will venture a bite of you, Ann Smith," said Catherine.

The men retreated into the barn and Catherine's knees went liquid with relief. They retraced their way through the yard and house and out the front door, where they stood with Barnaby, who pointed south down the road, shrugging again. Finally, they mounted up and, at the gate, deliberated a few seconds, gazing toward the south, but decided on the other way, back toward the town.

"Safe for the moment," said Thomas, collapsing to the ground. "And you see, no altarpiece. You may be sure their search was thorough."

"What do we do now?" said Catherine. "We mustn't darken Barnaby's door. They might have an eye on the house."

"I'll ride with you," said Thomas. "But not back to Mount Grace. Not yet."

"We have no choice," said William. "If my brother thinks me a thief, I will answer for it."

"Kimbolton," said Catherine, and they all looked at her.

"Have you lost your faculties?" said William.

"No. We go to Kimbolton. I have pledged my word to Mother."

"The Dowager is there," said William. "You know this. Why have you not spoken of it before?"

"I have a letter from Mother Christina," said Catherine. "She means for us to plead our rights to the queen. I made her a promise that I would not speak to you of it until we were here."

"She is no longer queen," said William. "Her title is Dowager Duchess of Wales. Catherine, I have been charged as a traitor. If I am seen at the dowager's court, it will add kindling to the flames."

"Who will see you? We will separate to avoid detection. I will make my visit alone if you prefer. I will make the entire journey alone if I must. I will not go back and tell Mother that I failed even an attempt. And I must see how she does with my own eyes. If her condition is queenly or no."

"I will go with you," said Ann.

"Catherine, you are as stubborn as any woman I know," said William. "I cannot permit you to ride that way alone."

"Then you will go with me? It is my promise to Mother Christina. I have made it and mean to see it through."

William threw himself onto his horse. "It could mean my head if I am seen."

"It may mean the same if we go straight back." Catherine got on her pony and pulled it around to face him. "Are you a betting man?"

"What difference does that make?" he said, irritably.

"Here is a wager for you," said Catherine. "If we go to Kimbolton, and the queen refuses to give us a sign that our convent is to be spared, I will consider your reform. Not for your king, mind you. For reform."

He brightened a little. "You will subscribe to the new succession?"

"I said I would study the reform. I will see if it changes me. I will need to find a way to reconcile my soul and my mind with the work of my hands."

"That's not much of a wager," grumbled William.

"It would mean altering my life thoroughly. My way of following my calling. So. I offer my life as a balance to the threat against your own."

"You tax my wits," William said, shaking his head. "All right, then. I will go. I suppose I have no choice."

"There is always a choice," said Catherine, turning her pony's head westward.

They travelled through the woods for a mile, then Catherine and William took the road, while Thomas led Simon and Ann across country. "There is an inn at Kimbolton," Thomas said. "Sign of the Rooster and Mare. You will see it."

"Thomas fears something in Mount Grace," said Catherine, when she and William were beyond anyone's hearing. "Or someone." They kept their horses going a steady pace away from Huntingdon, and Catherine looked over her shoulder now and then, but the road was empty.

"Arrest, no doubt," he said, clipping off the words and not looking at her. "The executioner, perhaps."

"It's something more than that. I thought his eyes showed shock when we told him how Nicholas died."

"I don't see a murderer in Thomas Aden. Nor a thief, neither," said William, softening.

"Nor I. Then why did he run?"

"For fear. A man does foolish things when a noose swings before his mind's eye. Any man might." He glanced at Catherine.

"There is much to fear these days."

A pair of riders came along and Catherine pulled her hood tight onto her face, but they went by with a mere word of greeting. The horses had barely worked up a lather when they came into the town and more travellers came into their way, but no one hailed them or asked their names.

"Do you see aught of Thomas?" said Catherine.

"No, but I see the Rooster and Mare," said William, pointing ahead. "I hope there is food."

"Your appetite is strong. A sign of good health."

William smiled and they were friends again. "My physician."

Inside the inn, a group of men sat at table, drinking, in the large public room, and they barely lifted their eyes at the newcomers. The innkeeper brought a pitcher of ale and a loaf with a thick slice of cheese beside it. William examined his knife blade and cut into it. He ate without ceremony, while Catherine said her silent blessing.

"Your lady wife refuses the cheese," said the innkeeper. "She would prefer something else?"

William swallowed. "She has less appetite than I have. She is unused to riding."

"I will find some fresh butter for her bread," the man said and disappeared into the back.

"You cannot maintain I am your wife," whispered Catherine, leaning over the table.

"I cannot be responsible for men's assumptions," said William, with a grin.

She reached across him. "Give me that cheese."

The innkeeper returned with butter and a plate of strawberries. "Ah, the lady has recovered her strength," he said, setting the fruit down.

"She has the fortitude of a lion," said William, taking a handful of berries.

They had ruined the loaf and most of the cheese when the others came through the door. Ann winked at Catherine, and they sat at another table, calling for drink. The innkeeper came scuttling with another pitcher. "This couple here has spoken for my last room," he said, gesturing at William and Catherine. "I have only one other."

"I will bed with the gentlewoman," said Catherine, rising. "And these men may share the other room with my . . . ."

Ann raised an eyebrow at Catherine. "That is most kind of you," she said quickly. "My brothers will be content with it."

"A splendid solution," said the innkeeper. "My wife will make them up for you." He went, rubbing his hands together like a stage miser.

The other group of men paid their reckoning and left. "Did they lay eyes on you?" said Ann softly to Catherine.

"Hardly noticed us." The innkeeper's wife beckoned them to follow her, and Catherine took Ann's arm. "Come, then, friend. Our chamber is ready. And what is your name?"

Fast behind the closed door, Ann fell on the bed laughing. "He is passing you as his wife now?"

Catherine sat beside her. "He was caught by the innkeeper before he could make up a story."

"Mm. Indeed. I think I've heard that one before." Ann sat up and nudged Catherine. "He watches you like a hungry falcon."

"Oh, Ann," said Catherine, laying her face in her hands. "What will I do?"

Ann pulled off her shoes and rubbed her feet. "You will do what comes natural to women, I suppose. Just make sure you are safe from charges. It is no sin if you are his wife. Nor no crime."

"I am no man's wife."

"Times change, Catherine. Times change. And you have wagered with the man. I believe he means to collect."

Chapter Seventeen

The road to Kimbolton was not long. Catherine had fallen into dream as the sun rose and slept like a mower in June with the broad day shining through the window. It was still morning when she came down, but the others had finished breaking their fast and sat waiting, the men pretending to have gotten caught up in a game at cards.

"The sleeping princess has awakened," said Ann as Catherine walked yawning into the room. "I had thought we would have to get a prince to kiss you awake." One corner of her mouth lifted, but Catherine was too muddy-headed to think of a retort.

They left the inn as they had arrived, assembling again at the big old house. It was surrounded by a full moat, and when they loitered at the gates, two windows flew up in the higher stories and women leaned from them, shading their eyes. William regarded the forbidding exterior. "We will not simply walk into her rooms, I assure you."

"The bridge is down," said Catherine. "And I have the letter."

"A letter from a prioress?" said William. "That may go so far as to get you tossed into that water if her keeper doesn't have you arrested outright. We need us a stratagem." He looked around, his eyes finally landing on Catherine. "Can you feign sickness?"

"Why?" Two men were striding across the yard toward them.

"Lean forward." He pressed her back. "Do it now. Ann, you act as her woman. Hold her head. Vomit if you are able, Catherine."

There was no time. The men were almost upon them, and Catherine leaned over her pony's mane, sticking her finger down her throat to make herself retch. Ann patted her back. The men came through the outer gates and Catherine groaned.

"What ails the lady?" said the man in front. He eyed them all suspiciously, his hand on his sword.

"She is my wife," said William. He jumped from his horse and whispered loudly to the man, "I believe she carries my first son." He winked and nudged him, and Catherine wailed. He went to her and helped her to the ground. "Come, sweetheart."

Catherine struck him across the head. "Don't you 'sweetheart' me. I need me some horehound to ease me." She groaned again, dramatically, and Ann hopped down as though to assist her.

William turned to the two stewards. "Have you got any of that, my man? The woman knows her plants and stuff and what may cure her. I see we will ride no further today."

"Where do you hail from?" said the chief of the stewards. They still blocked the gates.

"From Norwich," said William glibly. "We go to my wife's sister, where she will bide for the summer. I am bound on to London."

"What business are you on?"

"My father's business," said William, rubbing his thumb against his forefinger. "He owns a part of some ships that are due. But he lies ill and his business must be mine now. I must get my wife and her woman to the country. Now, have you got that, what was it, whore's hounds?"

The two stewards consulted privately, and Catherine, standing on the far side of Ann, made herself gag again and screeched, "Horehound, you vulgar monkey." Finally, they called back toward the house, and a servant came running to take the horses.

William bragged and laughed all the way inside, and when they were led to the kitchen, he sat with the others until the stewards left them in the care of the servants.

One old woman studied Catherine closely. She eased herself from the stool and regarded her with narrowed eyes, then bent and stretched Catherine's eyelids, one after the other. "You are not with child, girl. What do you do here?"

Catherine took the withered hands in hers. "I am here to see the queen."

"Dowager," said William, nervously checking the door.

"I have a letter from the prioress at Mount Grace," Catherine continued, handing the missive over. The woman took the message but did not open it.

"Wait here, and hold your tongues," she said, shuffling off.

They stayed near the outside door, looking anxiously at each other. "She can do nothing, whatever she may want. You understand," William said. He settled onto a rickety wooden bench, throwing one leg over the other. He looked up at the ceiling and whistled to hear the echo.

"How can you be sure?" said Catherine, pacing.

"She can do nothing at all. About anything. Even her daughter is kept from her."

"I need to see for myself. For Mother. There are still servants about her."

William laughed through his nose. "For all the good that does. I hope that old crone is not bringing the law down on us, any more than it already is." He whistled a few notes again. "In for a penny, in for a pound, as I suppose."

The woman reappeared through the door, waving her hand madly. "Come, come, hurry."

Ann lowered herself onto a stool and said, "I will wait here," and Simon, sitting beside her, nodded. Catherine and William followed the woman up a narrow winding staircase and through room after room. "I can scarcely see," complained Catherine, but their guide continued without speaking until they arrived at a carved door, where she lifted the latch, pushed, and stepped out of the way. "Do not stay long," she whispered as they passed.

Catherine delayed on the threshold, and a woman's voice said, "Enter, if you mean to speak to me."

The queen sat near a hearth, but the air was damp and Catherine could smell old soot. There was no fire, only a moldy-looking pile of ashes, and the Spanish Katherine huddled beside it, a cloth in her lap and a needle in her hand. Two old women sat in far corners, also embroidering, their gaze bright upon the visitors. When Catherine approached, with William behind her, the queen laid down her work. Her hair shone with silver, and her eyes, hung with dark circles, looked deeply bruised. "So you are the foundling of Mount Grace who came to me so long ago. Am I correct?"

"Yes, your Grace," said Catherine, kneeling. "I am much grown since we last met." She drew out the locket. "You gave me a token and I carry it to this day."

The queen bent to the small necklace and wedged it open with her thumbnail. "And do you still practice your copying and illuminations, Catherine Havens?"

"I study physic. I keep my own receipts, and my writing and illumination serve me well in that."

Katherine of Aragon rested her head against the chair back and her eyes drifted upward, far away. "My mother kept a woman doctor once. Many years back. And yet I can see her face as though she were here beside me." The queen readjusted her gaze and put her hand on Catherine's head for a moment. "The letter says you have taken the veil. But you go without your habit."

"Yes." Catherine looked up. "We are in danger at Mount Grace and must conceal ourselves. I fear I will no longer be allowed to practice my calling." She pulled off her gloves. "But you see I wear my ring."

"Your calling." Katherine slid the letter from under her needlework. "You are to be dissolved."

"The lands will go to my family," said William. "My brother."

The queen glanced up sharply, still clutching the paper. "And who are you?"

He bowed slightly. "William Overton. Younger brother of Robert Overton, who is heir to our father."

Katherine nodded. "And he will be leased the lands that Christina Havens' great-grandfather gave for the priory."

"It seems so," said William. He was not boasting now.

"And the goods?"

"Yes," said William. "There is a matter of a missing altarpiece that hangs over us."

"I know of your altarpiece," said the queen, turning her eyes back to Catherine. "It was considered quite beautiful. Quite valuable."

"We cannot determine who has taken it," said Catherine. "And Robert Overton is vexed at us for its absence."

"It seems that your priory has been charged with unchastity and immodesty," said the queen, reading again at the letter. "How is it that Christina still abides there?"

"William was taken with the smallpox," said Catherine. "And the men who came to remove us fled. Two of them contracted the disease and died along the road back to London."

"I see." The queen's eyes met Catherine's. "And what am I to do?"

"Mother Christina hopes you might intercede with the king and prevent our dissolution so that we may continue as we have been."

The queen put her head back and laughed. The loose skin at her neck quivered and Catherine could see rotting teeth in her mouth. "My dear girl, you have travelled a long way for this." The queen cast her hands out at the room. "This is all the realm I have now. And those walls are as far as my power extends. You want my advice? Go home, find your altarpiece, and use it to buy your lives. Put some money in your pocket before you leave, because the king's pensioner will charge you for his services. Then catch the first boat you can to Rome." She took Catherine's chin in her fingers, and Catherine could feel the nails driven upward, into her skin. The queen twisted the younger woman's face to the light. "The foundling, eh? You are grown into quite a beauty." She bent forward. "Yes, you grow lovely women in Mount Grace. Women of talent and great skill." She let go of Catherine's face and caught up her hands. "Flee while you have freedom to do so. And may God be with you, Catherine Havens. Catherine of Mount Grace. Because I assure you that, in this kingdom, few others will."

The queen's eyes fell to her needle again without acknowledging William a second time. Catherine stood silent for a moment, then backed from the room. William shut the door as they departed, and Catherine ran down the galleries in search of the narrow stairway to the kitchen.

Ann and Simon jumped up, but Catherine ran on through and out the door, tearing around past the side garden and toward the front gates. The other three followed more slowly, as they had to gather the horses, and Catherine was leaning against a tree, weeping, when they emerged.

They sat their horses in silence, plodding slowly along until they were clear of the grounds. "You have your answer," said William finally.

Ann was riding behind Catherine. "He speaks the truth," she said, but Catherine did not look up.

"There is nowhere else to seek help. We will have to return to Mount Grace," William said.

"Perhaps the altarpiece has been found," said Thomas.

"Yes, and perhaps Nicholas Hale has risen from his grave to hand it over," snapped Catherine. The words tasted sour, and she sank her teeth into her lip. "Forgive me, Thomas."

"We are all at the ends of our wits," he said gently.

"The queen looks ill," said Catherine. "You should have seen her, Ann, as blue under the eyes as a corpse. She is not long for the world."

"The world has already bid her farewell," said Ann. "I wonder she has stayed in it this long."

"We should travel a different way home," said Simon. He was studying the sky. "We could make Corby by nightfall."

"They will be searching for us," said William.

"What difference can it make if we are taken?" wailed Catherine. "We ride toward danger any way we go."

William said, "It is not far to Lynn. Or the port at Yarmouth. You women could take a boat to the continent."

Catherine jerked her face toward him. "And leave Veronica and Christina alone to face those men? Where will they go? Who will protect them? No, I will not do it."

"Nor I," said Ann behind her.

"I have lost the wager," she added. "I will do my thinking with my feet on English soil."

"Very well," said William, pulling his horse around. "We had better find a road north, then."

They rode on, cutting westward, then turning northerly again, guided by the tilt of the veiled sun. They kept to narrow paths, overgrown with young trees and dappled with light, when they could, and sometimes William and Catherine galloped ahead. But no one halted them along their way. No one even looked at them, and the rain only wetted them once. Catherine's mind worked too much for speech, and William let her alone in her silence, except to direct her when they changed roads. They passed through villages, where barefooted children ran alongside them, waving little wood switches and holding out their hands. They stopped once at suppertime for drink and rode on.

By the time the sun rested in the treetops to the west, they had come to Stamford. The town was still alive with shopkeepers and women with babies slung against their hips, and an inn on the high street boasted a freshly-painted sign. Catherine was almost asleep in the saddle, and by the time she realized they were stopping, the others were on their feet and William was reaching to help her down. Her stomach lurched at his hands on her waist, and she shuddered with a pleasure she didn't seek as he pulled her to the ground. She was so tired that she clung to him and for a moment they were pressed together full length. She seemed to feel his skin against her own, and in the shock of it her knees weakened and she struggled to stand. He backed away as soon as she gained her feet, but she could not meet his eyes.

Catherine had no appetite, but the others ate everything the innkeeper put before them, fresh roasted chicken and a joint of beef, bread, and salad from his garden. The innkeeper's daughter came to watch. "I swear I have never seen folks put away the victuals so fast." She took up an empty pewter platter. "Shall I kill a couple more chickens for you?"

"We did not stop for dinner on our way," said Simon, leaning back and patting his stomach. "We have a long road before us yet."

"Are you all kin?"

Simon regarded his companions. "Kin and near kin. We have a rich cousin who is getting married in York and we aim to be there for the feast."

The girl nodded. "They had better lay in extra butchers." Thomas belched, and she added, "Let me see what we have for puddings."

"The pox has not slowed you down none, either, William," said Ann.

He flexed his arms. "I was wasted to a stick. Do you see how I wax and grow fat now? It is Catherine's doing that my appetite is returned."

Catherine felt her cheeks flare, and she could not help but stare at his body. She ducked her head and busied herself pushing a chicken leg around.

"Catherine studies day and night," said Ann. "She will be a famous surgeon some day. She is a scholar and will not be content with being a mere mortal." Catherine still did not answer, and Ann clicked her fingers under the other woman's nose. "Snap, Catherine. Are you dreaming?"

"Stop," said Catherine, waving Ann away.

"Do not tease her," said Simon. "She is a scholar, indeed, and her mind is as full as her heart. Let her be."

"Forgive me," said Ann. She spoke in earnest and Catherine lifted her eyes.

"I am a poor companion," she said. "I am the one who should ask forgiveness."

"We are all melancholy," said Thomas, as the girl came out bearing stewed apples and custard. The sweets were set in the center of the table and the conversation ceased again.

They retired early to their two rooms, the women being given a boarded-in porch with a dirt floor as every other room was taken. Catherine fussed back and forth, wiping the table and flicking away every speck of dirt she could find. A broom was stuck in the back of a small press, and she toiled over a small hump in the earth.

Ann watched her work. "You will make yourself an old woman fretting over that broom, Catherine. If you think it so bad, call the girl to do the labour. That lump is not so large that we will break our necks on it. A fly would not stumble on it." She cleaned herself in the basin, rinsing out the bloodied clouts from between her legs, then propping one foot on the table to pare her toenails with her hand knife. "I beg you leave off the cleaning. You make me itch."

Catherine looked around. The room was plain but spotless as an altar and she was ashamed of herself. She tossed the broom back in the press, dropped on the bed, and stared at the rafters. The timbers were old oak, gnarled and knotty, like the dark limbs of some protecting spirit. "I could lie here forever."

Ann switched to the other leg. "You are up one minute, down the next. You wear yourself out, body and soul. Your fancy is eating you from the inside." She finished and sat on a stool. "My feet look like an old hen's."

Catherine finally laughed and it felt good. "Perhaps you can peck the soldiers away when we are home."

Ann made claw-shapes of her hands. "I will take out their very eyes." Catherine stretched, and Ann said, "I am full of sprites this evening and they will make me wicked if I do not work them out. I will go downstairs and see if the girl will show me her poultry-yard. You rest. I will not return soon." She put on her shoes and, taking up the basin of filthy water, left.

The bed was soft with feathers, and Catherine put her hand on her breast. Perhaps she was full of wicked sprites too. The queen was not the queen. She was just an old woman working her needle, no more monarch than Veronica. Father John had been right all along. And William too.

But King Henry. Catherine could not bear the thought of him. Under the dark rafters, it was all so far away that both king and pope were as faceless as God. She lit a taper and held Christina's crucifix tight in her hand, but all she felt were the sharp fingers of Christ, pricking the soft flesh of her palm.

Catherine rolled to the floor and put her forehead on the soft bed to pray, but still she failed. All that came was the image of William, and she was without words. She walked a turn around the room, trimmed the candle, and fell onto the bed again. She could hear Ann in the house somewhere, laughing. Where were the men? Catherine rubbed her face, trying to blot her mind's pictures. She pulled off the crucifix and held it a while, but then she laid it aside. Her hands went over her belly and under her skirts. She put her fingers to the secret places of her body, and she knew she was not saved.

A footstep creaked outside the door, and Catherine shoved her clothes back into shape, but the latch did not lift. Instead, a light knock sounded, and Catherine opened up. William stood in the doorway.

"Ann is just gone out with the girl to the poultry-yard," Catherine stammered. Her heart was working its noisy business in her chest. "It is already dark. She is likely back any second." She made for the window, stupidly tripping over her shoes.

"I am not here for Ann," William said, and he walked straight to her, putting his arms on her waist and pulling her to him. Catherine laughed suddenly, an awkward sound that came out of her like a cry. William closed the shutter and her heart

125

clogged her throat when he backed her to the window, dragging off the hood, then the little coif, and running his fingers through her hair. The door was standing ajar behind him and Catherine whispered, "Ann. She will return."

He stepped away and fixed the latch. "That she will not." Then he was with her, wrenching the skirt from her and pushing her toward the bed. Catherine heard the crucifix hit the ground just before he bunched the linen around her small waist and pulled the shift over her head. She watched the top of his head as he worked, and the room was brighter, darker, moving, and then his hands were on her skin, it was hot where he touched, and her mind spun away. His hands were between her legs, and she closed her eyes, hearing through the rush of blood in her head the unfastenings and cloth moving. She felt the heat of his skin against her thighs and he pulled her suddenly toward him, his hands lifting her and his head on her shoulder. Then he was inside her, hard, and she was falling, her strength all undone, and he moved against her and moved against her, then groaned and held her tight and leaned on her, heavy as any stone. Her hand was on the back of his head and she could feel the sweat between them. Her head was gone from her, she was floating, then she was so hot she would burst, she was aflame, then they were in a pile on the floor and he was pulling the fabric down from the bed to keep her bare skin from touching the earth.

Her breath still came shallow. He was heavy upon her, but she slept and he slept, tangled there. A minute perhaps, or a quarter of an hour, until the light in the room settled itself back onto the table and stools and the dark timbers above them. William's hand moved over her bare head and he pushed himself away, moving first to his knees, then to his feet and offering an extended hand. "Will you rise, lady?" he said, and Catherine found herself again, scrambling up and twining the dusty shift around her. She would not look in his eyes, but took up her rumpled skirt and shook the dirt from it. She could feel the wet on the back of her legs and ran her hand down over it. Catherine took up the crucifix and put it over her head. Only then did she look up at William, who was staring down at her with his hands out, both palms up as though he were asking for absolution. "Catherine, have I done aught that you did not crave?"

She shook her head but could not speak. He went quickly, leaving the door slightly open.

Chapter Eighteen

When Catherine opened her eyes, it was morning and Ann lay next to her, thrashing at a dream. Her nightdress was wrapped around her and the bedclothes were on the floor. Catherine sat up and shook Ann's shoulder. "Wake up. You're in the grip of a demon."

Ann flailed one more time and her eyes opened halfway. "What hour is it?"

"The sun is up," said Catherine. "And the men are probably cursing us for lazy cows." She stripped. The basin was full of fresh water, and she washed herself all over, drying with the clean end of the soiled shift. "I have slept like a stone."

Ann stretched and trudged over to stare at the water. "I will bathe at the next stop," she said, scrubbing her head with her fingertips.

The men had already eaten and saddled the horses. William was bridling Ann's pony when the women came out, and his eyes slid to their feet.

"I see you have decided to join us for our journey," said Simon, tying his bags to his horse. "We thought you had taken up residence in the blankets."

"Some of us have difficulty sleeping in strange beds," said Ann, leading her pony out. Catherine's face went hot again, and she reached for her reins. William was holding them, and their fingers touched. She could not but look at him.

"I hope you have slept," he said. "You were much wearied yesterday."

"She snored like a sailor," said Ann. "You could have rolled her to the next town."

The corner of William's mouth twitched upward, and Catherine jumped on her pony. "I feel very well."

Ann smiled and pulled her hood down against the rising sun. "I would say you do."

"We will make it back to Doncaster by dark if we press on," said Simon.

They kept their horses moving at a clip, taking the broader roads now and planning how to arrive. Thomas Aden waxed bold. "I will take off the ears of the constable with my bare hands if he thinks he will clap me into his gaol." His voice rose. "No one can prove that altarpiece against me. No one. And I will brew my own ale if I must. No one will be stirring any venoms into my dinner, I warrant you."

William rode beside Catherine, his face sober. "They may be waiting for us outside the village. If we come on the main road, they will see us a mile off."

"The way can be seen plain as your hand from the porch room in the church," said Catherine. She looked at William. "Robert will not put his own brother into gaol."

"Men have done worse," said William.

"I will have you at the Hare and Hound, William," said Simon, riding up to them. "They will have to have swords to take you."

"I will not hide," said William.

"I'm just saying," said Simon.

The rainclouds rolled in from the west and hovered over them again, and they bent their heads against the storm when the sky opened up. Catherine pulled her hood down and bent her head, but still she was drenched. Ann rode silently behind her, also hunched into herself. They stopped quickly at midday for food, and the afternoon grew hot, hot as chastisement. The road steamed and thickened, and the animals struggled to lift their hooves, but still they pressed on.

They came into Doncaster at suppertime, and when William slowed, Simon and Thomas rode up on either side of him. Ann was next to Catherine. "We have ridden like bandits," Ann said. "I can still see my hand before me."

They dismounted to search out rooms, separating into two groups again, Ann and Catherine with Thomas and Simon with William. Simon took a pallet in the hayloft to prepare the horses at first light, and Catherine stayed in with Ann to sew the remainder of their coins into the hems of their skirts. They worked until their eyes ached, and then Ann absented herself again.

"I need to walk. Tomorrow may bring gaol for us all."

"It's too late to go. You should come to bed," said Catherine, but she knew Ann would say no. Catherine sat by the window, but Ann did not walk outdoors. She was still somewhere in the inn. She should go seek her out, Catherine thought, but her mind struck her down with images of William, of the feeling of him. How far into Hell she had consigned herself she could not determine, and when she wandered downstairs and found him reading to Thomas, she did not turn to go. She nodded at them all, listened a while, then, when he reached a stopping place, she left with a yawn and a nod, saying she thought she would go to bed.

128

So they met again, Catherine stripped, as he would have it, to her very skin, so that she could feel his upon her. The weight of him seared her mind and the heat overtook her entire when he ran his fingertips or his tongue along her bare flesh. He was scarred just a little on the torso, and Catherine looked wholly on him by candlelight as he lay beside her. She pulled at the small hairs on his chest and stomach, passed her hands down the muscles of his arms and legs, took his member in her fingers and stared at the changes in it. She knew of male animals and the breeding of them, but she had never been so close to a man, and had never seen a man full naked. He began to move again in her hands and she wondered that she felt no word of guilt speak inside her.

"Would you anatomize me?" he said, taking her hand in his. "I should know better than to make love to a physician." He rolled to his side and looked hard at her. "Have you done your thinking on the reform?"

"I have thought. I have not decided. They are not just words to me, William, you must understand. I will not be a common servant to anyone. I must have my work."

He lay on his back and crossed his arms behind his head. "I will not make you my whore. I am free to marry." He put one hand out and touched her shoulder, ran his fingers down to her breast. "I am not Robert and I will not shame you." He smiled. "My surgeon."

Catherine's stomach slid sideways and she stared at the rafters, imagining them as newly wedded in their marriage chamber, and soon William began to snore. He sounded in sleep like Ann. "William," she whispered in his ear. "Ann will be wanting to come to bed."

He opened his eyes and blinked. "Let her get her own bed."

"This is her bed."

"I may not have its like again for a while," he said, throwing his legs out and pulling on his breeches. He blew out the candle and listened at the door before he opened it. "I mean what I say, Catherine. I will settle this matter with Robert, and then I will take you away." He slipped out and was gone.

"I will study an answer for you," she said, into the dark. But she lay back onto the bed and decided nothing, heard nothing until she opened her eyes at dawn and found Ann sleeping beside her.

The next day the little band rode almost without speaking. They knew what lay before them, and as they plodded up the last long hill, they could see the men above them, even through the rain that lashed at the gorse on their sides. The constable sat huddled in the muddy road with four men outside Mount Grace and both parties could see the others as the last mile closed between them. The Mount Grace men did not give chase, and William led his group on toward them, Catherine at his side.

"Robert is not among them," she said.

"Nor is Michael Hastings," said William.

"Who is Michael Hastings?"

"He was first of the men Robert brought to remove you. You may remember, he is quite tall and wears his clothes like a dandy."

"I recall him well enough. Do you think the soldiers are returned?"

"They are mostly not real soldiers, Catherine. They are just men Robert has whipped up in his cause." William lowered his voice. "Have you thought what you will do?"

"I must see how it stands with Mother Christina and Veronica. Mother will not be happy to hear the news from Kimbolton."

Thomas said, "Where is Elizabeth? She should be allowed to walk out and greet her husband."

"She has given birth not three weeks ago," said Ann. "You don't want her with those rascals, anyway."

One of the men pointed at them, and William raised his hand as though in greeting. They stopped a few feet short of the village boundary, and the horses all whinnied and pawed impatiently.

"William Overton, I arrest you for the theft of the altarpiece in the sanctuary of Mount Grace church," said the constable. "Please will you ride with me." He backed his horse to make a space for William to join him.

"On whose warrant am I arrested?"

"Mary Margaret Overton and Mary Frances Overton."

"What?" said Catherine. "Our sisters? His sisters? They have not had their own brother arrested. Their own blood. Tell me they have not."

"Madam, they have," said the constable without expression.

"What of my brother?" said William.

"Robert Overton lies sick of the smallpox. He has been inside a fever for near a week. Three of his household have already died."

"And for this I am to blame?"

"Your sisters charge that you waver in the matter of the king's authority and the new heir. That you protect the corrupted women of Mount Grace. That you had men given you to question the nuns and to turn them out and you dismissed those men instead. That you might have used these same men and the opportunity afforded you to seize upon your brother's property."

"I need to seize upon no property. I am no beggar. Nor a thief."

"Bet you done it for a little bit o' cunt," muttered one of the watchmen, and the constable grinned.

Catherine blushed ferociously, but William ignored the man. "Do they accuse me of murdering the sexton, now, as well?"

The constable looked from William to Thomas, whose face was blanched and damp. "You, Thomas Aden, are accused in the death of Nicholas Hale by his sister Maud Peters, and now we see that you have conspired with Master William in both crimes. Come with us." One of the other men took hold of Thomas's reins and led him up to William.

"Where is my wife?" cried Thomas. "Has anyone done aught to my wife?"

"No one has molested your woman," said the constable. He turned his attention to Catherine and Ann. "You two ladies must resign yourselves to the new order. Your absence gives proofs to the charges against your convent. Men will arrive at the church to remove you and the old ones. Robert Overton has sent the orders. You, Catherine Havens, have been spoken for a witch and if evidence is brought forth, you will make yourself available for arrest. You may thank John Bridle that we do not clap irons on you now."

"How long do we have before they come?" said Catherine. Her hands were shaking and she gripped her reins tight.

The constable gazed down the empty road. "Don't know. Can't say. They'll be here soon enough, mark me."

"Where are Mother Christina and Sister Veronica?" said Catherine.

"In their nunnery. I pray they are making arrangements to be gone." The constable was already tired of this conversation and was leading William's horse on. William jerked the reins from him.

"And Father John Bridle?" said Catherine. "What has become of him?"

"He is in his house, where he ought to be. You might go give him thanks for your freedom. And you, Simon Stubbe," the constable said, lifting his chin to look over the women. "What do you do with these outlaws?"

"I ride with them," Simon said. "They are no outlaws nor neither am I."

"Get you to your inn," the constable said, "and stop playing the jester. You will ride yourself into a noose."

Simon hurried his horse down the road without looking back, and William went on. One of the watchmen led Thomas behind the constable. Catherine and Ann were left in the road alone.

"What should we do with the ponies?" said Ann.

"Tie them in the road outside the church, where Simon can find them," said Catherine. They waited until all the men were out of sight, then they trotted up to their front porch where Christina and Veronica rushed out to meet them.

"What says the queen?" Christina asked, pulling on Catherine's skirt. "Are we to be spared?"

"The queen says little," Catherine answered, jumping to the ground. "You should not stand out here." She pulled the prioress inside, and the others followed. In the cool nave, Catherine pulled off the borrowed hood and threw it across to a bench. "Mother, the woman looks sick almost to death. I think she will not live long."

"She read the letter?"

"She did, every word. She laughed at us."

Christina's face flushed scarlet. "So nothing?"

"Nothing but what we can do for ourselves." Catherine took off her outer cloak and squeezed the water from it. "We must make ready. Robert's men are coming back."

Veronica collapsed onto the bench and Christina dashed to her side. "We will find us a way somehow, Veronica. Do not fall into despair."

"Thomas Aden is returned with us. He and William are arrested," said Catherine.

Christina whipped around. "The carpenter is here? In Mount Grace?"

"They are both here, in the gaol by this time. We will have to carry them dinner."

"The stupid gull. He should have stayed where he was," said Christina.

"The Marys have accused William."

"I know well enough. The constable has been here searching for him," said Christina. "Robert Overton is in a fever. He sent a boy here for physic." She patted Veronica on the shoulder. "I have sent him a draught that will cure his sickness." Veronica glanced up, and Christina touched her again.

"The constable says it is the pox," said Catherine, "and that others have died already."

"It is God's judgment in either case. I will take the men their dinner. You and Ann bathe and put on fresh clothes. You stink like pig-women. Come with me, Veronica."

132

"We must see Elizabeth Aden first," said Catherine, retrieving the hood and shaking it out. "We would wear dry garments if you have them."

It only took a few minutes to throw on fresh clothes and their old black headgear. "They all stare," said Ann as they walked the road back to Elizabeth Aden's cottage. "The shutters are closed but I can feel their eyes."

"Let them look," said Catherine.

The rain had left off. Elizabeth's door stood broad open, and Catherine hailed her as they came up the walk. Richard Mundell appeared from inside and ran to meet them. Elizabeth came more slowly, the child bundled in her arms. "Where is Thomas?" she called as Richard hugged Catherine and Ann. "Where have they taken my husband?"

"To the gaol," said Ann. "We would have stopped them if we could."

Elizabeth sat heavily on the soggy threshold, moaning into the child's swaddling. "They will kill him, for certain," she sobbed. "He is a dead man already."

"Now no, Lizzie," said Richard, pulling her up. "These ladies have come to tell you different. Haven't you?"

"Inside," said Catherine, shooing them all before her. She laid the hoods and skirts on the table. "The constable says Maud has signed the warrant for murder."

"She cried him down in the street after you left. Said he poisoned Nicholas for the altarpiece."

"He hasn't got it," said Catherine. "He had nowhere to keep it."

"Did I not say it? Did I not tell you?"

"Yes, you said so and we know it," said Ann. "Maud likely has it herself. Have you heard anyone say that Catherine is a witch?"

"There was such talk after you left. John Bridle spoke for her in the open green. It quieted people some. What charges will come next? People see the devil under their own beds these days." The child mewled, and Elizabeth gave it her breast. "Thomas may never lay eyes on this child." She murmured to it, "Then what will you do for a father, girl?"

"I will go and see how things stand," said Catherine, "and bring you back news."

Christina was at the church door with a pot of dinner for the men, and Catherine took it as she went by. "Stay inside. Ann, will you stay with Mother and Veronica?"

Catherine walked on, and at the edge of the sheepfold, a ragged figure scuttled around the corner. Maud was shutting her door when Catherine caught up to her and called. She stood on the rock and pounded until Maud opened a shutter enough to show her face.

"Back where you came from," Maud growled, pointing at the church tower. It looked like the keep of a fortified castle against the bleak, darkening sky, with one shred of cloud floating behind it. "Go back there." Maud's eyes glittered with meanness. "Go back to your *mother*. This place is mine."

"Maud, you cannot accuse Thomas Aden. He is innocent."

"No one is innocent," she sneered.

"They will condemn him to death. They will hang him and it will be on your hands."

Maud slammed the shutter and opened the door. Catherine thought for a brief second that she would come to the constable and withdraw her accusation, but Maud began to beat at Catherine's head. She ran, and Maud came behind her, Catherine carrying the pot as best she could. At the main road, Catherine, sliding in the mud, almost fell, and Maud brayed.

"You. It's you who condemns us." She shouted, and people opened their doors up and down the road to listen. "Damn this village for that damned church. You," she said, pointing at Catherine. "You're the guilty one. You and that filthy convent. That fraud John Bridle. Damn the earth it's built on and all the poisons and priests it grows." She jabbed her finger into Catherine's face. "And damn you most of all. Things were all of a piece in this corner of the world until you came. You changed things. You think yourself persecuted. But I know how pure you are. I *know*."

Catherine had no words to this. Maud brayed again, tonelessly, and reached for the pot. "Got some victuals for me?"

Catherine snatched it back, sloshing her tunic with the broth. "This is for William and Thomas."

Maud called to the open road, "You see? She takes food from the poor to feed murderers and thieves." She stomped back down the edge of the sheepfold, her long breeches catching on weeds as she went. The braying laughter grew louder and louder, even as her figure grew smaller, until Maud turned the last corner and was gone.

The gaoler saw Catherine coming and opened the door. His clothes were greasy and his teeth were black. He smelled like wet dog. "Got yourself an enemy in Maud," he said, grinning.

"This is from the convent," said Catherine, passing over the pot. "Be sure William Overton and Thomas Aden have something to eat."

He took it and set it on his hearth, toeing aside a pile of broken kindling. "They can't have no visitors. Not tonight."

"Can Elizabeth Aden come?"

"She can come whenever she likes, but she won't be seeing Thomas."

Catherine thought of the coins in the skirt. She had left them there when she returned it to Elizabeth. "Can she buy a few minutes?"

"No visits on the market. Not tonight." He lifted the lid and sniffed. "Constable is taking informations from the accusers tomorrow for the Justice, and the prisoners aren't to see no visitors. He'll be calling on you first light, too."

Catherine's heart tightened. "Me?"

"You. Be ready for the summons, 'cause it's a-comin'."

"Margaret and Frances Overton are here?"

"Can't say yes. Can't say no." The gaoler crossed his arms and pressed his lips together.

"Can they see light?"

"All they got to do is tell the constable what they know."

"The men, I mean. The prisoners. Can they see the sky? Have they got windows?"

"Not tonight. Don't know what good it'd do'm nohow." He dipped his finger into the pot and licked it. "They're dead men already, far as I can see it."

CHAPTER NINETEEN

The next morning, the four women sat with John Bridle in the refectory. "Someone must ride to Overton House and see how Robert does," the priest said. "Only he can put this mess to rights. It must be done now, before the soldiers return. And return they will."

"I have to give my testimony today, Father. It would go better with us if you were with me," said Catherine. "The Marys and Maud speak today, as well."

Veronica and Christina silently listened, and John Bridle consented. "I will sit in the gallery, then ride to Overton House."

The Court of Assizes would not meet its summer session in a town that had suffered smallpox, and no Court would convene again before Lent, but Kit Sillon, a Justice of the Peace, lived in Mount Grace and would hear the charges against the men in the village hall. Catherine sweated, even in the needling rain, as they walked up the road, wondering what Maud would claim against her, whether anyone had learned of her work with blood and open wounds. Kit Sillon claimed to hate Rome as he hated the plague, but Catherine had retrieved the brown skirt and modest gabled hood from Elizabeth and when she walked into the court and took her place, he seemed confused at where his wrath should fall. The chamber was large, and after Catherine and John Bridle, the twins, and Maud entered, people still crowded the doors to be admitted. Elizabeth Aden sat at the back, her hands twisted in her skirt.

William and Thomas were brought in another door, shackles on their ankles and wrists. They sat across the room, and Elizabeth stood to wave at her husband. The twins sat, Mary Margaret with her face in her hands. William's eyes found Catherine and she nodded briefly to him.

"What have you to say for your actions?" Kit Sillon asked the men, silencing the chatter. "Serious accusations are made against you, that you have conspired to steal from Robert Overton. That you have murdered a man. And you," he said, pointing at William, "have acted treasons in maintaining your allegiance to Rome against your king."

"Who charges that I have gone over to Rome?" said William. He did not look at Catherine. "And what am I alleged to have stolen? All I have done is follow my brother's commands in seeking the truth." He shouted at the Marys, "My sisters there, do you mean to see me beheaded for a traitor? Your own flesh? For nothing?"

The twins did not look up and did not answer. Mary Margaret's shoulders trembled. She could have been weeping. Mary Frances's face shone with sweat, and she wiped her brow. Her lips moved but nothing came out.

In the silence, Maud Peters leapt to her feet. Her hood slid off in her haste, and everyone could see her hair. She had taken to hacking it off years ago, and in her breeches and patched shirt, she looked like a mad Joan of Arc. Her head was uncovered except for a smudged, torn coif and she waved her arms. "See what happens to you when you turn yourselves over to their lot?" Her finger pointed south, toward the church. "That convent is a black spot on us all. You wonder that people fall sick?" Her voice rose ever higher. "I know, I know what they bring. They will chain you to their rules, they will take your goods and your coin, and what do they give in return? They give you death. You believe me, I have seen where this will end." She spun and spoke to the people in the gallery. "You will die. You will all die and that priest and his whore will be the ones to bring his God down on you." People began to edge away from her but there was nowhere to escape, and Maud continued her harangue. "Those nuns are women as all women are, they are vain and weak and proud, they wear gold and jewels under their robes. They're not brides of Christ, they're whores. They've got an underground passage to the priest's house. He's had all of them, they're frisky as any bitch in heat." People were looking at each other, and she laughed wildly. "John Bridle will see you all into your graves. He's a son of this town and so you want to think he prays for you. He prays for no one but himself. And those women shield him. They are a pack of lying sluts. They are all evil and they have brought you to this." She pointed at Catherine. "And that one. That one is a witch, black as any demon in Hell."

She was shouting now and Kit Sillon yelled back, "Be quiet, Maud Peters! Have you lost your mind entirely? Christ's wounds, woman, control your voice." The gaoler took her by the shoulder and shoved her down. "Why do you go about in men's weeds?"

Maud looked to the right and the left. No one spoke for her. "I am a poor woman, and I have nothing but what is upon my back. That one has taken my custom and my means of putting food in my mouth. That witch. You have to stop her. I will file a charge. There must be a charge I can file!"

The Justice sat back and folded his hands in his lap. "And what is that in your hair, my poor woman? There are laws against woad-making. Have you a license?"

Maud's hands flew to her head and she realized that she had lost her hood. She began stuffing the frizzy strands under her coif, and Kit Sillon said to Catherine, "And you. You dress like a housewife, Catherine Havens. Have you left the convent?"

Catherine was shaking. William was watching her, and she took up a handful of the wool. "I wear what suits me. If the convent is dissolved by order of the king, I will accustom myself to it."

The Justice looked from Catherine to William and back to Catherine, but he addressed the entire chamber. "I cannot see how this woman has lured the man to Rome when she has left the Romish church herself." He looked back at Catherine. "Do you subscribe to the new succession?"

"There has not been time," said Catherine. It was true enough.

"Have you concealed the altarpiece missing from the sanctuary of Mount Grace?"

"I have not, and I have not seen any such item in the possession of either William Overton or Thomas Aden. Upon my word, I have done a thorough searching."

Sillon now looked to the Overton sisters. "Which of you will stand and accuse William Overton of theft?"

Mary Frances got to her feet, but she was unsteady and she licked her lips. "I . . ." she started, but she leaned over the rail and vomited. "Sick," she whispered. "I'm sick." She fell backward onto the bench, and her sister fainted onto the floor.

William leapt toward her, but two watchmen grabbed his chained arms and dragged him and Thomas Aden away. William was shouting Catherine's name, and Elizabeth was against the back wall, calling for Thomas. The crowd rushed the doors, women screaming and crossing themselves and men waving their daggers as though someone had attacked them, and the room was soon empty of observers, the dust of their leavetaking swirling in the grey light. Elizabeth remained for a few seconds, cowering, her apron over her mouth, then she fled.

"See to these women," said Kit Sillon to the gaoler.

Wiping his face, the man hauled Margaret to a bucket by the open door, where she vomited. Mary Frances lay still on the floor, and Catherine scooted the bench back and turned her over. The woman's eyelids fluttered, and she disgorged flecks of food and drink, though she had no strength, and the awful stuff dribbled down her cheek. John Bridle hovered behind her, and Catherine said, "You must administer the unction of God. You must do it quickly."

Father John drew from his robes a small bottle, then knelt and with the oil traced a cross on Frances's forehead, saying *"Through this holy anointing, may the Lord in his love and mercy help you with the grace of the Holy Spirit."* Then he touched her hands. *"May the Lord who frees you from sin save you and raise you up."* Father John touched her with the oil on the eyelids, the ears, the mouth, and the feet. *"By this holy anointing, may the Lord pardon you whatever faults you have committed by sight, by hearing, by speaking, by treading upon this sorry earth."*

The priest rose from his knees, and Catherine closed Frances's lids.

Margaret had crawled, still retching, into the weak sunshine, where she lay on her back under the cloudy sky, weeping and sweating. She called for Catherine. The gaoler sat on a stump nearby and hung his hands. Christina was in the road walking slowly toward them, and Catherine palpated Margaret's neck and armpits through her bodice and sleeves. Margaret screamed, but there were no pustules or blisters. Catherine pulled down her shift to look more closely. Margaret's skin was smooth as milk, but she twisted and heaved again, pulling herself to her hands and knees to empty her stomach. Catherine shouldered her arm and dragged her back inside. John Bridle knelt at the side of Frances, who lay quite still.

The gaoler followed them in and Catherine asked, "How long have they been thus?"

"They were just as hale as you please right before they come in. You seen it for yourself. The one started in sicking up, and then the other." He regarded the scene in the chamber and backed up a step. "An' I ain't feeling so good myself." He swiped back his slick hair. "I don't want to tend no black death."

"It is not the black death," said Catherine, kneeling beside Frances and examining her as she had done Margaret. She felt through the cloth for growths in the groin, too, but found nothing. "This is something else."

"The pox?" said John Bridle.

Margaret was bent over, arms extended and face down, and Catherine put her palm on the woman's forehead. "No fever. Margaret, can you hear my voice?"

The woman nodded and sighed. "Is that you, Catherine? They said you ran away."

"Who said?"

"The boy." She closed her eyes and leaned back on Catherine. "He said you and William ran away, that you were going to Rome."

"The boy who took physic from Mother?" asked Catherine, but Margaret was sleeping in her arms. "Help me, Father," said Catherine, and they laid Margaret on the cool floor. The desolate remainders of Frances would have to be removed, and Catherine straightened the hands over the still breast.

"What have you to say concerning these women?" asked Kit Sillon, coming up behind her. He was holding a cloth over his face.

"I say poison," said Catherine firmly, looking up at him. "I have not been anywhere near these women before now."

"I know," said the judge. "They were sequestered from you and the other convent women at my command."

Maud Peters began to cackle from a corner, and the gaoler backed away and pointed at her. "She's been at 'em. She's the one, not the nun. It's witchcraft, sure as I stand on this earth. You, Maud. You're the one. You said it yourself, I heard you, you was all afire, saying you'd get you some justice for your brother." He spoke to the Justice. "Yessir. That there Maud, she said William and Thomas should die. Life for life. Maybe she brung the sickness. I got to feeling peaked myself just after she got here. Feel a mite hot." He put his hand to his own brow, then looked at his palm. "She's been at the Marys too. I seen her a-talkin' to 'em."

"Maud Peters, have you practiced aught of black magic?" said Kit Sillon. "Catherine Havens, come here. You know of this woman," the Justice continued. "What do you say to her? What do you say to save William Overton. And yourself?"

Catherine stepped up to the Justice. "I cannot answer for Maud Peters," she began, and Maud snapped her head up at that and glared. She had stopped laughing. "Nor can I understand why she has fixed on Thomas and William." Catherine did not look Maud's way. "I will maintain, however, before God, that she is no witch, that there is no witch in Mount Grace."

"She deals much in herbals, to you knowledge?" said Kit Sillon.

"She did at one time," said Catherine, "but it wasn't William and Thomas who fell here. And her brother had nightshade growing in his own garden."

"I got that from him with his permission," screeched Maud. Everyone turned to her in surprise. No one had yet accused her of keeping nightshade. "He knew I had it. I am still the one who knows of herbs in Mount Grace. She knows nothing. I'm the healer in this village."

"I see," said Kit Sillon. He looked down at Catherine. "So she keeps herbs that can kill."

"It seems so," said Catherine. She took a breath. "But so do I."

"Catherine heals, she does not bewitch," said John Bridle, stepping between Catherine and Kit Sillon. "I will maintain that in any court."

"That will do for now," Sillon said. The Justice squared himself to face Maud. "Maud Peters, your behavior has disrupted the peace of a town that already endures a pestilence that beggars our mortal understandings. You are known to deal in poisonous herbs and you have reason for taking your brother's life. You do not dress in the manner that suits womankind and you deal in unlicensed substances." He beckoned the constable. "You will search her hovel, and you," he said, motioning to a watchman in the corner. "Lock her in the gaol with the others."

Maud struggled and cursed. "You will not hang me for your murder. I will not let you hang me." She spat and tried to bite, but she could not free herself.

Sillon said, "I will slice your guts open with my own hand and hang you with them afterward if I see fit."

She snapped again with her teeth, but the man got hold of her and wrestled her out. Maud was screaming, "You won't, you won't!" and Sillon remained silent until she was gone. Then he excused the others, saying "I will take this matter to prayer. You all get you home. And, John, get that dead woman out of here, will you?"

The gaoler and the other watchman hoisted Frances. "What did she eat before the trial began?" said Catherine.

The gaoler almost dropped the dead woman's shoulders. "She et nothin'. There weren't nothin' for her. Nothin', I say. She et nothin'." He pulled at the body, and the watchman came along, followed by Father John and Catherine, who supported Margaret between them. They passed a small group of men standing in a doorway, and one of them said "more sickness" as they passed. A woman stood at a window. "They's plague in the gaol," she called out.

"This is no plague," Catherine answered, but the woman closed her shutters against them. Margaret collapsed, panting, and they let her rest for a minute before they dragged her on.

Christina came to Catherine's side. "I will carry Margaret."

Ann met them halfway. "Let me do that." She took the feet from the watchman. "You go back to the gaol."

"Take Margaret to the infirmary," Catherine said. "I will have a look at Maud's."

Catherine followed them as far as the sheepfold, then veered off toward the croft. This time, she went around back and found it a few feet into the woods. The pot, with a long stick pointing from it, sat like a cauldron over a small open hearth, and even with the fire decayed and the urine gone cold, Catherine could smell that it was the woad solution. She squatted to pick through the remains of the charred wood, but there was nothing that resembled even scraps of their altarpiece. Maud had been trying something new to make money and a name for herself. It hadn't worked out any better than her work with physic.

Claws scrabbled at the door, and Catherine went around to a window, where she peered through the closed shutters. Maud's old dog was standing guard, but he wagged his balding tail when she pushed open the shutter. Catherine went back to the door and unlatched it. The farrier's shears Maud used to hack off her blue hair lay in the dirt next to the sorry mattress.

Catherine let the dog out. She found belladonna and monkshood enough, but all of it was dried and dusty. She found the nightshade in a bowl, both withered berries and leaves, but it was coated with a film of dirt and it crumbled between her fingers. The pots and dishes were empty, the only food in the entire room a moldy heel of bread and a jug of water with a fly floating in it. This could be me some day, Catherine thought. This could be any of us.

Men and women were outside their cottages as Catherine walked back to the church, hanging sacks of rosemary over their doors and nailing garlic bulbs over the windows. She could smell the honeysuckle gum they'd rubbed on themselves with wax and the sage they had stuffed into their nostrils. Someone would already be making angelica tea, she knew, or grinding dung beetles to make an ointment. They ignored her when she called out, "It is not plague," and she went on alone to the convent and down the walk to her infirmary. Margaret lay on the table, quiet, and Catherine gathered aromatics to make a wash for her.

"How does she?" said Christina at the door.

"She sleeps."

"How were Thomas and William?"

"It surprises me that you ask." Catherine loosened Margaret's bodice. "They looked well enough, for men in chains." She put her hand on Margaret's forehead. "This looks to me like the same poison that took Nicholas. Monkshood is my guess. Maud has a shelf full of it but it's old as Methuselah. I will take the constable down and show him. She's been making woad behind her cottage, and she's blue as a Scotsman."

"She came to the court stained?"

"She seemed to think no one would notice. Will you walk with us down to her croft, Mother?"

"I have no need to be on the road again today. Maud can take care of herself. She knew what the risks were when she began handling such things."

By the time Catherine led the constable and John Bridle back down to Maud's home, the people of Mount Grace were burning their belongings. Bedding, cloth, and rope were being thrown onto a great bonfire in the green, and still more goods were being dragged from houses and set to the flame. Catherine grabbed a basket of woolens from the hands of an old woman. "It is not plague! I tell you, we do not suffer from the pestilence. Save your things."

"Then what is it?" growled the blacksmith. He was tending the fire and he jammed his pitchfork handle into the earth. He looked like Mephistopheles. People stood around him with their linens and thin straw mattresses, their faces slick with grease and sweat, waiting for her to answer. Someone had thrown a cat onto the fire, and the stench roiled Catherine's stomach. She almost wished it would start raining again.

"God is punishing us," said another man. "For keeping them nuns." He pointed at Catherine.

"No," said a woman. "It's for bringing them Overtons in. We've let them put the good sisters out and we see now the hand of God against us."

Catherine studied the crowd. She had thought herself that the weather was God's punishment. Now she saw it clearly. God sent the rain and the cold on the good and the wicked alike. "It is the hand of man, not God," said Catherine. "It is some kind of poison." But few could hear her over the flames and the chatter and the wind.

Purgatory was suddenly on everyone's lips, and they fell to arguing with each other. Catherine and the men left them to their destruction and hurried on to the croft in the woods, where Catherine quickly gathered the poisonous plants and the constable secured them in his bag. "If it please you, Father," she said, "I will go see how the prisoners do."

The priest nodded, and Catherine went on by the great fire, unnoticed. The gaoler, a handkerchief tied around his face, let her inside. "That stink will drive us all out of Mount Grace," he said. "Did the other girl pass?"

"She is still sleeping," said Catherine. Even with the window shuttered, she choked on the thin stream of smoke that flavored the air. "You must let me see how William Overton and Thomas Aden do."

The gaoler's eyes rounded over the cloth. "Constable says no visitors."

"Does the constable know that the Justice has put Maud Peters in prison for suspicion of her brother's murder?"

The goaler thought this over. "I suppose he would know of it."

"If Thomas himself is ill, we may see he is not the murderer of Nicholas Hale. It was he Maud threatened, not the Marys."

"We may at that," the gaoler said. "Wait you right there." He slipped through a side door to the adjoining room, and Catherine listened to the voices down the road. The smell of the fire was stronger now, and she scented more flesh in the smoke.

CHAPTER TWENTY

The gaoler had been gone less than a minute, and he shot back through the door, crying, "Lady, lady, you must come, the witch has combusted in her bed."

Catherine ran after him. The door to the cell was open, and Maud Peters lay in a thinning swirl of smoke. When the gaoler unlocked the shutters to let in more air and light, they could see her clearly, unmoving on a filthy smoldering pallet. The straw was damp and had refused to catch fully aflame, but the air was unbreathable. Maud's dyed hair lay matted around her ears. Her fingers were discolored, too, and she looked like a wind-wrinkled old Pictish scarecrow, bruised and flung into a forgotten corner.

"I couldn't smell it, 'cause of the burnin' down at the green," said the gaoler. "She's done it to herself, lady. It's none of my doin'."

"No, not your doing." A flint and some kindling had rolled out of Maud's hand into the dirt. Catherine touched her face, but Maud was gone. If she had set the flames herself, she could not be buried in consecrated ground.

"No one else around. No, not nobody but me and I've not been back here since the trial let out. You ask the watchmen, you ask them yourself, I was in the front room."

Catherine got on her knees and traced a dry cross on Maud's dirty forehead. She said the prayer for the dead, not knowing whether God would hear her female voice. Or would care. "I will fetch Father John." She covered Maud with the scorched cloth, made fast the shutters again, and, letting the gaoler go before, latched the door on her way out.

The bonfire made a hell of the village. People were now throwing quicklime over their young gardens. The sun, welcome in the morning, was now a great hole scorched in the fabric of the sky, blazing larger and larger until it seemed to have burned an immense track through the heavens. John Bridle was in his house, its glazed windows protecting him from the thickened air, with his Galen and Arnold of Villanova. Catherine knocked on the front door.

"Daughter." The priest pulled her inside. "You see what we come to. Villanova suggests here that we suffer under the possible influence of a malevolent alignment of planets. The air will stagnate and rot if they continue this burning. You and the others need to claim yourselves true Englishwomen. Subject to the king. You must do it now."

"Maud Peters is dead. Come to the gaol and judge for yourself. It is not a good death, Father."

He sat with a thump and, shoving the books aside, gazed out the window. "You see? She warned Kit that she wouldn't let him hang her. What will come next, Catherine?"

"What, indeed? Father, I don't believe Maud had any hand in the death of her brother. Nor of Frances, neither. She was in a rage, but her demon had his eye on us, not them."

John Bridle followed Catherine heavily back to the gaol, and they found two watchmen to carry Maud to the church. They laid her in the nave next to Frances, but John Bridle left, saying he would not speak for a suicide. Christina stood by Maud's side, with Veronica next to her.

"You should pray for her, Christina," said Veronica. "She was driven to this by fear of prosecution. By her hatred of us. If the death of Nicholas Hale had not occurred, this would not have followed. The Justice terrified her to this end."

"I cannot do it. I will not. The woman has delivered her soul to perdition, and she will have to pay the reckoning. There is nothing I can do for it." She left, too, and Veronica reluctantly went after her.

Catherine and Ann prayed over both of the dead women through the smoke and the sounds of the burning outside. By nightfall, the village had quieted. Catherine and Ann remained in the nave with the bodies until the sky was full dark, then they walked back to their dormitory together.

Catherine climbed under a thin blanket. "Mother showed as little compassion as Father John. As little as the king. Ann, I cannot see the road before me since our return. We seem all to have become monsters."

"Monsters," repeated Ann. "I think we mortals likely always were."

A big gibbous moon climbed their window glowing with menace, making ghosts of the curtains, moving softly in the smoky air, and Catherine slept fitfully under its light.

Next morning, the bonfire was still going, and the heat descended upon them. Now of all times the rains ceased and let the villagers burn. Catherine stirred early from her sweat-soaked pallet and woke Ann. "I should see how Elizabeth does this day. This sun feels as though it means to devour us, skin and bones."

"You had better go now, before people are about."

"They don't all blame us."

"Enough of them do. Suspicion could fall on you as fast as it did on Maud."

Catherine could hear Christina behind her chamber door, praying aloud. She put on her brown skirt again, and pulled her plain Englishwoman's hood down against the sun as she hurried down the road.

"Will they hang Thomas now?" Elizabeth said at the door, anxiously searching Catherine's eyes. "Tell me he is safe for the moment."

"We have pandemonium out there and Kit Sillon will have to sort it through. He won't decide anything today, but Thomas was locked up when the Marys went sick. The Justice is not blind. Nor is he superstitious. He will look somewhere else."

"Someone will say he bewitched them from his cell. Or that I did. Maud will say it."

"Maud is dead, Elizabeth."

She gasped and sat, covering her mouth. "How? Are they pointing the finger at Thomas?"

"No, but the death is doubtful. She may have foredone herself. The gaoler found her and he will call it suicide."

"My God." Elizabeth got the baby from her cradle. "Catherine, the skirt—have you decided to leave the convent?"

"I feel safer just now in these weeds." She took the baby and laid it on her thighs. The child kicked and Catherine played with the tiny feet. "What of you? Will you approve the king's changing one wife for another?"

"Only if it will free Thomas," Elizabeth said. "I have prayed and prayed to the Virgin for him. I will pray to King Henry if they require it. I will pray to Kit Sillon."

"William wishes me to reform."

Elizabeth raised an eyebrow. "Only you? Why is he so particular?" She narrowed her eyes at Catherine and examined the skirt once again. "Or do I already have an answer to that?"

Catherine's mouth was smiling despite her. "He . . . he has promised to marry me."

"What? What are you saying? Catherine, he sits under accusation of theft because of you. You can't think his brother will let you marry. They could hang him before the next full moon. Do you love the man? Are you insane?"

"The word has not passed between us. We have had more dangerous oaths in mind." On the wall over Elizabeth's head was a small image of the Madonna holding the infant on her knee. Catherine dropped the baby's toes and shoved the infant back at Elizabeth. An icicle of fear plunged through her and the words came out. "What if I should be with child?"

"Are you truly out of your mind? You have been abed with him?"

Catherine worried a thumbnail with her front teeth. "Yes."

"Surely you have taken precautions, you with your knowledge of potions and waters." The baby cried and Elizabeth held it to her breast. "When did you last have your flowers?"

"William says he will settle the matter with his brother."

"His brother means to have him in a noose. You cannot believe that he will marry you," Elizabeth said. "It will not be allowed. If he is ever freed to ask."

"But what if there were to be a child?"

"Catherine, do not be simple. His brother will not agree to it." She called to her father to come from the back. "We are in need of counsel."

"You will not reveal this to him?"

"Catherine, my father is not too meticulous in these matters, nor is he no hypocrite."

Richard was at the door, scraping his soles with a stick. "Well, as I am Rich in name, I am rich in wisdom, and what of it may I impart to you women?"

"What do you think of this sister leaving Mount Grace for a room in Overton House? An upper room? She says he has promised it."

"Who? Robert?" Richard said, suddenly serious.

"William," said Elizabeth.

Richard took her by the arm. "Catherine. What are you saying? The man may be on his way to the scaffold. Can you see it, now? 'Yes, bring home the nun and we will bed her down here amongst us.' Some people already whisper witch when you come down the road." He shook his head. "Do not deceive yourself. And Christina . . . my God I can't even imagine it. She will disown you even if she has no home of her own."

"She believes she may be with child," said Elizabeth, bouncing the infant.

Catherine was nauseous and she felt her face aflame. Elizabeth finally said, "We know what has to be done."

Richard said, "I will leave you women to discuss that matter, but, Catherine, think of this." She did not look up, and he continued. "You have some authority, you have bodily ease. As you are, you have some small freedom if you bear yourself rightly. Do not go crying this aloud in the streets. Preserve what you have. Do not tie the noose for these people to hang you with. And that is all the wisdom this old man has in him." He trudged back to his workbench.

"When did you last have your courses?"

"In faith, I can't say," whispered Catherine, quivering with shame. "We are not in the habit of marking them. Christina prefers to pretend that we do not have them at all."

"Fut, girl, go, you know what to do." Elizabeth took her by the sleeve. "Go on, check your stores. When those soldiers of the king's return, you must not be found with child. You will not end your life for a mere man. At once, now. Go."

"But if I should decide to accept the reform, Elizabeth, I could marry."

"Who will marry you with your belly sticking out? If William is hanged, you will be alone. And if he is released and his brother says nay, you will be alone. You know what you must do. You do it now. Don't wait until it undoes you."

Catherine, head down, walked straight back. She pictured herself with a baby in her lap. William, riding away, home to Overton House. William, dead in his grave. Father John. Mother Christina.

She would make herself a laughing-stock.

She would be whipped for a whore.

She would be hanged for a sorceress.

William would not marry her. Of course he would not. But she remembered his body, too, and, pausing inside the church, she ran her hand down the woolen skirt, feeling her breasts and flat stomach. Wondering if a child floated there. No matter. If she sent a child to God, the better for them all.

Margaret opened her eyes when Catherine came into the infirmary. "I would like to rest in my old chamber, if I might." Her tone was contrite, but Catherine scarcely heard it.

"Go, if you want. You do what pleases you anyway." Margaret sat up, hurt, blinking at her, but Catherine felt no pity. "Go, I said. If you are well enough to be in your own room, you are well enough to walk there."

Margaret slunk to the door, and Catherine felt a twinge of guilt as the latch clicked on her leaving. But it passed. Margaret was the reason William was in the gaol. "Tell me what I should do," she said to the empty room, but the infirmary was as silent as the nave. She got a stool and reached to the back of the highest shelf, where, there, her fingers touched them, were the sheets in which she kept bracken and the little crock of juniper berries. Dust sifted onto her face as she pulled them down and blew across the linen. She had not found use for them in months, but there was still plenty of green in the fronds. They would do.

Ann came to the door. "Veronica is fallen into a melancholy and I cannot rouse her."

Catherine folded the cloth. "Does she want to go? Cry yea to the reform?"

"Not on her life, she says. It will do her no good, she says. What do you have there?"

"Nothing." Catherine laid the packet on the shelf. "I am going to sound Mother on this question of reform. One last time."

Ann raised an eyebrow, but she let Catherine go by.

Catherine found the prioress reading in her chamber, and she stood before Christina's chair in the posture of a true penitent, head slightly lowered, hands behind her back. She was sure that her offense showed on her face clear as the thumbprint of Satan, but Christina closed her book and smiled. A tiny grasshopper, translucent green, pure and pale, had been making its way up the wooden finial of the elegant chair and Catherine kept her eye on its advancement. Finally it achieved the summit and whiskered the air with its delicate feelers, in an attitude of prayer. And just as it did, Christina lifted her hands to stretch, and reaching behind her, clasped both carved knobs in her fists. Catherine's mouth opened at the motion, but the palms came down too fast, and she remained unspeaking, without petition for the killed animal—such a small thing, after all, Christina would say. Catherine kept her eyes fixed forward, and Christina drank from the wine goblet at her elbow, emitted a small burp, and, discovering the small mess in her palm, wiped her hand on her skirt.

"What is the matter, Daughter?"

"Mother, do you not think of the soldiers? They will return anon."

"Robert is down in his bed. I predict he will not rise soon. We only need time for the king to come back to God. We will be patient. They will not come before he does."

"There have been many deaths of late, with Robert down in his bed."

"It is the way of the world."

"We must make our own way. Sometimes I fear we must bend to the world."

Catherine sat at the older woman's feet as though in a meditative mood, smoothing her skirt and tucking in the hem.

Christina bent and tucked a curl into Catherine's hood. "What troubles you, child?"

The mildness of her tone almost broke Catherine's will, but she gathered herself. "Mother, I have been thinking of late. Sisters are leaving their convents. There is a pension. Father John assures us that the king will not withhold it. What is your judgment on such doings? Can a sister return to the life of a married woman and live that way in felicity? Without warping her soul beyond recognition? Without incurring the anger of God?"

Christina was silent as a midsummer sky above her. Finally, she said coolly and steadily, "My judgment? You ask for judgment? What is this about, Daughter?"

Catherine raised her eyes at the controlled tone. "The followers of Luther believe that the church is corrupted. Others agree with them. William Tyndale, for one. We have read of these misdoings. We have agreed that some change was in order."

"That Luther and his lot will rot in Hell," said Christina, her voice quavering and lilting. Her eyes rested on Catherine's, then narrowed. "Your studies take you to perilous places, child."

"My studies have led me to wonder—" Catherine began, but Christina leapt to her feet.

"Is this the device of that Overton boy?" she said, low at first. Then her voice went up like a whirlwind. "Do not think I have been blind to the way his eyes follow you about. He believes you have saved him and now he means to have you, is that it? You are dull as dishwater. Do you mean to produce an Overton heir? Would you whore yourself to that scarred younger son when you are wedded to the perfect son of God?" Catherine began to quake. She had never seen Christina so furious. "Would you so demean yourself so? And us? You will place yourself in the bottom of Lucifer's boot, my girl."

Christina's face suddenly went white as a toadstool. "Are you carrying that man's bastard?" She grabbed Catherine and the hood slid from her head, but the prioress got her by the coif and began to shake her. "You will confess it. You will get on your knees and confess it. Who do you think you are, girl? You are nothing. You are nobody. Without me and Mount Grace, you are without kin or name, you are without family or friend. You have not begun to pay for the trouble you have caused, for your keep and your education. Whom do you have to thank for that education? You have me. You have me, and you will have no one else."

Catherine was shrieking and struggling to release herself, but the prioress had hold of just enough hair for a good grip, and Christina in anger was a strong opponent. "Are you with child? Have you polluted yourself with that scabbed, that pitted cripple? That younger son? That nothing?"

"No, no," Catherine cried out. It was done, and she would say the words that would save her, whatever they were. "I was simply studying the changes over the sea. Mother, I am innocent."

"You had better be. He will cast you off as easily as he has cast off God. You were better never born than to bewhore yourself in my care. You have no idea what I have done for you." Christina let go and Catherine dropped in front of her. "Now go pray and cease your studies for a time. They do you no good just now."

Catherine ran to the nave. She would pray, for forgiveness, for her courses to begin. She knelt in front of the skeletal Christ and closed her eyes, but she saw only William. Then she looked up again and saw the fleshless figure above her and thought she would be sick. When she'd first gotten her monthlies, she had fallen on her face before the Virgin and had lain there until Christina had come to gather her, saying "Child, child, you are Mary's daughter more than Eve's" and leading her to her bed. But now there was no Madonna, and Catherine prayed to the gap before her, *O blessed Virgin, Mother of God, look down in mercy from heaven, where thou art enthroned as Queen, upon me, a miserable sinner, thine unworthy servant. Although I know full well my own unworthiness, and from the depths of my heart I praise and extol thee as the purest, the fairest, the holiest creature of all God's handiwork. I bless thy holy name, I praise thine exalted privilege of being truly Mother of God, ever virgin, conceived without stain of sin, co-redemptrix of the human race.*

But the more fervently she prayed, the more the hungry Christ seemed to gaze not in her eyes but over her head, at some higher place on one of the pillars behind her. Catherine's eyes travelled the nave, but she saw nothing of note beyond the countless stones of the walls and the broken saints in their many postures of humiliation. She stole back to her infirmary in the silence and communed with herself, a host of juniper berries pounded to a flat pulp, a bloody infusion of the bracken raised to her lips in hope of some private salvation.

CHAPTER TWENTY-ONE

They gathered late for a sullen midday meal, except for Margaret, who kept her bed. Veronica had no appetite and Christina would not look at Catherine. Catherine felt hazy, and the meat on her plate seemed to move under her knife. She excused herself, but, back in her infirmary, she was unable to sort her herbs. She stumbled to the nave and stared at the corpses. They seemed to breathe and she laid her face first on one shroud, then the other. But the bodies were cold, cold, and already smelled like rot and loam. She wobbled up to the sanctuary and appealed to the Jesus there, but he squirmed on his cross, and Henry's middle swelled before her eyes.

Father John came in with Ann and Christina, and Catherine, hearing their voices, hid herself behind the rood screen. Ann asked, "Where is Catherine?" but the answer was muddy, and she couldn't think who they all were, some strangers she had seen in a dream. Frances was carried out, and Catherine slid across to the convent door and ran through her garth, where she could hear someone breaking the earth on the other side of the wall, in the church graveyard.

Maud's corpse was gone when she went back to the nave, but the front door was open, and Catherine went to the road to watch Father John and Simon Stubbe carry the body back toward the croft. The sun seemed bladed, and Catherine dropped to her knees with the sharpness of it. She couldn't tell what hour it was.

"Catherine?" It was Ann, behind her. Catherine jumped up and almost fell. Her head kept turning and she floundered for balance.

"What ails you?" Ann put her big hand on Catherine's forehead. "I don't even know what I feel for. Let me take you to Christina. She'll know."

"No, not Mother." Catherine croaked. "You will care for Margaret. You must wash her with plantain in clean water. You must make her take rhubarb and lettuce to purge her."

"Tell me," demanded Ann, shaking Catherine by the arms. "What have you done?"

"Swear." The word felt soft in her mouth, like a slug.

"I heard you with Christina. You must not listen to her. They will release him once Father John speaks to Robert. There is no evidence against him."

"Men have had their necks stretched on lesser words than Margaret's."

"She has gone to their old room. She asks for you. She's asked for you all afternoon."

"Let her ask to her last breath. She will do what Robert has told her to do, whoever suffers for it. You care for her. Swear to me you will." Catherine stumbled back to the porch and they stood at the corner of the small enclosure, watching the sun crackle down toward the horizon. "Your word is the only one worth the breath anymore."

"You must have sustenance. You aren't well. All this business is breaking your spirit."

"I'm well enough," said Catherine. "I will see if I have anything else that will ease her." They went inside and lit candles against the dusk, but when Catherine closed the door to her infirmary, she administered the poison to herself again.

The next morning she woke feverish and delirious, the dormitory lit with an otherworldly bright light and haloes on her sisters. "She lies too still," someone said. Lie. Lie. The word squirreled away from her and she felt herself chasing after its meaning. When Catherine woke again, someone, Veronica or Ann, was bent over her pallet and the face had grown bulbous and pink, a horrific blossom, and the voice bubbled into Catherine's ears as though she were under water. "What is it? What do you say?" she asked, but the big flower shook itself and went away, returning with a cup and forcing Catherine's head up up up into the vast whirring air where she entered the sun and was flooded with cleansing water, then was dropped with a cold wind blowing in her ears onto the hard and scratchy mattress.

"I fear for her life," said the flower to something dark standing beside it. Catherine laughed at it, thinking she was a child again splashing at the edge of the river. Then her guts turned over and turned over and she was on the floor, vomiting blood and foam. The flower was beside her then, its halo swelling and shrinking, and someone was wiping her mouth. "We must change these linens." It was Ann. "See how she bleeds. And she has beshat herself." Then Catherine lay back and the room was dark.

Father John was there and it was light again. He was a hazy smudge, he was laying something oily across her face. Catherine felt it run into her hair and she shook her head back and forth to get it off. The room whirled and she could not stop the motion, clinging to the cloth at her fingers. The dark smudge was rising, it was huge, a black cloud in the sunlight of the room. It rose straight through the ceiling and was gone. Dark, and in the dark something flapped its wings at her ears, she threw herself to the floor to get away and vomited again. Hands at her sides, lifting her.

Someone was praying, and the convent began to sound as though it had been invaded by the lowest ranks of the damned, the stone walls echoing with high-pitched wailing and weird speech. Hoards of the sick came at her from her infirmary, begging for help. They staggered across her vision naked, their unwashed legs smeared with the filth of their own loose bowels. They spoke to her in unfamiliar tongues and when she tried to raise herself to hear, they flattened her, their faces coming close, pressing her down with their gibberish. She lay on hot stones, panting from exertion, and then she felt someone carrying her back to bed. Someone was massaging her limbs and she cried out that she was covered with boils and they would break. The hands went away, and she implored God to grant her death, her skin swelled and bled and she felt like a decaying body, curled up against the cool stone of her own grave.

Then Catherine opened her eyes again and it was broad day, the air shimmering but soft in her face. Her hair was wet against her flat mattress and she was big with coverlets. She tried to lift an arm to wipe a sweaty strand from her mouth but she did not have the strength. She must have called out, because Ann was beside her, saying "all right now, all right" and lifting the offending hair from her lips. The hand that touched her smelled like sweet milk and Catherine smiled and said "bless you" and Ann dropped her forehead flat on the covers, saying, "You have returned to us, thank God." Catherine closed her eyes and thought, yes, and she hoped she had returned alone.

CHAPTER TWENTY-TWO

Some small corner of heaven opened to them at last, and the next morning the weather turned cooler and dry. The sun withheld its attack, drawing farther away as the day came up like an aging despot. Margaret was walking daily again, though slowly, and she came to Catherine's infirmary and asked for a draught of something. Catherine had lain down on her pallet and startled awake. She walked with Margaret to the kitchen and poured her a cup of feeble ale. The woman's delicacy frayed her temper.

"Catherine, how are you? They tell me you tended me until you fell ill."

"Yes, Margaret," she said coldly. "I cared for you as well as I knew how." She poured a drink for herself.

"And Frances?"

"There was nothing to do. The poison took her quickly."

"And my brother? Would you go to Robert and give him some care? He wastes, despite the tonics Christina has sent. You could help him."

Margaret was still thin as a weasel and ashy-faced. She looked desperate, and Catherine was ashamed to remember that she had been jealous of the twins, their higher rank, their whiter hands, their neater features. Catherine had always been the favorite, and she had always known it.

"Catherine? Would you do it?"

"Margaret—"

"Catherine, no one else can save him. No one." She struggled to sit on a stool, but she was too thin and her balance was bad. She leaned against the wall. "You are the only one. You must tell me yes. I beg you."

"Robert must bear God's will as you have. Mother knows as much of physic as I do."

Margaret tried to leap to her feet, but her legs failed her and she dropped down again. "Catherine, no. He will die. Like Frances. I will have no brother nor sister."

Anger shot through her again. "You have a brother," said Catherine through her teeth.

Margaret held the cup against her forehead. "It is too hard. Too hard. I cannot endure it."

Catherine's chest swelled. "You cannot endure it? Think what William endures. And he endures it at your hand."

"I was unkind." Margaret wept against the wall with racking cries. Catherine touched Margaret's shoulder, but she shrugged free. "Catherine, go from here, please, leave me to myself. Go now." And she raised one hand. The knobs of her wrist bones stuck out like young mushrooms in the woods, sprouting near a rotting and wasted log. "Go," she repeated.

"You could reverse this course. William sits in gaol yet. You could petition the Justice to release him. He has not spoken a word against you. You owe him this. Think what you ask of me and weigh it against what William might ask of you if he were given the chance."

Margaret turned, first shoulders, then hips. "Catherine, listen. I cannot speak against Robert. I live under his roof, and without Frances there is no one between me and him. He is sure William has taken his property, and if he hears I have had the thief freed, where will I go? I have not meant to mistreat my brother, but I am just one woman in the world. Frances was stronger. I would have all of our sisters together again if it cost me all the brothers on this earth, I swear it. But I'm too late. Robert told me that I must speak against William. And that is what I must do. He won't have me back in the house if I disobey."

Catherine held her hand, a little too tightly. "Father John will go. Perhaps he will bring a man changed in his mind as you are changed."

"If I hear the order from Robert's own mouth, I will retract my testimonies."

Catherine still clutched the hand. "Margaret, do you recall the day of the trial?"

"A little. It's like a nightmare to me."

"Do you recall what you ate before you fell ill?"

Margaret closed her eyes and Catherine thought she had fallen asleep, but she finally said, "I remember. We had meat and broth. From the gaoler."

A cold thread tickled along Catherine's heart. "The gaoler made it for you?"

"Maud Peters had come. She might have made it. But she wouldn't eat it."

"Why not?"

"She said she only ever et at her croft." Margaret's eyes drifted closed again. "I am weary. I must sleep now."

Catherine walked Margaret to her room, then went to the dormitory, where she dropped onto her pallet. But before she could sleep, the priest pounded on the door and walked in.

"Come sit with me, Catherine, before I ride," he said. His tone was sober and she rose to follow him into the nave. The sun was leaving the east windows and the room darkened as it lifted into the sky.

Catherine took a bench. "You have not been to Overton House yet?"

Father John sat beside her. "You fell ill, Daughter."

Catherine tensed for the lecture, but he did not upbraid her. He was silent, patting her hand, and she said, "There was a time, Father, when you thought I would be at court by this age, do you remember?"

"In service to the queen. You had the manners for it, child. And the beauty." He studied her eyes, lifted her fingers, and looked at each one in turn, holding them between his own thick ones. "You have many talents, my daughter. Those court days are ghosts, apparitions that hang over my dreams. You might have had another way of life." He put her hand down and turned her face to him. "You will have one. But not at the court. A home, Catherine. You might choose one for yourself." She looked at him in the slant light. He was getting heavier and there was grey in his beard.

"Catherine. Daughter. You could make a home with me if you wanted. You could take my name and we could live as father and daughter. I have always served you in that way. It would honor me to own you as my child."

Catherine's stomach danced a little at that and she put her hand on it to quiet herself. "I could still practice physic?"

"I would not prevent you. No one in the village would dare accuse you if you were called Catherine Bridle." John Bridle sat long and stared at the door. "But henceforth you must practice physic on yourself as well as on others."

Her guts skidded and she looked at her hands. "I fall ill as well as others."

"You are mortal as others are. I know how it is." He put his hand on her head and pulled her to him. He kissed her on the temple and she thought she would weep.

"What of Mother Christina?"

"She will be in a rage whatever comes. I fear she will continue difficult. I think she might follow if you led."

"I have never led Mother," said Catherine. "It does me no good even to mention reform in her presence."

The priest sighed. "I expect not."

"And what will you do? Will you be a priest in the reformed church?" Catherine swept her arm to indicate the building. "Will you be Robert Overton's priest? When he despises us?"

Her voice had shrilled upward, and he shrank back, startled at her vehemence. "I am already Robert Overton's priest. I have always been. We are not told to leave our callings. I am a priest and that is what I will be."

"And I am a nun. I was a nun. That was my calling." Catherine stopped herself.

"Was it?" he said. "We would have sent you off to the court with our blessings."

"And I would have gone," she admitted.

"For Christina, the change will go harder. She is older. The land was her family's. She speaks truth in that."

"Can we do nothing for her? Before she goes too far?"

"We could do a great deal if she would have it done."

"And the others?"

John Bridle looked out the door. "I will ride with them to collect the pensions if they are offered. Beyond that, I can do little. If they are found guilty of corrupt living, there will be nothing for them."

"Veronica is an old woman. Neither she nor Ann will live under Robert Overton."

"I would take her on in the household but she will not stoop to that, I think. It has always been contentious between us." He looked down and shook his head. "It's all a dismal business. But the words must be said. Catherine, they are just words."

She laughed a little. "That is precisely what William told me. Just words. So our mouths need not speak our hearts any longer. I've learned that lesson, but it tastes sour."

"It grieves me to hear you say it so direct, but that is how the world turns."

"So."

"And you will say these words."

"I have promised William to consider it."

"Daughter, I must ask you this. Do you love the man?"

"He's a man who can match wits with me."

"A true miracle," said the priest. Catherine laughed, and he laughed. In the old easy way. "But can you love him?"

"His brother will not permit it, I am told. I must have been in a kind of fit to believe he would. Robert will want a wife and son of his own before his brother. But William has spoken to me." Her voice shook and she bit back tears. "How could Robert do it? Have William sit accused in public of theft." She swallowed hard and waited until she could speak clearly. "But, as you say, words are just wind nowadays. There need be no soul behind them." She looked at her hands. They looked frail. "I believed him, nevertheless."

"Well." John Bridle pulled a whip from his belt and fumbled at it, seeming to want to unwind the leather from the handle. "Would it please you to have him? If we could save him?"

Catherine watched the light, broken through Christ's passion, paint the floor gold and red. "I will have to consider that as well. I will not be a servant in Overton House neither." Her voice leapt a little. "I fear a marriage will not be permitted."

"Is that all you have feared of late?"

"I would be ashamed to throw myself at a man who could not take me up. Or would not."

"I will speak for you to Robert, if you want."

"In what way?"

"I am his priest. I act as your father. Robert Overton is a boy in his mind. He is spoilt and selfish. But he might have his brother wived if it takes him away from Mount Grace." He raised his eyes. "If he thought you would ask no part of the land or the goods."

"And what then is William to do? Father, my mind is not turned against you. Nor am I resentful. I have had a good life here. I have studied and had the company of the sisters. I have been blessed with the leisure to study and draw and record my receipts. Mount Grace does not cast such fair looks at us as they did, but we are not so very different than any other village. But for William it's different."

The priest looked hopeful. "You could make a home here. William could go to court. He will be a great diplomat. A soldier. If his brother turns him out, the king will take him up."

"His brother turns him out and his king turns me out," said Catherine. "Where is the justice in it?"

John Bridle looked over Catherine's head. The window let only a dim mottled light onto his face. With the south windows behind him, he looked like some dark angel come to deliver an unwanted message. "There is no justice in it. But you cannot murder yourself for justice." There was no triumph in his voice.

Catherine's face was hot, and she was glad for the low light. "I will use my physic for my health, Father."

He was looking around the nave. "These men will come back. And they will expect to be rewarded for second labours."

"And then it will be Robert Overton's private chapel. And he will buy you to administer it for him."

"Now your words are vinegar indeed. We may not have a church here at all."

"And what will belong to you?"

"Very little." He scanned the nave again. "'When Adam delved and Eve span—'" he said.

"'Who was then the gentleman?'" Catherine finished the old rhyme for him. They both laughed quietly. "Will you take up a shovel, then, and reverse the course of the world?"

John Bridle pulled at his beard. "Perhaps I will. But I fear what would happen if you and Christina took up spinning."

Catherine laughed with more heart. "I am no better with a thread than I ever was. Mine would be a wheel of fortune indeed." They both looked at the open door. "Though I do still dream of a perfect garden now and then." John Bridle laid his hand on Catherine's, then removed it. She took a breath. "And do you believe God smiles on this change, Father?"

He forced a short snort through his nose. "No, Catherine. It scars my soul to bow to this king." He looked quickly up. "But it keeps my head on my shoulders. And so you see your father as he is, Catherine. Meat gone bad, that is what I am."

"You have ever been a good father to me. And you are alive."

"I will return as quickly as I can, but if they come while I am gone, do not attempt to take or hide too much. They will seize what they want as spoils. Keep what seems modest. Keep it on your persons. Anything that says Rome will inflame them. Anything that Robert will use they will likely leave for him if they are under direction. Anything too large for them to carry. Do you understand?"

"Yes, Father."

"And no more harm to yourself, do you hear?"

"You must bring him back or bring a letter with his seal."

"I will bring one or the other."

"How much will the king grant us?"

161

"It depends upon the commissioner's report. If no scandal is found, Christina will get a larger pension as prioress. The others will receive a fixed sum."

"Of how great?"

John Bridle shook his head. "It hangs upon the report."

"And whose office is it to deliver this report?"

"The heir of Overton House. I'm afraid it may be one he relishes." The priest looked her in the eyes now. "You will all have to go to York to receive the monies, if there are monies to be had. The commissioner there is charged with dispensing the payments. You will have to pay the tax and you will have to pay their scribe, as well."

"But how much might we hope for?"

"Enough to feed you for a year. Perhaps a few years. But, Catherine, if there is a trial, there may be nothing. Worse than nothing. I will see to you." He paused. "Where do you want to go?"

"I have never seen the sea."

"I will take you. You may put your very toes into the waves if it pleases you."

She smiled at him.

"Submit to the change, then come to me and I will decide what is to be done with you and William."

The light in the room was fading as the sun rose beyond the windows, and John Bridle's face was disappearing, dark at the center. Catherine said, "Can you convince Robert to hurry back here in the morning?"

"I will raise him from his bed before the sun does if he is ever to rise again."

"Look for the altarpiece while you are there. William has had no part of it, and I would gamble my right hand that Thomas has not made a penny on it."

"I always thought you tended to favor the sinister side, anyway."

Catherine gasped a little. She had thought no one knew. She rose and John Bridle followed her lead. She took his hand and led him from the bench to the door. "Do you think Maud Peters killed her brother?" She was staring at the road.

"He is dead and buried. She is dead. What do we gain by torturing their memory?"

Catherine nodded.

The priest tugged her hand. "Daughter, I will bring Robert Overton or a sign from him. And when I return, you will leave this place and then life begins new."

"Not so new. No never very new." She kissed his cheek. "Now go ride after Robert so that we do not face these soldiers alone."

CHAPTER TWENTY-THREE

John Bridle went, and Catherine wandered to the starving Christ at the altar. He was spangled with deep colors, smiling complacently at the images of his own humiliation and death in the windows. She knelt and tried to pray, but the twisted picture above her had his own wounds to tend, and he stared out hungrily, over her head, and did nothing.

He would give her some answers, she thought, if she waited long and patiently enough. She stayed on her knees while the sun arrived at its zenith and began its descent. It slowly retracted its light and then lit the west windows, streaks of red and gold turning the stained glass images of Christ's passion and crucifixion and resurrection lurid and hostile. The sky darkened to the inky blue of early night and yet Catherine remained at the altar. Ann called her to supper, and Catherine waved her away. Christina came to her side and murmured, "Child, you need not mortify yourself," but Catherine continued to stare at the painted face above her. Veronica stuck her head through the door, sometime after dark, but she did not speak.

Through the late hours, then the wee hours, Catherine listened for the still voice. But what she heard said nothing of kings or convents. She heard a dull sound, like bored chastisement. The room went dark and darker and the voice splintered into many, the susseration of a delegation of demi-devils, a liturgy of Hell, until Catherine covered her ears with her hands. They were all sinners, the voices seemed to say, and they were drowned in an ocean of human failure. She knelt, her back to the portraits, in the empty hollow of the nave. The angels cast their eyes down on her, but Catherine did not see them. Only the blank expanse before her, and, if she held them close enough to her face, her hands. Her own hands. They were clean and capable, God-given hands that had pulled children free and pushed bone and muscle back into place. Catherine squeezed her nails into her palms, but she kept them trimmed short and could not pierce her own skin.

The room became silent but for a series of notes that rang in Catherine's head, a melody like the sweetest of psalms. The voice now sang that the world would turn under the changeable moon, whose sphere marked the brink of the heavens. *Prepare yourself,* came into Catherine's mind. Every act was part of a net that spread like a dewy spider's web over humankind. Glistening and beautiful. Deadly. Words would fail, but God was not to blame, nor the Mother who had held Him in the space of Her starry lap and with whom the saints wept for the follies of men, who festered under the weight of their yearnings. The yearnings of men. Worse is to come, she heard, always to come, the sagging flesh and loosening teeth of mortality, the clouded eyes, the knees and elbows that snapped and cracked with movement. Catherine opened her hands. Her fingers were long and straight. Strong. Her abilities were the Christ in her, and she would bear them as the Mother of God had borne her Son, whatever else befell her.

Catherine must have slept, because the voice continued to echo in her mind when she opened her eyes and saw the new light etch a beam across her sight from the east window. She sat up. Someone was in the porch and the front door stood wide open.

A basket of rotting pigeons had been tossed at the church, and Ann was loading them into a wheelbarrow when Catherine came out. Ann held her apron over her nose and mouth while she scraped some feathers from the stones. "Yesterday it was a chunk of rancid cheese." Catherine gagged and covered her face. "Who would turn to tricks like this?"

"We haven't enough parchment left for the list." Ann threw the last carcass on top of the mess and hefted the handles. "What will it be tomorrow? A pile of steaming horse shit?"

The day promised brightness again, and Catherine thought she heard murmuring in the air, like the buzzing of a faraway hive of bees. "Some of them will hate us even if we fall in the mud and renounce ourselves."

"Be sure you have sanctuary from Christina before you say anything about renunciation out loud," said Ann, trundling the stinking pile of birds toward the river.

Someone shouted Catherine's name, as if through an early morning fog. The call came again, and Catherine turned. Elizabeth was running up the road, her head covered in only her coif, and she fell into Catherine's arms on the threshold. She was hysterical, panting and coughing, and Catherine scarcely recognized her friend's voice.

"Get your breath, Elizabeth. I can't understand a word you say."

"The soldiers, I say. The king's men. They are coming up the road."

"No! Not yet. It is too soon." Catherine scrambled up the ladder to the porch room, and through the window she could see. There they were. Catherine flew down again and fled to the back door of the convent, shouting at Ann. "Come and help me hide the linens," she said as Ann came puffing back up. "The king's men are on the road."

Ann tossed the wheelbarrow aside and hitched up her skirts to run. "Where are Christina and Veronica?"

"I don't know." Catherine bolted the door behind them.

They ran back into the nave and Ann brought out the cloths while Catherine threw the bar over the front doors. "Here, Elizabeth, take these home with you," said Catherine, gathering a bundle. "Put them where you will."

"I will be accused of thievery," said Elizabeth, backing in horror. "No, you must keep them upon you."

Catherine hunted for a spot, but nothing would do. "What think you of this?" she said. "We wear them, wrap them around ourselves." Catherine chose the piece on top, designed to cover the Overton dining table, and threw off her clothes by the altar. Ann watched unbelieving. "No one can get in from outside," Catherine said, wrapping the linen tight around her. She began at her breasts and wound the cloth down to just below her buttocks, twisted the ends up and tucked them at the waist. "I believe I could manage a second. Quickly now."

A second cloth, this one a small coverlet, went on flat over the table cover. Ann followed suit, soon standing bare skinned and sifting through the coverlets and bed linens to see what she could twist around herself. "Come on, Elizabeth. Have a few. Take them. We can't wear them all. No one here will charge you with theft, for God's sake."

Elizabeth undid her woolen skirt. She slipped it down and threw off her shirt, then her shift, and stood between them, choosing, just as Christina came through the convent door behind them.

"What in God's name is happening here?" She strode across the room and struck Catherine, who was closest, from behind, a hard blow. "Have you no shame, you bunch of bawdy baskets, having your filthy games here before God? Stripped like a bunch of plucked geese here in His house. You are worse than the doxies on the high road, showing off their instruments to any Dick that happens by."

"Christina, listen to me. The soldiers—" Ann began, but Christina would not be

165

silenced. She grabbed up an armful of the linens and slung them to the floor. Her voice levitated with passion.

"Do you think these will go to sale after you have soiled them with your bodies? God's wounds, is any of you bleeding? Do you think this is a brothel? An alehouse?" She lifted one cloth in her hand and shook it at the other women. "My sweet Jesus, we are a small house, my young madams, and we must keep our reputations." She threw the linen down again. "Wasted. Ruined. Now get your disgraceful selves to the dormitory at once or by my troth I will bring the wrath of God down upon you all, mark me. Get you gone, now, the lot of you, you shame me."

"Mother," said Catherine. "The men are coming. They are on the road. This is the only way to conceal these. Elizabeth will take some to her cottage and wear them until the men are gone. We will need them to sell. Later."

Christina blinked. "Men? Where are they?"

"Not a mile down the road. Soldiers. We have no one to step between us and their wrath. We must hurry."

The prioress faced the altar where the king frowned upon her. She seemed to shrink. "Very well then. Do what you must." She patted Catherine's cheek and silently left the nave. They sifted through the linens, and winding and fastening each other's choices, reclaimed their own shifts and quietly replaced their outer garments.

Ann held up her skirt. "Should we change into the brown skirts? That might confuse them, at least."

"There's no time to fetch them," said Catherine. She helped Elizabeth with her sleeves, then steered her out the back. "Cut behind the sheepfold and come around down the road that way. No one will stop you." She watched until her friend, waddling inside the folds of linen, was almost out of sight, and by the time she could get to the porch room again, two soldiers sat under the window, their horses munching at each other's harness, speaking so softly that Catherine could not make out the words. One or the other would cock his head toward the church and the other would nod or shake his head. She pressed her face to the opening, and they looked up, hands cupped at their foreheads.

"Oho, there, lady, won't you welcome us back? We're a couple of helpless horsemen in need of a warm bite and a soft bed."

"Or a soft bite and a warm bed," said the other. They snickered together. "Haven't you got something we can share in?"

"To hell with you," muttered Catherine. She felt fingers on the crook of her elbow. It was Christina. Ann was just coming up the last steps.

"How dare they speak to you from the road? The common road, and such words from them." Christina was rigid with rage, and she jiggled Catherine's arm. "I still have the force in this arm to shake the devil from them." Ann stepped to the window, where she gazed down at the men below, her arms crossed and her face impassive. Another knot of them ambled up.

Catherine put her arm around Christina and called out to the soldiers. "Mary Margaret Overton lies here recovering from an illness. You cannot mean to disturb her. Is this what Robert Overton has commanded?"

The men were joined by three more, who came dawdling on their horses. They conferred in whispers for a while. "Let them send to Overton House about that," said Catherine quietly. "Come on, Mother, you needn't be up here." She dragged the prioress to the steps and they went down together.

Christina tightened her wimple. "I am the face of Jesus, Mary, and Joseph in this convent. I will fight them to my last breath. And so will you, my daughter. We have a station here. It is mine. It was my father's." Her face had grown pale and the air grew still as a tomb around them. Then she whimpered. "Where is John?" She crumpled and was suddenly an old woman.

"Gone," said Ann, backing down the steps to join them. "Do you want me to run to the gaol and see if William might be released to these men?"

Something hard, a pommel or a hammer, rapped on the main door and Catherine jumped. The wood boomed and groaned, but the big latch did not give. They waited, and the blows came again—three solid knocks.

"We need word from Robert," whispered Catherine. The nave suddenly felt hot as Purgatory, and she itched to move the shutter on the eye slit. She tiptoed to the door and listened.

"The village is with us," said Christina, bold again. "They will come to our aid. You wait and see."

"Mother, shh," said Catherine in a low voice.

Christina walked away, without reply, at a sovereign pace. In the sanctuary, she turned, her hands clasped before her and withdrawal in her slate-colored eyes. Then she smiled and quietly left the church.

"Ladies, you must open the door for your king." A man's voice, a young man.

It was difficult to move without being heard, but crouching, they could see boots beyond the threshold and the muddy feet of dogs. "For your king, sisters," said the youthful voice again. "He requests your obedience and your testimonies as his loyal subjects. We wait upon you, sisters." There were a few beats of silence. "But we cannot wait forever."

The tone was honey and the pounding came again, louder this time, and longer. The door shuddered in its frame. "Ladies. Sisters, please listen. We are here on behalf of your king. We are required to inquire into your behavior. Don't leave us out in the weather. It threatens rain, sisters, and we will grow moldy." Hoots of laughter from the others. "We are your penitents. We seek your help. Your king seeks your compliance. You do not want to dissent." The knocking came once more, yet louder, and shadows darkened the narrow crack between the panels. Someone was attempting to see into the nave. The latch was rattled gently. "We come in the name of God."

Catherine coughed out a laugh. "The name of God?"

"Yes, sister. We come to bring you to confession. To bring you to God."

Catherine slung open the eye slit. "So you fight for God? Is that it? Tell me this, then. For whom does God fight? For you?" She was almost spitting on the door. "Did God fight for Thomas More? Do you think He pays any more attention to us?" She stared into the eyes of the young soldier.

"Catherine." Ann closed the eye slit and whispered, "Do not voice these opinions where they may hear. Will you be posing questions while they skin you?"

"Come on, girls. Open the door," came a voice from the porch. It was less plaintive than the other. They were becoming impatient.

Catherine rested her forehead on the wood, then put her lips to the space between the doors. "What shall we do with Mary Margaret Overton? We must know what is to become of her."

Ann went to peer through the body of a sheep in the stained glass, but there was little to see from that angle. "They must all be in the porch. Fewer than before." They looked at each other. "We'll have to unbar sooner or later."

"We must get Mother and Veronica to agree to a course of action. We might send them out the back way. They know the fields better than the soldiers."

"You truly think Christina will go?"

The men outside continued to shuffle and call out. They hit the door a few times and tried the latch again. After a few minutes, they seemed to have lost heart for the useless knocking, and Catherine and Ann heard them withdraw, laughing among themselves.

Ann dragged Catherine away from the door. "Before God, I will prepare myself. You come help me." They went swiftly to the kitchen, and Ann gathered up a handful of knives. "Whatever happens, those men do not mean to be easy with us. To my mind, a well-tempered blade is now the thing."

CHAPTER TWENTY-FOUR

Christina and Veronica were in the back of the pantry, hiding the claret in a large hole under a stone, and they emerged at Ann's voice, the prioress shaking dust from her skirt. She wore a velvet purse at her waist, and her fingers shone with gold rings. "Is there anyone we can send after Father John?" she asked. She seemed herself again. Angry and certain.

"Mother, take off that jewelry," said Catherine. "You will make them run mad."

Christina slid the rings off and dropped them into the bag, pulling the drawstring tight and tying it into a slipknot. She lifted an eyebrow at Catherine.

"That won't do," said Catherine. "They will have that bag off you in a second."

"Go to, you talk like a silly girl," said Christina, tucking the bag into the folds of her skirt. "William Overton directed them last time. You heard him yourself. No one is to touch our personal goods. No one has ever questioned my wisdom in the management of our house. Twenty-five nuns in my care, little children, infants I have cared for." Her eyes lit for a moment. "Hmmph," she concluded, folding her hands.

They had not been twenty-five in twenty-five years. The knocking began again. They could hear it even in the kitchen, and Catherine said, "Get Margaret out here. We need her to speak to these men." She needed to keep the prioress out of their sight.

"I am right here," said Margaret. She was in the walk, listening.

"You could go speak to those men in Robert's name. Then go to the Justice and have William released. Do it now before these men cause trouble they will have to answer for."

Margaret hesitated, chewing on the inside of her cheek, and Catherine said, "Margaret, we need you to do it. There is no word from Robert. We can't wait any longer."

Still she worked the cheek, and Ann said, "Your brother can make sense to them.

They'll abide by what he tells them. Margaret, do you want to die here because Robert was late sending word?" She was tucking the knives under her tunic.

This moved Margaret's feet toward the back door. "I do not wish to speak to those men. They look like thunder."

"Then fetch William. This way is safest."

Catherine checked the window. "Keep your head down until you get to the end of the sheepfold, and stay close to the buildings on the high road. And, here, cover your hair." She pulled a heavy black hood from a hook where someone had left it on her way indoors and plopped it onto Margaret's head, shoving the straw of her hair under the edge of her coif. Margaret struggled against the old head covering, and Catherine gave her a light slap on the arm. "It's just for this minute. My apologies that I don't have a French one in my pocket. Now hurry and don't call attention to yourself." Margaret cast one worried look back, then bent almost double and scooted along the narrow path.

They watched until she was out of sight. The pounding began again, in grave notes, and Catherine and Ann ran back to the nave. It sounded as though the men were heaving the end of a wooden post against the door, and the bolt that held the bar jolted. "Sisters, listen. We will escort you from here to your next home to keep you safe. It is your choice, as you are free Englishwomen. You may begin new. A boundless world is before you."

"It is a lie," said Ann under her breath. "They will kick us to the road and let us starve."

Other voices shouted from a distance. "Come on out of there, girls."

"Get you gone now," yelled another. "You've brought too much trouble on our heads today."

"Out of there now, you old whores. We have need of these stones as well as you." This last one's tone sounded more ominous. The rain was beginning to patter down.

Mother Christina joined them, furious at the noise and swaying in her rage. She was white as a spring birch. She moved as though she meant to slither right through the crack between the front doors and attack the men herself. "Curse them, the pits of filth," Christina said, loudly enough to be heard. She bent to the door and added through the crack, "They will drag me cold from this church or I will stay."

"Mother, stay back, I beg you," said Catherine. She thought a second and added, "These men aren't fit to lay eyes upon you."

"Indeed. Very true," said Christina. And with that, she whipped her slim frame around, stalked through the church, and disappeared through the convent door.

Catherine put her face to the window and squinted southward, but the priest was nowhere.

Suddenly a man's voice sounded across the vault behind them. "Catherine, Ann, are you girls both here?" It was Richard Mundell. "I have tended to the birds this day, and they have thanked me with twelve eggs, which I have here in my pockets. Yes, I am Rich indeed, in the royal crowns of the roost. Come here and greet an old man and receive your reward. "Catherine? Ann? Are you here?" Bent and grasping his walking stick for support, Richard made his slow way through the nave.

"How did you get in?" Catherine said, while Ann took the eggs in her apron.

Richard winked. "I have a key to the garderobe's back entry, and them soldiers don't care about old men. Walked right under their foul noses. Don't worry none, I locked the door behind me." His eyes in the withered face glittered like a falcon's, and he hugged Catherine to him. "Elizabeth is fast in the cottage, and she's put the linens in the rafters on the dry end." Richard hobbled to the door and peered through the eye slit. "They're a rough lot, I tell you." He called out, "You boys be off, will you? These ladies haven't done a thing to you."

Someone grumbled and a rock struck the door. But the soldiers began to move off again, and soon she heard the sound of their boots on the road. "I have thought and prayed all night, but I have no answer from them." She flicked her fingers at the two portraits. "I will have to fashion a solution for myself."

"Ah, well now," said Richard. "God's mighty quiet these days. Maybe you should keep your converse with His mother."

"If I knew where she was, I might," said Catherine. "Did you see Margaret? We sent her to the gaol."

"I passed her on the road. She's dressed half like a nun and half like a lady. But what's she going to do there? See if she can get her brother hanged while there are soldiers handy to build a scaffold?"

"I hope she is friendlier to us than that. He is her brother, Richard."

"She has another more powerfuller than that one."

"Feeble vermin," Ann said, returning from the kitchen. She spat on the floor. "Robert Overton would consign his soul to a wood rat if it wore a little crown."

"And little thanks he has gotten for it. There is a tall soldier amongst them who has sworn he will burn the buildings down."

"Michael Hastings." Catherine said. "William told me."

Richard said, "We lack their accustomed London entertainments. The sun won't set again on their patience if the elder Overton does not show his face amongst us."

"Mother and Veronica may need some time yet."

"To these men's minds, you have had time. God's plenty of time."

"Or the king's," said Catherine.

"Christina will see some trouble before this is over," Richard said. "And how does the Face of God on Earth fare this day?"

Catherine smiled despite herself. "Fair as the sun, shining and benevolent as always." She looked over his shoulder to make sure Christina had not reappeared. "It will gleam upon us any moment now."

"Well, as I am Rich in spirit as well as in name, I will greet such an eminence as required." He laughed his reedy laugh, then broke into a cough. Catherine wished she could force even a chuckle from her belly to match his.

"Come this way, Richard," said Ann, tugging at his arm. "We do need your help now, as you are rich in cunning as well as in name."

"And so I am, my girl, and willing to do your bidding."

"I want you to take whatever you can carry from the kitchen back to your cottage. We have some good spoons yet." She added bitterly, "A few women too if you can fit them somewhere. I am not precisely what marriageable men are seeking."

"So you will live as you lived before you married," said Richard.

"On what, Richard? My old cottage is gone. My father's fields are gone to pay debts. There is nothing out there for me anymore." Ann indicated the door with her head. Catherine had never heard her speak so angrily, not even on the road from Kimbolton. "They will take what profits we have here and my dowry is long spent. I will not go to the Overtons as a servant. I suppose I can beg for my supper."

"The king has promised you pensions," said Richard.

Ann snorted. "The king. The king. He promised the pope that he would defend the church, too, did he not?"

"He promised the queen that she was his wife," Catherine put in. They stood a few moment in silence, then Catherine said, "And what of Thomas, Richard? Have you laid an eye on him?"

"Oh, lady," he said, "he is kept behind a locked door, and I can only speak to him through the keyhole. I took meat from Elizabeth to him, good meat, but the gaoler had his eye on it when I left." He touched her arm with one veiny hand. "I fear he won't taste a bite of it."

Catherine felt as though she'd swallowed a hot coal. "Did the gaoler keep the meat in his room?"

"Right on his own hearth. Said he'd 'see to it.' And I expect he will."

"Come on to the kitchen and gather these things." Catherine checked the bolt and led them to the kitchen.

While Ann piled up the remaining silver for Richard, Catherine counted the pots. "Are we missing a couple of these?"

"I don't know," said Ann. She was rummaging in the cupboards for anything of value. "Why?"

"What became of the pot Christina took to the gaol? The one she took the day of the trial."

Ann looked at the hooks. Several were empty. "God's foot, Catherine, I can't keep an account of every pot and pan. The other girls took some when they went."

"Maybe it was one of these," said Catherine to herself. "Where is Mother?"

"In her chamber. She's likely stuffing whatever she can into that bag of hers," said Ann.

"What about these hooks?" They were carved oak, shaped like leaves and branches, and Nicholas Hale had made them especially for the Mount Grace kitchen. "Can you get them off, Richard?"

"By the blood of Christ, yes, my madam." He straightened up part by part, first his back, then arms, then legs. "Let me find some tools. Have you girls got a drill?"

"There are tools in the altar," said Catherine.

"The altar? Is that how John catechizes the innocent children nowadays?"

Ann guffawed, and Catherine said, "I believe you left it there yourself, Richard."

Ann said, "When you altered the altar."

"Ah, yes, the altar. Reformed, you might say. Closer to God, as I recall."

"It has raised all of John's prayers," Ann said, with a perfectly straight face.

"Hmm. I seem to recall an issue of original rot at bottom." His white eyebrows went up, but Catherine still could not laugh. "Well," he said. "I will go and fetch it. Mine own to gather again to my bosom. Catherine, will you walk with me?"

Catherine went, her feet dragging and her head lowered, Richard put a hand on her arm. "And how do you this morning, lady?"

"I have scarcely shut my eyes for thinking."

"They will not execute him while the brother delays."

"Do you have any words of wisdom for me?"

Richard nudged her. "Just what I would ask you. Who is the holy one here?"

Catherine put on a smile, but she could not hold it. "Who indeed?" And then Richard slipped his head into the altar in search of the missing tool.

They'd removed the hooks and piled everything into an old leather bag for Richard when Margaret came rapping at the back door, calling, "Let me inside." They opened up, and she pushed her way into the kitchen. "Why do you bother with locks and bolts?" she said, irritated and haughty again. "The men are going to come in. You will answer for the charges against the convent." She yanked off the hood and slapped it to the floor as though she'd found a spider in her hair. "They will not release him. He has been charged and the altarpiece is still missing. They will free Thomas Aden, if that lifts your heart."

"What? Are you sure?" Catherine grabbed Margaret's arm. "When?"

Margaret jerked away and swiped at her sleeve. "Of course I am sure. Didn't you send me on just such a mission? There is no evidence against Thomas no more. The suspicion is fastened upon William and Maud and Maud is dead." She looked at Richard, then at the bag. "Is that my brother's property you have there?"

She sounded like the Margaret of the trial day and Catherine felt her muscles toughen. "How is it that Thomas is released and William is held?"

"There is no one to speak against Thomas." Margaret's eyes were still on the sack.

"Did you not speak for William?" Catherine's chest and face grew hot. She wanted to slap Margaret. Hard this time. "That was the reason we sent you."

"What is in the bag?"

"It is just some old bent spoons," Catherine said. "They are too twisted for your brother. Your older brother, I mean to say."

"Mm, charity, I suppose," said Margaret. "Come, bring me something to drink in the refectory." She crooked her finger and went ahead of them, perching on one of the benches. "I have spoken to the men outside and they are sent to perform a task. That is all they are here for. You two are addled to keep pretending that you're fighting a heroic battle. Come, come, you can ride me back to Overton House and we will settle all this."

"You spoke to them?" said Ann, astonished.

"Why, yes. And wherefore should I not? Come, I will be generous. You may live with your other reformed sisters in our cottages."

"Your very skin was trembling at the thought of those same men not two hours ago."

Margaret shrugged. "They hailed me as I was returning. They are gentlemen. Quite gallant. All very mannered. It was you who frightened me, telling tales like you do. They are just men."

"And a sword is just an instrument for cutting meat," said Ann. She sat, poured wine, and slugged it down. "And what will you do with me at Overton House?"

"You've learned to bake, haven't you? I've seen you do laundry as well as any woman I know. You're strong enough. You can't be seen, that's flat, but you can work."

"How can you sit here and discuss your domestic arrangements when you have left William sitting in the gaol?" said Catherine.

"What would you have me do? He has gone against his brother and his king. And if you won't leave this place, you will be charged yourself. There is much talk of you, Catherine, and your conjuring."

"I did not take you for such a heartless viper," said Richard. "I will not sit at table with you."

"Then you have leave to go," said Margaret, drinking off her draught and waving him off with the cup. But before he could put the bag on his shoulder, she rose. "I will retire to my chamber now. Let those men in, Catherine. Now. Or I will."

CHAPTER TWENTY-FIVE

Margaret swished out, past Veronica, who was standing on the threshold, bothering her old beads through her fingers. "Christina is very quiet and her door is barred. Richard, might you think of breaking it in? She may be ill."

"That woman has never been sick a day of her life," said Ann. "Let her be. If she refuses to come out for dinner, we will see to her. She is likely safer where she is."

Veronica frowned, then she shuffled away, tiny and gnomic, down the walk.

Ann said, "There is not a bite of food to be had in the kitchen, I suppose?"

"How can you think of eating at such a time?" said Catherine.

Ann scratched at her cheek and raised the shadow of a pink scar where Frances had struck her. "A last supper. Come, let's sit us down like the apostles and drink to death."

"There is bread in the pantry. And there's more wine. We might as well drink the best of it. Richard?"

"As I am Rich in name at my work, I am rich in thirst afterward. Ann, if you would find us the victuals?"

Ann brought out a jug of the hidden French claret and two loaves of bread. There was a large pat of butter left and some apples, though they were withered and soft. "Richard, you have arrived like the knight in the tale, just at the calamity, and we must honor you with repast." By the time they had finished one loaf, Veronica had appeared in the door again.

"Are there victuals enough for an old woman?" She was already easing herself onto the bench.

"Enough for scores of old women. And old men, too," said Richard. "Will we always be brother and sisters, you girls?"

"Where will a shrunken old thing like I am go?" Veronica lifted an apple and swung it by its stem. "I am more decayed than this." She dropped it and it splatted softly on the boards.

Catherine wondered if she might consider the continent. "There are boats to Florence from Durham, or from Yarmouth."

Ann lined up some crumbs with the back of her hand. "Everything I had is here." She motioned to indicate the room as the center of the convent, but Catherine knew her wave extended to the graveyard too. "Catherine, you could go. Have a new home. Be a famous doctor to a queen somewhere. Veronica, you could go with her. Christina, too."

Veronica knocked on the top of the table. It was smooth, well-worn and well used. "It would never be home to me. And what if the church breaks again and cannot be repaired and we are in a strange land with no one to protect us from their soldiers and no one offering us pensions?"

Catherine looked down at the silky grain, the glossy heads of the pins like horn buttons. She would be loath to eat anywhere else. "What if God has turned his face away from us all? Clashing and scrambling for position. The pope, then the king. What if Henry is a scourge to the English people? The king claims to fight for God, the pope claims to fight for God. Is it possible that, in such times, God may lose?"

They sat in silence until Richard hefted one end of the table. "It was better before they did the repair. Better-looking anyway."

"Maybe its ugliness will keep it safe," said Catherine.

Richard flung the canvas from the original legs and examined one at the window. It was good oak and he had done the carving himself. He winked at Catherine. "Made by an expert craftsman, that's clear as your young eyes." Then he got to his knees, feeling the vines and flowers. "Hate to see these go to the Overtons." His hands ran the length and he laid the piece on the pavers. "I would have them myself if I dared."

"If Robert comes back before we are turned onto the road, I will plead for you to take them," said Catherine.

"As I am Rich in name, so have I been Rich in craft." He pushed himself to his feet. "I can be patient until then."

Suddenly, they heard screaming. "That's Christina," said Veronica, and Catherine's joints went watery with fear. The wailing became a keening and they were at the prioress's room in seconds.

"What is the matter?" Catherine called, but there was no answer. Her head felt cobwebby and her knees trembled. "Margaret! Come help us."

"That little bitch can stay in her room," said Ann. "Come, we may have to break this door."

Richard stood nearby, a hammer in his hand. He was looking down at it, shaking his head. "I must find an ax."

"Go to the barn," said Ann, turning him away. "You will find one by the wood pile there. But take care not to be seen."

Veronica was knocking hard on the door, calling to Christina to open and let them inside. The door was flung open and Christina seemed to hover before them in the dark room, wildly disordered and red-faced, one hand at the red velvet bag. "There was a man at my window. Almost beating in the shutters. Where is John?" She wailed and tried to push past the other women.

Catherine said, "Margaret has gone to the gaol and says they will not release William." She held the prioress firmly by both shoulders. "Let Richard take your goods and hide them. When they have taken what they want and are gone, we will retrieve them for you."

"They will not dare to touch my personal goods. William Overton will see to it. This is still the house of God, child, and I am still its prioress." She shook the belt as if to show them.

Ann touched Christina's shoulder, and the older woman began to shriek. "Take your hands off my tunic. I will bring a wrath down upon you if you do not remember your place."

Ann's face flamed. "I have done. She's going to get us all killed for a few damned trinkets."

Veronica crossed her arms. "I wonder at you, Christina Havens."

"What is the great wonder? That I know what is mine and mean to preserve it?"

"That you can be so old and so dull." Christina's eyes kindled but Veronica held her place. "What makes you think that because you wear those things that they are safe? Has your memory deserted you in the last few weeks? Or is it your reason? You have overstepped, Christina, you have overstepped badly."

"The soldiers are prevented from laying hands on our personal goods. You heard William Overton. They are not to touch us."

"I fail to see a William Overton here," said Veronica, looking around at ceiling, floor, and corners. "Have you hidden him somewhere, Christina? Have you got him under your tunic? For once in your life, will you see things as they are?"

Christina glared at Veronica. "I know what I do."

"So you say. So I have heard you say. And I have believed you. But the times change, Christina. And we shall see." Veronica beckoned for Catherine and Ann to follow. They left Christina, who was busied tying an additional knot in the silk handles of the purse.

By the time the three women entered the nave, the knocking had begun again. They opened the eye slit and were met with the gaze of Michael Hastings. "Let us in, woman." His voice lilted socially. "Time to go."

"We wait for William Overton," said Veronica. "He is to watch over your men."

"Let us in. There is no Overton available. Neither of the bulls anyhow. We have seen the little heifer and she is very tractable."

"We will wait."

"You will not. Open the door or we come in another way. We will wait no longer."

Veronica shut the eye slit. Her hands were shaking. "We had better retreat to a safer place."

But before they could move, a stone shattered the window next to the door, then another, and men were spilling through, bashing out the sharp stubs with their sword-butts. Two of the small, shabby ones led the way. They lifted off the bar and let in the better men through the door. Michael Hastings strutted in last, tossing back his glossy cloak and smoothing his beard. He sought through the dark space until his eyes landed on the three women. "You there. Get over here."

Two men prodded them in the backs with sword-points, and they shuffled up to stand before Michael Hastings. "What will you have?" said Ann. "You have already robbed us of everything we own. Perhaps we have a plague we could loan you."

The man flinched but did not step away. "You think you frighten me with your threats. I see no sign of pestilence on you."

"Then why do you study me so?" asked Ann. "You have broken that window for naught."

Christina entered the nave, shouting. "What in God's name was that noise?" Two soldiers were at her elbows in a second, and they dragged her into the light.

"Mother, do not speak to them," called Catherine.

"What is it you fear she will say?" said Hastings. He motioned his followers toward Christina. The prioress was surrounded by soldiers, and Catherine could not see her.

"Get you gone, William Overton will have you on the block," Christina yelled. They did not relent. Hastings watched from a distance.

Then Christina began to shriek and a few of the soldiers backed away. One of them had the tip of his sword at her underskirts, lifting them while she tried to free herself and smooth them down. The man was dirty and his black cloak was shiny with age, but he was smiling as though demented, agitated by the degree of the pleasure he discovered in his power over the prioress.

"Stop him," said Catherine. "She will not endure it."

"She will. She has no choice." Hastings crossed his arms and watched. "You want him to step away? Have one of your familiars nibble his heels, witch."

"Heathens! Sons of the devil!" Christina howled. "You will not touch the bride of Christ in his Father's house." When he lowered the sword, she shoved the offender in the chest with both hands. He tottered like a young tree in the wind but did not give ground. She shoved again, this time with more force, and he took a step backward, dropping the sword. He looked at his patched and scabbed companions, a grin wobbling onto his face, and fell dramatically to the floor.

"Oh see how I am wounded, gentlemen! The bride of Christ has felled me!"

They broke up in hilarity, slapping their own knees. Two more fell to the flags beside him.

"The Virgin Mother has assaulted me from on high!"

"And I, I cannot stand before the face of the bride of Christ!"

Then they all three jumped back to their feet, still laughing.

Christina's face was mottled purple and white. "How dare you, you demons. You rotten, festering onions. You sewage. Out of this church before I call down the hand of God on you."

"The hand of God? Would that be this hand?" The soldier who had had his sword under her skirts took Christina by the left wrist, raising her almost into the air. She was forced to stretch onto her toes and the purse at her waist jangled.

"Ah, and what is here?" The soldier shifted his hold on Christina to his left hand, and pulling out his dagger, cut the purse strings from her belt with one swipe. When the bag clanked to the paver, he let her go and stooped to pick it up. The other two moved in like ravens to see what he had gained.

Christina flew at the man with both fists out, screaming. When he looked up, she slapped him in the face, and in his surprise, he actually dropped the bag. She bent to regain it, and he bent with her. They came up together, he more than a head taller and twice as broad through the body, and she fought him with her nails. The other soldiers had stepped backed and were watching in amusement as the blood began to show on their companion's face and neck. He tried to elbow Christina away but she was not to be stopped. The two watchers were fully laughing now, doubled over.

Hastings stood by unmoving, and the others in the church had not even noticed. One young man, slender and finely dressed, leaned against the doorframe and stared at the scene idly, a grin lifting one side of his mouth.

Christina spit at the soldier, and the dagger in his hand flashed out.

Christina slowed her assault, then backed away and placed one hand gently on her stomach, as though she had just realized that meal time was approaching and she had neglected to break her fast that morning. Her expression had changed. She seemed to be witnessing a miracle, and her eyes fixed themselves on the glass of a window above the soldier's head as she walked slowly backward. The purse lay in his left hand like a dead rat. In the other was the blade, its tip stained dark.

"My God, you have killed me," Christina said, looking down at her front. The black tunic was blacker at the center, and in the fresh light coming from the door, the three nuns on the bench could see that it was shining. Shining wet. Catherine and Ann leapt from their seats and ran. There was blood on the floor now, pooling around her left shoe, and the ragged soldier had wandered to a statue. Michael Hastings covered a yawn and walked off.

Ann caught Christina as she fell and set her down on the flags. "Catherine, run to your infirmary and bring rags. No, run on and I will carry her there." Catherine looked up in horror at the soldier, who had emptied the purse and was picking through Christina's jewels, the dagger tucked under his arm.

"Do you see what you have done? She will die, do you see this?" Catherine cried out, but the soldier ignored her and then they were running to the infirmary, Christina whimpering in Ann's big arms. They laid her on the table and Catherine slit the tunic with Ann's hand knife to find the wound. "Go see if Father John is coming. Send someone after him if you must. Send Richard if there is no one else." Ann staggered off, and Catherine ripped open the layers of fabric, down to the skin.

The wound was small but black blood oozed out. The dagger had gone deep. Catherine probed the gash with two fingers, but the blood bubbled and she could see little. Christina said nothing, and Catherine began to perspire, the sweat running into her eyes and blinding her.

She swabbed her face with her sleeve and bent again to her task. A poultice of cobweb and lard slowed the bleeding, but the more she packed the wound the more it seemed to yawn open. Catherine took up clean cloths and pressed down, hoping to stop the loss by force, but the bleeding leaked through, under her palms, and soon the cloths were saturated. Christina's eyes were closed and she breathed like a sleeper. Her hand on Catherine's arm had gone slack and Catherine shouted her name. There was nothing else that she knew to do but kneel by the table. "*O Mary, conceived without sin, pray for us who have recourse to thee,*" she began. Christina's arm hung limp from the edge of the table and Catherine thought, "She is better this way."

It was an ungodly thought, and Catherine forced it from her mind, but now it came again, louder, after every verse of the *de profundis*.

"*Out of the depths have I cried unto thee, O Lord. Lord, hear my voice: let thine ears be attentive to the voice of my supplications*—I should have taken the purse.

"*If thou, Lord, shouldest mark iniquities, O Lord, who shall stand? But there is forgiveness with thee, that thou mayest be feared.*—I should have demanded it of her.

"*I wait for the Lord, my soul doth wait, and in his word do I hope. My soul waiteth for the Lord more than they that watch for the morning: I say, more than they that watch for the morning*—I let her cling to the old ways.

"*Let Israel hope in the Lord: for with the Lord there is mercy, and with him is plenteous redemption. And he shall redeem Israel from all his iniquities*—let her delude herself that we would be saved."

She listened to the rise and fall of words in her mind and finally said them aloud. "I have killed my mother."

CHAPTER TWENTY-SIX

The convent was overrun with men when Catherine opened the infirmary door and Thomas Aden was among them, running toward her.

"Ann says Christina is killed."

"Not dead yet. I have done what I can. Her body is much damaged." She burst into tears, and Thomas held her while she cried. One of the soldiers shoved them apart. "No lovemaking here. Get you gone."

"Find Veronica," Catherine said. He went, and she peeked into the dormitory. It was a doleful scene, pallets ripped open, their opulent feather stuffing scattered about, and the heavy frames, which Thomas had hewn, in pieces. The Deposition tapestry was gone, and the other two had been cut down and sliced through. The shelves had been knocked from the walls, the wooden bowls and cups left where they had fallen. The nuns' tunics and stockings were hacked and strewn. The room was empty of men, but Veronica sat on a stool, alone, wringing her hands and staring into the dusty space of the wrecked room.

"Have they touched you? Are you injured?" Catherine rushed to the old woman's side and knelt beside her. "Can you speak?"

"What is there more to say? You see what they mean to leave us. Nothing. Not even a cloth to fashion into a bag to carry anything away." Then she began to chortle, a horrible sound deep in her throat. Catherine thought she might hawk and spit, but even that gesture of contempt was beyond her. She looked up at Catherine. "I will not accept their new religion or their new heir. Not for anything they can offer. I will hide me until they are gone or they may kill me."

Catherine took hold of Veronica's hand. "Where is it?" Veronica looked up in question. "Your ring. Where is it?"

"Why, they took it from me, child. And they will take yours. We are no brides of Christ anymore, you know, nor no brides of any man. We are to fall upon the king's mercy or fall upon his swords and be content with that."

"Father John says he will see to our pensions."

Veronica worked her fingers into knots and said nothing.

"Where has Ann gone? Is she hiding from them?"

"Ann hides from no man. Leave me be for a while. Go on, girl. They have done to me all they want."

"As you wish." Catherine pushed herself to her feet.

The convent walk was a motley series of destruction scenes, the few small shelves knocked to the floor, the windows smashed out, shards of glass hanging from the sills and scattered into the grass outside. The soft rain blew though, and there was Thomas, on his knees, picking up the jagged pieces and stacking them against the wall. In her garden three soldiers were tramping across the vegetables and herbs, grinding them into the muck. One was picking the young radishes and placing them in his teeth, then chomping them and spitting them out. They all smelled like wet sheep.

One of them yelled at Thomas, "Ho, there, man. I have a use for you." It was the young, fine one. He was almost a boy. His beard was soft and fair as down, and he wore new, soft boots that looked too large for him. He came stomping across the green slush. "We are in need of satchels to carry our rewards in." He tucked a bedraggled blossom into his waterlogged cloak at the shoulder. "Run to your hovel, fellow, and bring us some. Go, now. These women have nothing for you to do anymore. That is, unless you can be their stallion and service them all." He roared out a great scornful laugh, too loud for his size, and Catherine could see the bits of stem and leaves stuck in his dirty mouth. Thomas did not move, and the soldier became grim, taking on the posture of an older man. "Go, now, sirrah. Bring me somewhat to carry our goods in." He was in deadly earnest, and Catherine nudged Thomas aside.

"Do as he says," she whispered.

Thomas bowed to Catherine, pointedly not to the soldier, and left.

"So you see, we are the masters here today. Your lady seems not to be able to protect you, her loyal daughters. Nor does your divine husband seem interested to come to the aid of his harem." He pointed to the ring on her finger. "That you may give over to my keeping, as you have no further reason to wear it." Catherine tried to remove it, but the ring was tight, and she twisted it up to the knuckle. Beyond that it would not go. "You women all seem to have welded the things to your hands. Give it a lick, or if you like I will do it for you."

Catherine drew her hand close to her body. She pulled, but the harder she tried to force the ring, the smaller it felt. Her finger seemed to swell, and she finally stuck it in her mouth. She ran her tongue around the silver and pulled again. It slipped a mite further, but still it would not clear her knuckle.

"You will need to grease it. Come, there is butter in the kitchen. You ladies surely have made good use of grease to slick up your bodies before now." He leaned into Catherine and smiled. There was too much broken glass for him to leap in upon her, but he shadowed her steps from the garden as she made her way back down the walk and joined her, shaking the rain from his cloak, at the door.

"Now we will go in together, like a pair of lovebirds on a breeze." He took her arm and dragged her along. There was noise coming from the refectory, and he stopped there, Catherine still caught by the elbow.

Ann was sitting at the table, elbows on the wood and chin in her hands. Her left eye was swollen almost shut and the cheekbone was purpling. Two soldiers were scuffling about in the small storage pantry, and a pitcher of wine sat on the end of one bench beside a half-eaten loaf of bread. Salad greens littered the floor. "I have arrived in time for victuals," said the soldier holding Catherine. "Let me just see to this small task. Ho, Michael, is there a dab of butter anywhere in the kitchen for my bread?"

Hastings backed from the pantry. "What you have there is meat, my man, not bread, but I can find you a sauce to it." Catherine felt her face flush hot and she looked at the floor. Ann said nothing, and Catherine glanced at her hand. No ring there, either, but an ugly red mark had formed on Ann's wrist where the sleeve had fallen back and her nails showed dark at the tips, as though she had attacked someone hard enough to draw blood.

Hastings returned from the kitchen with a butter crock and scooped a dollop out. The young man shoved Catherine toward him, and she stumbled, falling to one knee and hitting her wrist on the oak bench. She cried out, but the boy yanked her up again and the other took hold of her hand and began working the butter onto her finger. "Feels good to you, does it?" Hastings said. He snaked one oily hand up her arm. "You may get the ring off now."

The boy bent to the work, twisting until Catherine thought she would lose the finger as well. Finally it slid off, and he popped the ring into the air, catching it as it fell. "This one is mine." He rubbed it on his breeches to bring out the shine, then twirled the silver in the light. "This will not bring me much."

"If it means so little to you, perhaps you would grant it back to me," said Catherine, extending her hand.

He curled his fingers and the ring was gone. "I will have it set with a stone as a token for a whore in London that I fancy."

Catherine sat, defeated, and the soldiers continued their search, disappearing into the kitchen and returning to stack things on the table, pausing now and then to tear a morsel from the mutton or bread and swigging great draughts of wine. Someone kicked at the pans in the fireplace and one of the men came back in, wiping ashes from his hands. He must have been up in the chimney looking for anything that might be stowed there. Hastings came in behind him.

"We have some gold in our chamber pots that would suit you," muttered Ann, and the soldier whipped around to glare at her.

"That mouth of yours might be better used in prayer than in insults, woman," said Hastings. "You have need of prayer just now. Great need. But you had better be praying to God and not to those images of yours. The likes of you has been served up to the gallows more than once in recent days."

Ann's eyes flared at him, but she kept her seat, even as one foot began to beat on the floor.

"Impatient to be gone, sister? There is nothing holding you here. You may confess your crimes and commit yourself to the road." He raised his hands as though in surrender. "I did not come here to take me no prisoners." The young soldier joined them, and Hastings asked, "Do you find any more moveable goods here, Adam?"

"None to be seen." They had stacked the pans and the candelabra, the remaining spoons and the good cloths, onto the table and were sorting amongst them. Catherine noted with a small lift to her stomach that none of the wine hidden under the stone in the pantry was there, but the kitchen hourglass was, and Catherine reached out to claim it, a sorry compensation. Hastings thumbed it beyond her arm's length. Adam ran a hand down the arms of Christina's chair. It was finely carved but heavy, oak, as were all the furnishings. He leaned it back and smacked the solid seat. "This would be a fine addition to my house, if a body could think how to transport it."

"The Overton household may be entitled to that," said Catherine. "You don't want to fall foul of them." Her voice quavered.

"Oh yes. The Overtons. The mighty Overtons. The wooly men." The soldiers sniggered. "Sure we would not want to run afoul of them."

Ann began to rub at the spot on her wrist. "It is easy to say when they are not here. I would wager your tune would change if Robert Overton walked in that door." Her eyes were locked on the soldier Adam.

He lifted the chair by its arms and set it down, testing the weight. "I wonder if my horse could carry this along."

Hastings held out the hourglass. "Keep your desires to the small things, Coz."

Another man put his head in the door. He was heavy-jawed and chewing on something. "We want to be gone from here and push on, Michael," he said, "not travelling the roads like gypsies." He said to Adam, "Quick now, boy," then glanced at the two women. "Let Overton take charge of these."

His eyes went to the table, and Ann tensed as though she would rise, but she froze halfway, a sudden stone image. The soldier fingered the grain of the boards and peered at the pins. "This is a good table, lads, of a sort my own wife would be glad at heart to have in her kitchen."

Hastings shook the hourglass, and the grains began to count their irresistible passage through the slender neck. "Maybe you should hire a cart and take it to her. Might be she would let you into her bed then," he said, and Adam laughed with him. "I'll be sworn that old carpenter has a wagon and mule he would sell."

They all had a chortle but the eyes of the new one remained on the table, regarding its worth and the favor he might gain with such a prize.

"You will not have the table." Ann rose of a sudden. The bench fell backward with a loud thump but she did not stoop to reset it. Catherine motioned for her to stop, but Ann would not be silenced. "The table will go to the Overtons or it will stay here." She slapped the wood and leaned toward the soldier, glaring. "You will not have it," she repeated. "You have taken everything." She swept the room with her injured hand. "You have broken and stolen and torn. You have desecrated this place. Is it not enough? Have you not done enough harm?"

The soldier quietly raised himself to full height and stared at Ann.

"You have among you killed an old woman and there is another sitting over there," she pointed in the direction of the dormitory," whose life draws to its end because of your doings. Is this what your master has ordered? Your *king*? Do you among you set out to murder all the old women who are become inconvenient to you? Or are you just a pack of wild dogs that tear through whatever steps in the way?"

The soldiers had all fallen quiet. Ann stepped back and almost tripped over the fallen bench. She scrambled to right herself. "May God damn you all and your murdering king along with you." She sputtered the words out. "You will not have this table."

The soldiers exchanged looks, and Catherine sat, cold with fear. The muscles in her chest and stomach had begun to shake. "It is just furnishings, Ann," she whispered, gripping the edge of the board in front of her, but Ann shoved the table in her fury and Catherine was forced to grab at the edge of her own bench to keep from falling backward.

Michael Hastings stepped forward and threw back his cloak. The dagger lay like some hideous growth on his hip, and Ann snorted at it. "Will you murder me as well? On orders of your God? Or are you bent too crooked to look that high?" She laid herself face down across the table and held on to the side where Catherine's fingers rested. "Well here I am, an unarmed woman. Will you stab me in the back, like the dirty Judases you are?"

Catherine was motionless with fear. The soldier grabbed Ann by the coif and tried to haul her upright, but Ann was holding on, and she was sturdier than they anticipated. She was laughing wildly and two of them were at her now. Her tunic tore. "Ha. So you will strip me first, is that it?" Ann continued to cling to the table, and she scoffed at the soldiers. "Come on, then, you boys. You might want to see what a woman looks like before you crawl back to your obedient wives and boughten girls."

They were at her then in force, all of them, one at her head, another pulling her by the waist. She kicked backward and her right elbow went out like a shot, catching the one called Adam full in the nose. He bawled and reeled backward, his face spewing blood.

"She has broken my nose, the bitch! She has maimed me, Michael!" But he came back, locking onto the arm that now flailed and then they had her up, one pulling her chin up as far as her neck would allow, the others at her arms. She twisted her face as far as she could to see the ruined nose and began to laugh.

"Now how will you fight?" Hastings said, shaking Ann. His arm was wrapped about her head and she seemed immobilized. Catherine could hear her own breathing over Ann's wheezing, but none of them even looked her way. Ann was quiet for the moment, and the soldiers' chests were heaving with the effort of holding her. Adam's smashed nose was trickling and the sound coming from him was like the flopping of a dying fish. He was looking at Ann with scorching hatred but she acted as though she were standing in the room alone, saying a silent prayer to the empty shelves on the wall.

They stood in tense balance for some seconds. Suddenly, Ann pulled herself free with two jerks of her elbows. The soldiers jolted backward and Ann's hand dived to the pocket where she'd secreted her hand knife. The blade flashed, and Ann thrust across herself. Hastings was just within reach, and she jabbed at his middle with a practiced aim. It looked like she was gutting a calf, as her wrist snapped, the hand slicing forward, then back, the bright red splattering across the space between them.

Michael Hastings and Ann Smith stood, both wide-eyed at what had just passed between them. Then he staggered backward, smashing the hourglass, and the other two ran at Ann. She went slack in their arms, and Adam raised the hilt of his sword. Catherine slammed herself against the table, and it caught the soldier in the back, and when he brought the weapon down, it glanced off Ann's temple. She crumpled with the blow into the arms of the other one, who caught her from behind. Catherine shoved the table again, hard, as the soldier drew his short knife. He floundered as a corner caught his hip, and he slashed wildly at Ann's throat.

"That will stop your mouth, woman." He had hit her with the tip of the blade, and blood sprayed from the wound. Ann's hands went up, but she was in a shock and her legs wobbled, then went, and she folded into a heap, knocking against the tipped bench as she went down.

"And would you fight us as well?" Adam asked Catherine. He still had the sword out, and she backed away.

"Go. Get away from me. I have nothing else for you."

"You have a thing, I think," said Adam. He shoved Christina's big chair aside and sliced at the air. Catherine tried to back away, but the bench was yanked from behind her and she tripped. Adam was on her, tearing at her tunic, but her apron would not easily give way, and he threw the sword aside to dig at it with his dagger. Someone was holding her hands above her head. Adam loosened his breeches, then worked his way between her knees and began to thrust at her, but she had the linens wrapped tight around her and he had to hack them away. Someone high above her was laughing. "Go to it, man."

Catherine writhed and scrabbled with her heels. She was almost under the table by now, and Adam crawled after her. She kicked him savagely in the leg and he slammed her against the floor. She lay dazed until the pressure on her wrists let up, and she lashed with both fists blindly. Then he was on her again, but the space was tight and he panted over her, working her legs open enough to get fully inside her.

Catherine was pinned and she stared upward. She seemed to see stars, glinting in her face. Her eyes tried to find a focus. She was going to faint. She was going to be sick.

Adam's mouth was at her ear and she could smell his breath, rancid with ale and meat. He reared back and smacked his head on the table's underside. "God damn me but this bitch has got a whole wardrobe on under here." His eyes went to her neck. "What's this?" He had the locket in his hands and yanked it free.

"Come on, then," said a voice above them. "Bring her out in the light or be done with her. Michael is hurt. He bleeds like a stuck hog."

Adam wiped his broken nose on her apron, then shoved himself from Catherine and, pocketing her necklace, kicked her shin and backed away. The soldiers quickly gathered what stuffs they could and carried their companion from the room.

CHAPTER TWENTY-SEVEN

Ann lay against the wall, trying to speak, but the blood bubbled from between her fingers, and the words would not come. Catherine rolled to her stomach and wiped the dampness from her thighs. Ann's eyes were closed, and Catherine crawled over and tucked a hand under her hair, palming broken glass away to see the wound. Ann gurgled and opened her eyes. Closed them again. The blood continued to run from her throat, though more slowly now. Catherine bunched a corner of the torn linens that had come loose from Ann's body and pushed it into the gash.

The cut was not as deep as she had feared, but the blade had grazed Ann's windpipe, and Catherine tore the cloth loose from her own body, and wrapped it around her friend's neck. She pushed the bench and the table aside, straightening Ann onto her back. Then she squeezed in and they lay there together, Ann's eyes opening and closing. She was still trying to say something, and she pointed upward, but only a wheezing sound would come past the hole in her neck.

Catherine said, "Shh. They have fled. No speech. Be still until we know they are gone." Ann did as she was bidden, and Catherine lay quietly by her side while the silence settled into her ears, said a blessing—*Grant us a peaceful night and a perfect ending, O omnipotent Lord*—then closed her own eyes and let the hot tears run over her temples.

She must have slept. In her dreams, Ann walked with her but said nothing. Then she was in the dormitory with all the other nuns. It was morning, and she rose at the first pink petals of dawn, opening on the horizon. The cocks in the poultry-yard seemed to be crowing their morning rites and Veronica was there, a young woman, flinging on her veil like a robe.

Then Catherine stood with William in the high road of Mount Grace, holding his hand as though they were fast married. She carried a bunch of roses in her hand, but the sun was fierce, and when she wiped away the sweat with the back of her wrist, a large spider fell from the bouquet onto her face. She flailed with the stems, but the blossoms became hooks, of the kind that flagellants used. She was ripping the flesh from her own face and when she turned to seek help of William, his throat was swollen with the black buboes of plague. Catherine was snatched awake with a jerk and a howl and realized where she was. Her breath came shallow and fast and she placed her palm on her chest to steady herself. Ann lay beside her, and the gore cooling under her dress made her shiver. Catherine was afraid she was stuck to the floor, and she prayed—

Hail, holy Queen, Mother of Mercy, Our life, our sweetness, and our hope. To thee do we cry, poor banished children of Eve; to thee do we send up our sighs, mourning and weeping in this valley of tears. Turn, then, most gracious Advocate, thine eyes of mercy toward us; and after this our exile show unto us the blessed fruit of thy womb, Jesus. O clement, O loving, O sweet Virgin Mary.

Ann was awake and Catherine put a finger on her lips to keep her from talking. It was growing cold, and a taunting wind, not quite ferocious, toyed with the windows. Catherine eased herself up, peeling her clothing loose from the muck. She was listening hard. She heard someone calling her name but decided that her senses were being tricked. Her feet were numb in her wet shoes, and Catherine slid them off and rubbed her toes until they tingled.

"Can you stand?" she whispered to Ann. "Shake your head yea or nay."

Ann nodded slightly, and Catherine put her hands under her head. "You can lie on the table and I will tend this cut."

Ann heaved herself to a sitting position and began shaking her head, but the pain stopped her and she put a hand to the makeshift bandage.

"Come, onto the table."

But Ann protested again, a bubble of sound rattling from her mouth. She pointed to the hallway.

"You would go to your bed?"

Ann nodded more vigorously, scrambling to her feet. She wobbled with the effort, and Catherine caught her under one arm. "You're much weakened. Lean on me." They stumbled together back to the dormitory, and Ann fell onto her pallet. "Now let me see." Catherine unwound the cloth. The wound was long. "I need honey," she said, and fetched the small pot from the infirmary in a blur of a run. She smeared the gash, sealing the edges, tore a clean strip of linen from a cast-off sheet, and bound up her friend again. "You must keep this closed. Do you hear? No talking. No pulling the linens off."

Ann smiled, waving her off, and Catherine she fell onto her own pallet nearby.

"Catherine, do you sleep?" Catherine opened her eyes. Veronica was leaning over her, petting her hair. "What has happened to Ann?"

Catherine sat up quickly, but Ann's face was still rosy with life and she could see the woman's big chest rise and fall. "She was injured. Where is Margaret?"

"Nowhere that I can find."

Catherine stood. Her clothing was bloodstained and torn, but Veronica said nothing. Catherine's feet were still bare, and she padded to the kitchen, Veronica behind her. Catherine got a jug of claret and two goblets. "We need to see to Christina. Drink this. You will need your strength."

A worry vein showed in Veronica's forehead and she looked into the goblet of wine. Looked at the blood on Catherine's front. "My stomach has gone sour."

"Should I make you a physic? Lettuce juice will purge you." Catherine's eyes were heavy and hot, and she blinked to clear the haze.

"Not now." Veronica stared at the refectory door. It was closed, though Catherine did not recall closing it. "Let's go to Christina." The vein was worming down her face.

The prioress lay still, and the blood had stopped. Catherine swigged from her goblet and set it aside. "There is nothing more I can do. She will have to heal herself if she is to live."

"Every one of us will die," said Veronica simply. "Christina had prepared herself."

"I have seen people recover their health from worse," said Catherine, but the tears leaked from her eyes, and she swiped at them with her sleeve. "I must have a task. Will you help me clean the refectory?"

"You will ever be yourself," said Veronica, standing. But when they arrived and stepped into the room, the old woman sucked in her breath. "My God, there is blood," she whispered. "So much blood."

"Not so much to send Ann to heaven." Catherine got the bucket of water from the kitchen and swung it onto the table. "Not yet."

"Set it on the floor."

"It is easier to reach here." Catherine was already pulling away the bench.

"No. On the floor." Veronica struggled with the weight of it, and Catherine turned, impatient, but the bucket was already down.

"What imp has got into you?" Catherine asked, but before Veronica could answer, they heard a woman's voice, calling.

"That's Margaret," said Veronica. "She's outside." They threw down their cloths and followed the sound, through the church and onto the porch.

Margaret came tearing down the road, waving and pointing south. "He comes. He comes up the road."

"Robert?" said Veronica, pushing past her.

"John Bridle. He comes alone. Thank God, he will bring word from home and we shall all be saved."

"Not all," said Catherine. She could not look full at Robert Overton's sister.

Margaret peeked into the nave. "What is that?"

"It is the remains of our home," said Catherine. "Your brother's men have done a nice turn for him, have they not?"

"No!" said Margaret, running into the building. "They would not do such destruction. They are gentlemen." The broken statues lay all around her. Dust and chunks of stone were strewn amidst the slivers and slabs of broken glass. "You provoked them. You must have." She looked around her again. "It was your fault. This was a misstep."

"A misstep with drawn blades," said Catherine, turning away.

"I will speak to Robin of this." Margaret followed her.

"And will that bring our lives back to us again?"

They waited at the gate until John Bridle arrived. The horse lurched and veered and he almost lost his saddle. He threw himself to the ground and embraced Catherine. "Where are you hurt, daughter? Tell me."

"I am myself, Father John. The soldiers have been here."

"Dear God. I came as soon as I was able." He pushed her away and felt her arms.

"I say, I am not the one most injured. Do you bring word from Robert Overton?"

John Bridle saw Veronica and gazed beyond them into the dark nave. "What has transpired here? Where is Christina?"

"She lies in the infirmary, with a hole in her side," said Catherine. "She hangs between earth and heaven."

"But my brother," said Margaret, tugging the priest's sleeve. "What of him? Does he send a letter?"

"Not now nor ever," said John Bridle, pulling free of her. "I tarried only long enough to send him on his way. Margaret, your brother is dead."

She stepped away. "It's not true. He's ill." She glared at the priest. "You lie."

"I do not lie, girl," barked Father John. He lifted his hand as though to strike her, but caught himself on the backswing and refrained. "Robert Overton lies in the chapel at your home, cold as any stone." The look he fixed on Margaret was no warmer.

"Did he write before he died?" Margaret's voice shook and she had shoved her hands into her pockets.

"He wrote nothing nor could. He was in a fever when I arrived and he went without knowing I was there. I spoke to him. I prayed for him. God saw fit to take him just the same." The priest looked at Catherine and she knew he was concealing the details of the death. "Two of your convent sisters died of it before Robert, and the household is desperate. It was all I could do to keep his boy from leaping into the grave as they made it. He is Robert's parrot and will have no keeper now."

"I think he came here for physic," said Catherine. "He was surly and proud."

"The mimic of his master. He came to Christina when you were gone. He spent Robert Overton's last hours ridiculing the convent and promising to help his master tear it to the ground." The priest shook his head. "It was no good way to step into God's presence." He glared at Margaret. "Do you hear what I say?"

Catherine cleared her throat. "Father, we must see Kit Sillon about this. Margaret, you come with us."

"That I will not."

"Your brother will not condemn you, girl," said Veronica. "He is your flesh and blood."

"As I was his when I spoke against him," said Margaret. "I will tarry here and wait in my chamber for my doom."

CHAPTER TWENTY-EIGHT

"Kit Sillon will not see you," said the constable. "Not now."

"Why not now?" said John Bridle. Catherine and Veronica were behind him and the three of them blocked the gaol house door.

"The Justice is at his rest," said the gaoler from inside. "At his home. You may return before suppertime and he will speak with you then. I have orders not to waken him. He won't want to see these women no how. You have caused this village troubles enough." The constable held onto the open door as though he might use it against them.

"You tell Justice Sillon that Robert Overton is dead and see if that gives him any rest."

The constable's face went ashy and tight and he swung the door back and forth a little. "Who says Master Overton is dead?"

"His priest says so. I closed his eyes myself. Would you like to smell the infection on my hands?"

"You wait yourselves here and I will see to it."

"I will walk along with you, man," said the gaoler. He raised his chin as he came out. "You may rest yourselves here."

They were left to hold vigil with the gaoler's hearth, and Catherine lifted the pots and spoons to examine them in the light.

"Will you have his dinner things?" said John Bridle.

"I would like to know what all a gaol-keeper keeps," said Catherine. She made a careful circuit around the room and was still holding a pot when the men returned.

"The priest will be seen at the village hall. You females are to wait." John Bridle went with the constable, the gaoler trailing after, and Catherine began opening the small doors and looking into covered buckets.

"What do you think to find?" asked Veronica.

"I don't know." As Catherine she said it, she opened a dark nook next to the hearth. There sat the convent pot that Christina had sent. The meat for William and Thomas Aden was long gone, and the pot had been scoured to a shine. "This. Why is this here?"

Veronica took the pot from Catherine's hand and put her nose to it. "He has not had a moment to return it." Catherine watched Veronica's expression. She did not appear well, her face, broad across the cheeks, broken into the lines of an ancient woman's, the lines themselves cracked into fragments. The room was silent, except for the soft damp wind working at the latch of the door.

"Is there aught you know about this pot, Veronica?"

"I have nothing to say regarding pots." Veronica set the thing on the hearthstone.

Catherine paced her way around the room, running her fingers down the curtains and gazing into the placid eyes of Kit Sillon's portrait, hanging over the gaoler's table. The Justice was posed like a Roman, hands crossed before him, big nose pointing upward as though at some vision in the sky. He wore a velvety-looking robe with a fur collar, and his skin was ruddy with drink or sun. In the distance behind him was a lion, sleeping on some rocks, docile as a dog. Catherine wondered meanly what favor had occasioned such a gift.

The door opened and John Bridle came in with the gaoler. "He will bring William in for another hearing of evidence. It will be in two hours."

"Margaret must be here," said Catherine.

"The evidence will be heard whether she comes or no," said John Bridle. He shook hands with the gaoler and Catherine retrieved the pot.

"This belongs to the convent, I think?"

The gaoler said, "Take it, then," and waved them off.

Thomas Aden was in the road when they came out. "What is the news? Is William freed?"

"Not yet," said John Bridle. "But I have news from Overton House. Robert Overton is dead."

"Has he taken himself off in anger?"

"The pox."

"Eh. And you shrived him at the last, I suppose?" Thomas booted a small rock.

"I have done my duty. I would do the same for you."

"And so he kicks the earth away and flies off to heaven."

"As we all hope to. Thomas, you surprise me with this sullenness."

"And wherefore should I not be sullen? Robert Overton should have been made to come here to answer for his crimes."

"We will all answer for our failings, of that you may be sure," said the priest. "Now run and tell Elizabeth and Richard that William is to be tried again in two hours' time."

"I go." Thomas sped away down the road.

"You must come see to Mother," said Catherine, leading them toward the convent.

"What madness did she commit this time?"

"She did nothing but try to keep what was hers," Veronica said acidly.

No one stopped them along the road, and they entered the infirmary without words. The priest swept his hand over Christina, as though he were pronouncing her final judgment. "Nothing was hers to keep. And now see this tragedy. Nothing at all is hers. Do you hear me, Christina?"

"They were robbing her." Catherine could barely keep her voice steady. "We all saw it."

"What would you have me do, Catherine?" said John Bridle. "No woman has the authority to hold position in this building anymore. You are all trespassers within these walls. I have been lenient, too lenient, in allowing you the leisure to decide where you would go for yourselves. Those villains will ride from here as free as birds. They have a warrant beyond mine." The priest laid his hand on Christina's head. "Still, I am sorry for this." John Bridle looked closely into the pale face. "Christina, you were ever in my thoughts and this is how you answer my good offices."

"You will not abandon her," said Catherine. "Give her the rites, Father. She had no chance."

"She had every chance." John Bridle bent close to Christina's face. "Christina, you might have waited to tell me good-bye as I have waited on you all these years."

Miraculously, Christina's eyes opened and her vision wavered toward John Bridle. "You."

John Bridle put his forehead on hers. "In the flesh, Christina. You are not in heaven, to be sure."

"No, not heaven. You heard the child. Give me the rites, John. I have been killed."

He threw the tunic back. Catherine jumped forward to stop the violation, but he shook her off. "Let me see what has happened here."

Christina rocked her head toward Catherine. "You know it. You know it all. Surely you do. There is no need for me to say it." Her voice was weak but clear.

199

Catherine took her hand. Her mind tippled a little. "Mother, what do you say?"

"I am not Lazarus, child. I have not been dead yet. Look with your eyes and not with your heart. Use your wits as I have always instructed you. See what is truly before you." The prioress closed her eyes again. John's hands had stopped.

Veronica said, "You will give her the Eucharist now. I will bring the monstrance and chalice." And she left the room.

Christina did not open her eyes again. Nor did she raise her hand to reach for Catherine. She said, "You will be a fonder father now," and before John could stop her, added, "as I was never a fond enough mother." She laughed a note. John Bridle stood still. "She never owned a glass," the prioress went on, "but she can see if she looks. They all see. Don't deceive her any longer, John. Stop this pretending."

Catherine raised her face to John Bridle, who was staring down at Christina. His eyes were fishy and unfocused and when Veronica returned, carrying the Eucharist silver, he flung an arm at her and she almost dropped them. "Not now, Veronica. She is not dead." Veronica clanged down the pieces at his elbow, and he shouted, "Get out! Do you hear me?"

Veronica did not move, and Christina lay quiet. She looked like someone meditating. "You will give her the extreme unction," Veronica said. "You will do it now."

"Yes. Very well." John Bridle ducked his head and took up the wine and host. "Hold up her head, Catherine."

Catherine placed her hands under Christina's thin shoulders. "Mother, do you hear me? Say something to me, Mother." But Christina shook her head, or her head shook under Catherine's hands. The prioress wrapped one hand around Catherine's forearm and feebly held on, but she did not open her eyes or speak. John Bridle laid the linen on a nearby bench and poured the wine. He slid the host between Christina's teeth, which unclenched at the touch of his thumb on her lip, and tipped the chalice to her mouth. He got a few drops into her mouth and said the *de profundis* over her.

"That is as much as I can do." The priest bent close to her again. "Christina. Robert Overton is dead." The prioress did not respond, and he straightened. "Will you stay with her?"

Catherine nodded and John Bridle opened his mouth as though to speak. For a second, his eyes softened, and he raised one hand. But then he dropped it again and he scanned the earthen jars on the shelves around them. "There is no need for dramatics, Catherine. You must not anger the soldiers again. They will not let you out without molestation unless you promise to submit to the law."

"Will you never learn?" Veronica blurted. "Those men don't care a fig about anyone's law but their own. I had not thought you such a coward. What a quivering finch of a man." Her voice lowered. "You are not a man of God. You are not even a man." She spit on the floor at his feet.

"Just as I would expect from a creature such as you. Your manners were ever made for the barn. What has ever made you think that God would listen to prayers coming out of a filthy hole like yours?" The priest was shaken, though. His face was bleached, and small scarlet splotches rose along his throat. Veronica stepped forward and Catherine thought they might swing fists, but they both stopped, regarding each other with careful eyes.

Then the old woman slumped. "Are we come to this? We are worse than hogs. They only fight over slops. We fight over God." She spun on her heel and left the room.

"That woman belongs in a garderobe," Father John said, returning his attention to Christina, "with the piss and dung of which she is formed."

"Must we speak so? In the presence of this woman?"

John Bridle looked down at the prioress and his face flattened. He put his palm on her forehead and bent over her unmoving features. His eyes were red-rimmed. He took her hands and folded them over her breast. "My poor Christina." He looked up at Catherine. "I hope this speaks to you. I do not mean to spend the next week tending to dead nuns. Better to be a live woman, however unprepared." Christina's face had gone white, and John Bridle lingered at her side. The veins showed dark against the thin skin at her temples, and John traced the left one gently with his forefinger.

"I will go prepare myself for William's trial," John Bridle said. "Make the sensible choice, Catherine. Join me." He picked up the monstrance and chalice.

"I will stay for now."

Catherine held Christina's hand and after John Bridle left, the prioress whispered, "Daughter. Are all the men gone?"

Catherine bent to her ear. "Yes. What would you tell me, Mother? My mind is all upon you."

The prioress smiled briefly. "Your mind is worth a full village of sextons."

Veronica came back in with two sheets and laid them on a side table. "Veronica,"

Catherine said without taking her eyes from the prioress. "Do you know who my parents were?"

"We are all the children of God, are we not?"

"So I have been told, my entire life. You know this place. These two." Her throat closed up.

"I have told you the story many times, child. It was a January morning, black and bitter, so cold I thought the very stones of the church would crack. I found you in the nave, as blue as any thundercloud."

"And who would have left me?"

"Mothers left children at our door now and then. There was plague. There was a year of bad harvest and people starved in their fields."

"And there was sin, was there not?"

Veronica unfolded one of the sheets. "There is always sin, Catherine. Wherever there are men and women under the sun, there is sin."

CHAPTER TWENTY-NINE

"I will ask you without ornament," said Catherine. "Are John Bridle and Christina Havens my parents?"

Veronica tugged the ripped edges of Christina's tunic together. She took two small coins from her pocket and placed them on the table next to the prioress. "Those days are long past, Catherine. John was ever a fractious man. And Christina in those times was a sharp and incisive woman. You should have seen them. How they would argue, she demanding that monks and nuns work out their salvation in the world, John arguing that prayer was the only work fit for religious. He would quote S. Benedict until I wanted to punch him." Veronica blew a mirthless laugh through her nose. "I believe there was love between them. They were very alike, after all. These habits conceal much. No one needs an old woman to tell her that. Some folks in the village used to say we curled our devil's tails under them and pinned them up with ribbons. And in winter, with the robes and cloaks piled on top, well, who can say what might be concealed? No one saw who left you on the church porch. I know I saw no footprints in the snow. Why did I not find you frozen over as any little stream? It was never for me to say. Christina knew much of physic and the body. You were the only orphan she took in with no question, the only one she raised and taught at her own foot."

She stopped and looked sadly into the face of the prioress. After a few moments of silence, she said, "I am weary of this story. You want the real tale?"

"If you will grant it."

"Then here is the plain unvarnished truth. There were two others before you. Little boys, both. They lie in the graveyard. The priest could show you where, since he buried them with his own hands."

"Do I resemble him?"

Veronica leaned forward to look close. "God above, I hope not."

"Do not jest with me about this matter, Veronica."

"I'm serious. I cannot say. We are all such different beings. We all have our own appearances in the eyes of God. I have looked at you so long that you look like no one but yourself to me. I think John Bridle does not have the generous spirit to share even his features. But clear your mind of this, Catherine. You have been the child of us all."

Catherine put her ear to Christina's chest. She heard nothing, not even the flutter of breath. "Christina? Mother?"

The prioress's mouth had fallen slack and her eyes half-opened, seeing nothing. Catherine knelt and wept until Veronica pulled her up and laid one of the sheets gently across the still form. "Help me carry this poor woman to the nave. Let us lay her where she belongs."

Catherine, for reply, pulled the other side of the sheet straight and laid the pennies on Christina's eyes before wrapping a cloth around her head. "What else will you tell me?" Catherine did not look at Veronica. "Of Nicholas Hale. Or Robert Overton."

"You know all that is worth knowing. Ask me nothing more just now."

Richard's bent form appeared in the doorway and he crossed himself when he saw them tucking the cloth around Christina. He took up the shoulders and the women took the feet. There was no time for formal prayer. "Does Elizabeth have an apron?" said Catherine. "We must go to court soon."

"She will get the skirts for you."

"I will wear my tunic," said Veronica, "as I always have."

It took almost an hour to change Ann's bandage. The bleeding had slowed, and Catherine washed the wound with wine and olive oil before she reapplied the honey. Ann was a good patient, though, and didn't try to talk. Catherine shifted into Elizabeth's skirt, and by that time Margaret had planted herself at the church door, her head down. She hailed Catherine and Veronica with a raised hand as they came from Elizabeth's cottage and fell into step beside them but none of the women spoke.

The constable was all bows and foot-scrapings at his door, and John Bridle was already within, wearing a brushed coat and a clean collar and hose. He frowned at Margaret. "I hope you know your business here today, girl, is to tell the truth."

Margaret said, "I have always told the truth as I understood it to be. As I was told it was."

"No one will tell you what your truth is any more," said John Bridle. "You will have to determine it for yourself now. Even a woman must know her own mind and speak it. No brothers will stand between you and God, Margaret."

She bit her lip and they walked in before her, the constable holding the door as they went.

The gallery was empty. Catherine and Veronica sat with the priest, and Margaret sat a ways down the bench from them. Kit Sillon came in through another door and made for his chair without acknowledging any of them. Two watchmen came in with him, and once he was settled, he motioned to them. "Bring the man forth."

William was brought out, still shackled and dazed in the light. He was thin and his beard was uncut. His coat and breeches were filthy. He looked around the room, and when his eyes fell on Catherine, he smiled.

Kit Sillon banged on his table. "William Overton, you are brought here again to answer charges that have been laid against you by Margaret Overton and Frances Overton on behalf of your brother Robert Overton."

"I have done nothing," said William, but his voice broke and the last syllable fell away.

"Let me finish," said Kit Sillon. Catherine squirmed with impatience, and John Bridle put his hands firmly on his knees.

"Thomas Aden, your conspirator, has been released upon new testimonies given by your sister, Margaret Overton, and upon new discoveries against Maud Peters."

"What?" William stared at Margaret and she looked at her hands.

"Frances Overton is dead in suspicious circumstances and Robert Overton is dead of smallpox. Maud Peters is dead by her own power. John Bridle, will you stand and give your evidence of these events?"

John Bridle sprang to his feet and William moved toward him, but one of the watchmen seized his arm and he quieted. John Bridle cleared his throat. "I would like to speak on these matters. I have helped to bury Frances Overton and these same hands tended the body of Robert Overton in death. Frances Overton died of an illness that also struck her sister Margaret, whom you see here before you, recovered by the grace of God. I cannot say what the source of Frances Overton's sickness was, but I stood by while she fell ill and stood by when she died. William Overton was nowhere to be seen and could not have reached a hand to harm her. Robert Overton suffered the same illness as William himself, who is also recovered by the grace of God. Robert's body was less strong and a fever took him to heaven. I was at the bedside watching when he passed from this earth and I saw the marks of the pox upon him."

"Where was Thomas Aden during these occurrences?" said Kit Sillon.

"Thomas Aden was chained in the gaol when Frances Overton took ill. He was chained in the gaol when Robert Overton was laid down with the pox and when Maud Peters smoked herself to death. His hand could not have touched any of them."

"What say you to the death of Nicholas Hale? Was Frances Overton's illness of a kind as his?"

"My daughter Catherine may speak with more knowledge of that."

"Catherine Havens," said Kit Sillon, and she rose. "What have you to say to these deaths?"

Catherine's eyes skimmed across William to the Justice. "I can say nothing to the death of Robert Overton, as I was not present when it occurred. I attended both Nicholas Hale and Frances Overton, however, and in my judgment they died by a single element."

"That element being . . . ?" said the Justice.

"Poison. I would venture to say monskhood."

"And what of Maud Peters?"

Catherine glanced at the priest, then back at the Justice. "My understanding, like Father John's, is that Maud Peters smoked herself to death. I saw no signs of poison upon her."

"But monkshood was found in her cottage?"

"There was monkshood in her cottage after her death. Belladonna and nightshade as well. But it was all old and dried. There was no attempt to conceal it, and it looked untouched. Belladonna is often used for women who are carrying too lightly. For weak pregnancies it is sometimes deemed beneficial."

"Ah, but we have had no such cases in Mount Grace these weeks, have we?" The Justice leaned over his table.

"No, but . . . "

"That is all," said Kit Sillon. "Catherine Havens, you know a great deal of potions."

"I have studied physic under the guidance of the prioress and priest of Mount Grace, thanks be to God."

Kit Sillon regarded her with a watery eye. "You would do well to mind the fate of Maud Peters and confine your studies to predicting your husband's will."

"I have no husband, if it please you."

"It does not please me, nor should it you. We will endure no witches in Mount Grace."

"Catherine practices no black magic," said John Bridle.

"She had best not. Now sit down." Kit Sillon's eye was on Margaret. "Margaret Overton, rise."

Margaret wobbled to her feet. "I am here."

"Mary Margaret Overton, sister to William Overton and sister to Robert Overton and twin sister to Mary Frances Overton. Is that correct?"

"Yes."

"Speak up, so that I may hear you," growled Kit Sillon. "Are you kin to these folks or are you not?"

"Yes."

"I have sometimes heard that twins are only half a soul each," mused Kit Sillon. "That Satan has divided you in the womb. What think you of this, Mary Margaret Overton? Have you only half a soul? Perhaps half an intellect?" He sneered at her.

"My soul has ever felt whole, though when my sister died it felt as though half had deserted me."

"And Satan has left you the worser part, is that it?"

"I hope to God not."

"Well, then, my divided woman," said the Justice, "can you tell me what you say to the charges you yourself have made against your own brother, who stands before you in chains as a result of your words?"

"I . . . I do not know what to say." Margaret began to cry. "I have repeated what my brother instructed me to say. I have done as I was bidden to keep roof over my head and meat on my plate." She wailed, "William, if I have forsworn you, I say nay to it all, with all my heart." She put her face into her hands and dropped back onto the bench.

"With all of your heart," said the Justice. "But you only possess half a heart, woman, and we have heard how grimy are its contents." Catherine started up, but John Bridle restrained her with one hand. "Will you say your confession to your priest and mend your mouth in future, Mary Margaret Overton?"

She jumped back up, her face flushed. "I will say my confession here before you all. I was beholden to my brother Robert and he was in a rage at the missing of the altarpiece. He sent his boy here from our home at Overton House. I heard him tell the child to find out what his brother, my brother, did. Why he had not found out the thief. When the boy came home and said William was gone with Catherine Havens, Robert told me he did not give a damn for the death of the sexton but that his brother William would not ride off to the London markets with his goods and his whore and that as his sister and his householder it was my duty to give my testimonies in the matter of the theft and that I should add in the death of Nicholas Hale for good measure if I wanted to keep my place with him and that is what I have done and I am heartily sorry for it, of that I will swear on any Bible." She gulped for breath. Her lashes were matted with tears and she rubbed them away. "You may lock me away for a perjurer and strike off my head with the ax you have sharpened for my brother. But that is the truth and I will stand for it."

The corners of Kit Sillon's mouth lifted, and he glanced over at William. "And what says William Overton to this confession?"

"My brother was ever a hard man when it came to accounts, but I do not like to speak ill of the dead."

"And you have no altarpiece?"

"It is as much a mystery to me as to you where the altarpiece lies. I sought Thomas Aden, as my brother wished. He does not have the painting."

"Well," the Justice said expansively. "And who is now the heir to Overton House?" No one answered and the Justice banged his hand again on the table. "I will tell you. William Overton himself." Margaret began to cry loudly again. "Get hold of yourself, Margaret Overton. You will frighten my thoughts from my head with that wailing." She quieted, sniffling, and he began again. "Who, I say, is the heir to Overton House? William Overton, brother to the childless Robert Overton. That is, unless someone will produce a son to the late Robert?"

"My brother had no son, nor no daughter neither," said William.

"He speaks truth," said Margaret, lifting herself from the bench and sitting down again quickly.

"Then it is as I have pronounced it," said Kit Sillon, triumphant. "I see no evidence that you have had a hand in the death of your brother, your sister, or the sexton of Mount Grace, Nicholas Hale. And to charge you with the theft of the altarpiece is as much as charging you with the theft of your own sword and dagger." He hit the table one last time and stood. "William Overton, I absolve you of these charges and say you are a free man. Go see to your family and your new estate." He nodded toward Margaret. "That is a piece I would see to most closely." She blushed violently from chin to hairline. "Take the man back and find him some clean clothes," said Kit Sillon to the watchmen. "And for God's sake get those chains off him before he rots."

CHAPTER THIRTY

"He will not appear immediately," said John Bridle. "Back home with you, and I will bring him when he comes out. Give him a chance to breathe the air before you jump on him."

Catherine took Veronica back down the road, Margaret scurrying away ahead of them. By the time they entered the convent, Margaret was in her chamber with the door closed. "Will you see that she doesn't become frantic?" said Catherine. "We don't need any more blood this day."

Veronica rapped on Margaret's door and went inside, and Catherine stopped in the nave to make sure that no one had interfered with Christina's body. Richard waited there, standing sentinel. The prioress lay unmoved and still as an effigy in stone. Catherine put her hand on the cloth that covered Christina's face, hesitated, then turned it back. The prioress wore a regal look in death. Catherine could feel the tears beginning behind her eyes, but she was too exhausted to weep.

"So am I a child of sin. Daughter truly of Eve begotten by sinners." She looked up at Richard. "And you knew it. How many people of Mount Grace know this?"

"I would never venture to say."

"And I was let to go on as though I had a saint in me, saying my prayers as though they would reach the ear of God." Catherine shook her head. "My words have fallen to earth like wing-broken moths. Richard, do you think someone may be born bad? Beyond salvation?"

"Oh, Catherine, sin is in all of our blood. And whatever you are thinking, your birth is no more a great fault than a child is for any another woman who loves a man. And I would not have you damning this woman in her death, thorny as she was." Richard lifted her hand from the shroud. "Listen to me, lady." He was silent until she looked up at him. "Any woman may fall, and any man with her. Christina taught you your letters and she fed you and cared for you and gave you the paper and ink and pigments of your heart's delight. You wonder that Veronica has always been at odds with the priest, I know you do. What must she have thought, you stuck in the porch in the freezing winter and Christina taking you in and making over you? Like you were her own, she said it, right out loud. It was not easy for Veronica, the woman is not a clod, especially when the trouble came with the king. All the talk of corruption and Christina going about as though she could not be touched. John Bridle, too, with all his talk of doing right."

"I know that now. I wonder that I did not see before."

"And yet did Veronica ever do you harm? Did anyone ever do you harm? Even John, that old devil? He was a crusty one in his younger years. Don't think Veronica ever forgave him for you. But even so, did they ever do you ill, any one of them?"

"No, they did not."

"Have you not had the books and food and drink to feed you? And freedom to come and go as you please?"

"Yes."

"And warm wool in the dark months and forgiveness for however many needles you have broken over the years?"

She laughed a little, and he patted her hand. "Come now, Catherine, stop your hard thoughts. They mar your face."

"Hmph. There is no one here who cares for my face."

He put a finger under her chin. "It is a right nice face, you should know that. And not a thing like John Bridle's. And it's one that is ever dear to me. And not only me. Do you know that?"

"Yes, Richard, of course I do." She put her hand on the dead woman's shoulder. "I should have taken that purse from her, though. I should have demanded it. She would still be alive."

"Now you sound like your mother in full. People will be what they are, Catherine, and a woman like Christina Havens will do as she thinks fit. You could not have gotten that purse from her with a fortune's worth of predictions. So take a little of your wisdom for yourself. Leave this lady lie quiet, and go see if you can be of some help to your sisters."

Catherine went into the convent. Ann was sleeping on her pallet in the dormitory, and Catherine sat silently beside her until she opened her eyes.

"What news?" No sound came from Ann's lips, but Catherine could read the shapes of the words.

"William is to be freed. Robert Overton is dead."

Ann nodded and closed her eyes again. Catherine left her and, back in the walk, slipped up to Margaret's door and put her ear against the wood. She could hear the low voices inside and, looking over her shoulder to be sure no one had not followed, she continued silently up the walk and into Christina's chamber, latching the door behind her.

The soldiers had not done their destruction here. They must have thought it was the Marys' room. The bed was neatly made, with its silk coverlet and down pillow. The cupboard held four veils and several underskirts, all silk, and a bottle of rose oil. The underskirts were worked in colored thread, and they shone when Catherine pulled them into the light. Christina had kept several volumes on a small shelf on the wall, and Catherine riffled the pages. A Book of Hours. A breviary. Arthurian tales in French. She replaced the books and lifted the mattress. The bed sat on a frame of wood and rope, several inches from the floor. It smelled of roses when Catherine shook it and stripped off the cover. It was clean as Eden, and Catherine folded the coverlet and laid it at the foot. Then she pulled the entire bed away from the wall. She got on her knees and felt the edges of the floorboards until she found the loose one she knew had to be there. The men would never have discovered a seam this neat. Catherine dug into it with her nails and pulled the plank free.

The space was smaller than the hiding spot in the porch room, but it was big enough. The parchments were smooth, and when Catherine laid them on the bed, the stems and leaves of the monskhood slid free, freshly pressed and still green as the day they were harvested. Under them were juniper fronds, just like those Catherine kept in her store. And nightshade, both leaves and berries, fresher than Maud's. Under the plants was another book, a volume of Magister Santes de Ardoynes. Catherine knew what it was before she opened the well-thumbed pages. *The Book of Venoms.* Catherine leafed through the catalogue of poisons. Christina had not been fool enough to make notations in it.

"Sweet heart of Mary," Catherine breathed. She started to replace the things but tucked them back into the parchments, then into her shift, instead, and hurried back to the infirmary. She got on her stool and placed the herbs on a high shelf, then took the book to the kitchen and laid it in the hiding place beneath the pantry, as far back as she could reach. Her hands were shaking as she replaced the wine jugs and worked the paver back into its slot.

The refectory was still a shambles, and a chill shuddered down Catherine's back as she surveyed it, but she rolled up her sleeves and returned to the kitchen for water. The rain butt, just outside the door, stood astonishingly unbroken and almost full. Catherine fetched enough to slosh across the floor and got on her knees to clean the spot where she had lain under the soldier. She could not lift the stain of Ann's blood from between the flagstones, though, and she was sweating with her labour within minutes.

"Oh God preserve us, what is this?"

Catherine looked up. Thomas was standing in the door. He came in and leaned across the table to see better. "Catherine, oh girl, what have those villains done here?"

Catherine made room for him, and he knelt on the floor and helped her scrub. "This is a hopeless task." He sat on his heels. "What did they think, that they would break the very walls to the ground?"

"Ann fought with them over the table. They threatened to take it away. I think she has mutilated two."

"Over the table, you say. Well, she hurt them indeed. They are at the inn debating with the constable. I saw one with a broken face and they say one has died. They are in a fury to swear out a warrant against you all."

Catherine looked hard at Thomas. "We have been punished enough."

He nodded, his eyes on the blood running in watery rivulets to the edge of the floor. "For the table."

Catherine shoved half-heartedly at the cloth again. "I can finish this alone, Thomas. It is not a man's office."

"Nor yours. It belongs to the Overtons. Let them clean it." His face flamed, but he said more gently, "William has men. He will see to it. He would not want you on your knees like a washerwoman." He settled onto his haunches and thought. "Will you say the words now, Catherine? What is there to stop you? This is all at an end. Can you do it?"

"Let me finish this first. I want work just now."

Thomas shook his head. "I'll leave you to it, then, but it is not a task for a lady."

"I'm not a lady, Thomas. But I suppose you knew that as well as everyone else." She looked at her swollen hands and the anguish came up like a wad of pins in her throat. "Thomas, it is too much."

"You must not give way now, I tell you. The soldiers are still in a wrath and you must keep your head."

She nodded. "Go now and find out what they say. I will do here what can be done."

There was no way to wash the floor entirely clean. The blood that had seeped between the flags began to dry into dark veins. The stones themselves had begun to absorb it and would not give up their stigmata. Catherine pushed the rags into the pits and wrung them until her arms ached. She peeled bits of Ann's sticky linens from the corners and tossed them into the bucket. She dumped the whole thing out back and got fresh water three times, and finally the floor began to show grey again through the red. With the windows open, the stones bleached as they dried, and Catherine lay on the floor, listening to the beat in her head. The air smelled sweet from the crushed herb garden, and she gazed upward. The pounding in her arms and legs began to subside. She felt again the press of the man on her, the stars she had seen as he forced her onto her back. Something winked above her, and she squinted up at the underside of the table. The stars she had seen. A blink of something gold and blue. She put her fingers up and the star went out. She was looking at an eye, and as her vision adjusted, she saw it plain. A painted eye. It was staring down at her.

Catherine had studied it often enough. The altarpiece had lost its wings to rot years back, before they had fixed the piece to the wall. The Virgin dominated, hugging the child in her elbow's curve and gazing skyward, far beyond her. The child, wearing his inscrutable smile, sometimes seemed to meet her eyes with his own and sometimes seemed to be caught by a glory undetectable to humans, some radiant spot in the murky world of mortal decay just over Catherine's left shoulder. When Catherine was a child, the Madonna had been flanked by Mary Magdalene and John the Baptist. There had even been tiny panels once—a donkey grazing while Joseph picked cherries from a tree and foreboding mountains behind an ominous Herod. Catherine had spent many hours as a young girl memorizing the curve of each leaf in the trees and admiring the alabaster jar raised in Mary Magdalene's hand. She seemed to be offering it to the Virgin as a gift, and Catherine had thought of them as sisters. Joseph and Mary she had fancied as her own parents, giving her up to God.

But they had perished with the old wood, and now only Mary and the Child remained. One of the Madonna's eyes was just visible through the shrunken boards, and Catherine did what she had never done before. She touched the paint, tracing the dark eyelid, then the sliver of rosy cheek over the pale bridge of the nose. Catherine did not believe that pigments were divine, but she thought of the votive

213

stubs that had lain at the feet of the saints in the church, how many had come here to find their way toward a God whose face seemed so often turned against them. This face had always looked for her. It was not just the surface drawn on wood. It was what the picture pointed toward. God with a compassionate eye. God who contained creation, however heavy it grew, and held it gently in one arm.

A song from her childhood sprang into her mind, one Christina and Veronica had used to sing, and when Catherine opened her mouth the words came back to her—

> *Saint Joseph was an old man,*
> *and an old man was he;*
> *He married sweet Mary,*
> *And a Virgin was she.*
> *And as they were walking*
> *In the garden so green,*
> *She spied some ripe cherries*
> *Hanging over yon tree.*
> *Said Mary to Joseph,*
> *With her sweet lips, and smiled,*
> *"Go, pluck me yon ripe cherries off,*
> *For to give to my Child."*
> *Said Joseph to the cherry-tree,*
> *"Come, bow to my knee,*
> *And I will pluck thy cherries off,*
> *By one, two, and three."*

She hadn't heard it since she was a little girl, passed from one to the other like a favorite doll. A laugh spilled from her, but she stopped it before it could ring loudly enough to call anyone. She stared up, committing to her heart the eyes, the curved mouth, the colors of her skin. "Send me out safe, Mother, and you will be ever in my eye. You must stay in your tomb, and I must learn to make my way without you."

"Catherine?" said Veronica at the door. "Are you dreaming again?"

"No." She slid out from under the table. "I have cleaned the floor as well as I am able. And I have been talking to God's mother."

Veronica looked at Catherine. Looked at the table. "I made a vow, Catherine."

"Not every vow pledges a soul to goodness."

214

"I made a vow to Christina."

"She did wrong. Veronica, my worst enemy has been my own blood."

"I made a vow to God. I will break neither."

"I demand no explanations of you. Not now. Others have also been to blame." Catherine held up her arm. "And their sin runs through me. And I have spent my anger everywhere but here." They met Thomas in the nave and she asked, "What news of the injured soldiers?"

"There is a broken nose that will not mend any time soon and their leader is dead."

"So there is our justice. We cannot pursue them any more than we can seek a writ against the king," said Catherine. "But the table is still here, Thomas. Tell me truth. You aided Nicholas in this."

Thomas looked hard at Catherine. "I was warned. You understand why I meant to stay away? Why I was driven to return? I have a wife and child. There was no choice given to me."

"I judge no one," said Catherine.

His shoulders sagged with relief. "Then for me, it is done."

"Not done all the way through," said Catherine. "I will need you for a small task yet."

CHAPTER THIRTY-ONE

The porch door stood wide open, and the spring wind blew in, sweet-scented and clean. It had only taken a few swift hours. Inside, dust swirled up like smoke from the toppled icons and defaced tombs. Two of the stained glass windows had been smashed. Catherine and Veronica moved through the nave and aisles without making a sound, Thomas behind them, gathering shards from the floor. The story they had always told was of death, anyway, Catherine thought. One small scene showed Mary Magdalene and Jesus as a groundskeeper outside the empty tomb, and Catherine halted her progress there.

"Someone in the village will have this." Her voice sounded hollow in the newly opened space. "We are turned out, but you may stay as you are." Catherine took Thomas's hand. "I hope it will go well for you."

He nodded.

"You will see to the burial?"

"You know I will, Catherine. No man will prevent me."

"Thomas, you and Elizabeth have ever been my dear and faithful friends and I will always think of you with love. You should not have been drawn into any of this business."

"You speak as if you plan to go away from Mount Grace, Catherine."

She shrugged, looking again at the window. "Where in the world is there to go? I've heard it said that wherever a man goes, there he is himself. It is true of a woman, as well."

They moved on. The two tapestries still lay haphazardly rumpled. The church already looked abandoned, with the pale light slanting across it at an unaccustomed angle and the dust here thicker, moving like an uneasy congregation of flies in their midst. The corners now revealed themselves to be powdered with mold and the sills were mounded with bird droppings. Back in the Lady Chapel, Catherine shoved open the tomb where they had hidden the remaining linens. They were safe, and she scooped them into her arms. "Here is something, at least." She dumped them into Thomas's hands. "You will take these to Elizabeth."

"I am here." Elizabeth was standing in the nave with her arms full. "I have brought you clean garments."

"Then will we trade you," said Catherine. "Friend, I have a boon to ask of you. Ann needs care. She needs a pallet and soft food. She will need much rest."

"My home is hers."

"More than that. I need you to conceal her. And Thomas, you must make a second grave. Next to Mother's. You will mark it with Ann's name and we will put it about that she has died from her wound. She will die but for now, and when the storm has cleared, we may resurrect her." Catherine led them through the dormitory, and they found Ann lying down but awake. "Ann, will you rise and go with Elizabeth and Thomas?"

She said nothing, but let the others pull her to her feet. She was unsteady, but Elizabeth and Thomas propped her on either side. Catherine took her hands. "You will rest and mend and hide your head for now. Elizabeth and Thomas will keep you until it is safe for you to be seen." She turned to the other woman. "Elizabeth, you must keep honey thick on the wound until the skin begins to knit. When the edges are tight down, you wash it with vinegar or wine every morning. There are plenty of stores in the infirmary. She must have only drink and soft victuals. Can you do it?"

Elizabeth picked up the pot. "I will get me some bees if need be."

"Then you must die to live, Ann. And once you are whole, we will laugh as we have always laughed."

Ann opened her mouth, but no sound came out. Instead, she wept without speaking, and she stood on her own long enough to hold Catherine in her arms. "Come home," she croaked.

Then Elizabeth and Thomas helped her away, down the long stone dormitory walk, across the nave, and out the front door. "Go along the hedgerow," Catherine called after them. "Keep your heads low."

Suddenly, another figure appeared. It was William, and when he saw her, he ran. "Catherine, have you been injured?"

She took him in her arms. "Wherefore would you think me harmed?" She looked down at herself. The skirt was marred by the washing, and its folds were lacquered with streaks of thin dried blood. She touched a hand to her bare head. Her hair was dirty, and she started to twist from him.

"Catherine, you must not think I am concerned with the beauty of your dress."

"Have you eaten? You have lost flesh. Have you had meat since Christina sent food to the gaol?"

"I have had no bite of meat in these three days, from Christina or anyone else. John Bridle gave me bread and ale." He rubbed at his stubbly beard. "And the use of a dull blade."

So the meat had gone to Frances and Margaret. Meat meant for Thomas and William. Catherine held her tongue. Veronica was still by the door into the convent, looking at the floor. She already knew. Had known from the beginning. "Where are the solders?"

"Gathered at the Hare and Hound. They speak of getting a warrant against you women for violence against them."

"A warrant against which of us?" Catherine pointed toward the tomb, and the white form showed like a pale shadow in the gloom. "They have killed Mother."

"I will see to it that they are charged." He walked toward the body but stopped. Catherine had not followed. "You do want me to charge them?"

"I want nothing more to do with them at all."

Richard came tramping up, the folds and trenches of his skin dark with soot and age. She noticed the new growth of white beard patching his chin and cheeks, like some old hermit's. "You are just released from the gaol yourself, William. You want Kit Sillon against you again?"

"I have been cleared of it all." William suddenly looked around. "And where is this sister of mine?"

"In her room," said Veronica, but as she spoke, Margaret pushed through the door behind her.

"Is my brother returned?" she said meekly, though she could see him plainly, standing before her. She rushed across the room and knelt at his feet, taking his hand in hers. "William, pardon me. I have been a vile and evil sister to you. I will be your servant now."

William looked at the top of Margaret's head. She had removed the pearl-covered French hood and wore only a simple white coif. He pulled his hand from hers. "You were under orders from Robert. Swear to me that you were."

She looked up at him. "He was adamant that you had betrayed him."

"Perhaps he believed it," said Richard. "He must have believed it."

William lifted his sister. "We have much to say, Margaret. But no sister of mine will serve me." He looked darkly into her eyes. "You speak truth? For once, do you?"

"He drew on me and Frances. He was wild with it."

William shook his head. "The fever, maybe. He could not have been in his right mind. Still, Margaret. You have been greatly at fault." He let her go and turned to Catherine. "My brother is gone, and there is no more Michael Hastings to answer for this destruction." His eyes glided over the dead form and back to the living. "I will inspect the property. I will make my report to the commission, and then I will go to the constable."

"No, I say." There was a sound of horses in the road, and shouting. Catherine took hold of William's arm.

The knot of men was outside the door, the young one called Adam circling the others and calling out orders. There was some rearrangement of position, then Adam jabbed his heels into his horse's flanks and they rumbled by, not even glancing at the church.

"They have got no satisfaction from the constable. Now I will ride after him," said William.

"Please, let it be. Let Kit Sillon forget he ever saw your face," said Catherine.

Richard slid his cap onto his head. "I will go to the churchyard and make this lady's final bed." He nodded at Catherine. "With your permission."

"I have no authority here. Can you bring yourself to take the oath?"

Richard fingered his throat. "I am not sure what this old neck is worth, but I suppose I will say their words. Your words," he added to William.

"They are not mine," said William.

Richard blew into a rag. "I will begin this minute."

"Thomas will help you in that," said Catherine.

Richard looked into her eyes for a moment. Then he made a crooked bow and left.

"Your men have not even left us a mouthful of bread," Catherine said.

"They were not my men, Catherine. I have told you and told you. They were the king's men. Robert's. Not mine. Michael Hastings came from a family far greater than mine. His mother was a cousin to the Nevilles. I have been his servant in most things, even if he was a younger son, and am like to hear from Adam for this day, even if he is illegitimate."

"You see where his family connections have gotten him." Catherine thought a moment. "All belongs to King Henry."

"We are the king's subjects, every man of us. We make our way as we may."

"Ah," Catherine said. "Will you ride with them again as you have done in the past?"

"Do you see me here, or am I gone with them? Would you like to push a finger in me to test my flesh?"

"And they are just words after all. What will you do then? Live in peace at your brother's house?"

"It is my house now, and I will make it as peaceful as I am able."

"I am going to change these weeds for the cleaner cloth Elizabeth brought," said Veronica. She took Margaret's arm firmly and led her back to the dormitory.

William was alone with Catherine now, and he put his hands under her elbows. "Listen to me. We are here and we are alive. There are so few choices for you." He drew her into the confines of the porch. "I will make my report, and then we might live together happily for the rest of our years."

"But they are just words, William, your vows. And my vows as well. What do they mean?" She looked at his dark eyes and the shallow scars that still marked his skin. Her belly shivered and she felt the old desire moving in her. He pulled her to him, and she relaxed into the kiss. His beard was scratchy and coarse and its tickle made her draw back. But she accustomed herself to it by pressing in closer to his mouth and she put her hands on his back to feel his man's body against her. He eased her back against a wall, and a rushing sound rose in her ears, like the small waterfall down the river. The heat began to rise up through her, opening like a summer flower in her chest. What were words to this, she thought, letting herself ease against him.

But then she felt the ghost of Adam Hastings' body against her. She let her head fall back, breathing in the cool air, and pressed him from her. "William, not now. Not here."

He still held her. "You could be my wife."

She freed herself and drew him toward the steps, where the discarded books still lay, their pages fluttering soft as wings in the breeze. Catherine stacked them in her arm. "May I take these?"

William was watching her face. "They are yours."

"I thank you. Now, you walk on. I must change my skirt and I will meet you outside of these buildings." Catherine curtsied in her best court manner and went through to the convent. She could hear neither Veronica nor Margaret. The building was cold and silent and she listened at a corner of the walk. A wren was trilling from somewhere at the other side of the garth. The soldiers had likely shredded its nest. Four enormous crows were marching around in the remnants outside, scavenging for scraps, and a lark called from somewhere beyond the convent wall, across the river. She had not thought it was still so early but the light was different now and she could not tell. Perhaps the birds were bewildered as well.

Catherine slipped into her infirmary. The stores would have to be trusted to God for now. She stepped onto her little stool and ran her hand into the gap at the top of the wall. Her will lay there, unmolested, and she checked the wax seal before returning it to its hidden shelf.

In the dormitory, Catherine found a skirt and hood and a clean pair of sleeves laid out on her pallet, and she changed quickly. Then she scooted the bed away, and retrieved the rest of her library. It was a large pile and Catherine tottered as she carried the volumes down the walk and out the side door into the bright morning.

The village of Mount Grace looked as though nothing had transpired—people at their dwellings and skinny cats under the hedges. The smithy was at work, and the smoke twisted as it climbed above his roof, then dissolved into the blue sky. A man sat on a stump, cleaning his boots, a woman beside him, waiting, a pewter cup in her hand. The cook shop door was open, and Catherine could hear the baker yelling at her girls. The day was cool, and no one looked at her as she passed in her strange dress.

John Bridle and Veronica, in a housewife's skirt and gabled hood, were talking by the convent's smaller gate. William, beside them, was speaking to his sister, and at the sight of Catherine, Margaret ran away toward the inn. The priest looked like an old man, tired and wrinkled, and Catherine felt a great sadness at the sight of him. "Father, you are tired," she said, drawing closer. "You should be resting in your house."

His face was tight. "You will be shrewd now and subscribe to the king's order. Daughter, do not let your stubbornness become a stone in your path."

There was a long moment of silence and Veronica said, "I will stretch my old legs," and she headed away from them, toward the green.

John Bridle watched until Veronica was out of hearing. "You would be welcome to stay with me. You could live with me. You could serve as my housekeeper, you could be the lady of my house. You could read and study. I could give you my name. It would protect you."

Catherine shook her head. Two proposals in one morning after a lifetime in the convent. And she had thought her choice was between the pope and the king. "Will you secure these for me?" She handed him the books.

"If you will pledge to return for them."

Catherine smiled. "I will have to examine my conscience on the matter of pledges. The table in the kitchen is particularly fine, made pin and board by Richard and Thomas," she said to William. "The men were of a mind to take it, and Christina's chair with it. You might want to rescue it. It would do nicely for your kitchen maids. The doors being open, the rooms are vulnerable to thieves."

"I will see to it." said William. "They are young wolves, to a man. I marvel they left anything to recover." His dark eyes went black. "But can we speak of nothing but goods? A woman lies dead in that convent." He pointed at the door. "It might have been you." He put his hands on his face and rubbed at the scarred skin. "I am sick to my death with goods." He stomped off down the road and Catherine watched him go.

John Bridle glanced toward the convent. "Your man's spirits are ragged with watching. You should give him an answer. I will see to the table."

"I send it along to his home with my blessings, whatever those are worth. Good-bye, Father."

He hugged her awkwardly around the books. "Daughter. Do not keep your old father waiting forever."

Catherine walked alone to where Veronica rested on a large stone, waiting. "You knew the entire business, did you not?" Catherine said, her eyes on the long way ahead.

"I told you, I vowed," said Veronica. "Even after Nicholas Hale died, I meant to keep my word."

"What hand had Mother in the death of Robert Overton?"

"He was sick with the pox in truth. I could not say what took him off in the end. I never asked what was in the pots of puddings Christina sent with that boy. She sent more than once, of that I am sure."

"As he was Robert's weapon in life, the boy became the instrument of Robert's death."

"It would seem so."

"It is not an irony to please anyone."

"But spare Thomas and Richard in your thoughts, Catherine. Thomas helped with the work. He told Richard nothing. He had no hand in the matter of Nicholas Hale. Or Margaret and Frances. Or Robert Overton."

"I would not have believed it of them." Catherine watched the shadows of leaves flutter and shift on the ground before them. "But I did not believe it of Mother until the proof was in my hand."

A kite, circling above the spikes of gorse across the moors, cried out. Catherine had never liked them, unwilling to think of the poor mortal thing that lay waiting to be pecked into nothing, but now it calmed her to think that the flesh of one would pass into life again in the muscles of the large bird. She turned at the sound of panting to see John Bridle running toward them, holding out two bags.

"Stay and I will press for your rights. I will make your claim." He held the bags against his side.

"And we will have to take the oath," said Veronica. She rose and Catherine caught her by the elbow.

"You will not stay?" John Bridle asked.

"Veronica must find a place where she can live peaceably."

"Ah, yes. The niece." He held out the bags. "Very well. One is food. The other is money. It is more yours than mine, Daughter. But it is a long journey by foot."

"We will make us up stories along the way. I will be like Margery Kempe, but my pilgrimage will take me into Lynn instead of away from it. Weeping along the way, like her, perhaps."

"Ach, that woman. She had a devil in her that would never dare to touch you. But for all that, you may meet highwaymen on the road."

"Highwaymen." Catherine thought he might be considering whether to accompany them. "Father, if we meet with thieves I will give them what we have and hope they send us along. I cannot think we will be less safe than we are here. We will be just two poor travellers with nothing to seize."

"The king's soldiers are still on the roads and you are set down for an enemy. If you meet with them again, it will not go well for you."

"They took the road south, Father. To London. We travel east."

The priest thought a while and finally said, "Then God be with you until you return."

William was waiting at the other side of the green and Veronica walked slowly on. Catherine hesitated and he stepped into her path. "There is no need for concealment, Catherine. Their sin was not yours. I will set you down as spotless for the commission. John Bridle will own you for his daughter."

She drew back. "John Bridle will never own me, though he be the best of fathers."

"Then come with me, back to the House, and we will see to finding a suitable companion for the old woman. You will be my lady. Catherine, please. The times are dangerous. Who can say how many years we have before us?"

Catherine studied William's face, so serious, so handsome, even with the damage. She pushed his hair back and placed his hands on her back. Then she stretched onto her toes and kissed his mouth. "God knows how many years we have, William. Or what I will find in Lynn. Maybe a place for Veronica to hide her head. Maybe her whole family in the ground." She looked back, in the direction of the convent. "When I have finished this journey, I will be simple Catherine Havens." She heard herself say it. "Perhaps I will be Catherine Bridle."

"You may be destined to become Catherine Overton."

"Only God can tell who she would be."

"She will be a great healer. A teacher. That I will vow to you."

"No vows. You must tend to that sister of yours first. I make no promises, William."

"Nor am I in position to require them."

"Then we will talk of it at another time. But this day, William, I am going to take Veronica home."

The afternoon was still young and bright and Catherine easily caught up to Veronica, hobbling along the east road, and they walked along in silence. She could practice healing somewhere, Catherine thought, in Durham to the north or York or Yarmouth beyond the fens. She could send for Ann. Or she could come home. She slowed to match Veronica's pace. She tried to see into the future but too many endings rose before her, William in some of them, an empty place where he might have stood in others.

Catherine did not turn to see William standing at the edge of the green, watching them go, and she could not yet imagine the day, hundreds of years beyond her, when a maid at the old Overton House, thinking to clean an antique stick of furniture, would bend to scrub the underside of the oak trestle table and gasp at what she would find there. Catherine could only see clearly before her the shadows of two women—they could be any mother and daughter—laid out in the dust as the sun tilted into its long descent behind them.

Praise for The First Blast of the Trumpet

"Marie Macpherson's well-researched novel captures the period which led up to the Reformation in Scotland, in which decay and despotism led eventually to a new regime. She leaves the reader much better informed about the rivalries between the Scots nobility, and the way in which they used the late medieval church as a power base to consolidate their hold on power. In addition, she skilfully escapes the constraints of the known facts to give her readers an intriguing fictional tale of the early life of John Knox. The violence and brutality of life in sixteenth century Scotland is well captured, along with the struggles among the vying dynasties to supplant a weak monarchy. Her romances are earthy rather than ethereal, her nobles far short of heroic and the result is a book which portrays the main players in Scotland's Reformation as flawed human beings rather than the goodies and baddies which partisan history has often made them."

—**Rev Stewart Lamont**, *author of "The Swordbearer: John Knox and the European Reformation"*

"In this novel, set in one of the most turbulent periods of Scottish (and English) history, much historical, ethnological and linguistic research is in evidence, which - importantly - Marie Macpherson delivers with a commendable lightness of touch. Descriptions of contemporary superstitions, medicinal cures, and religious practices are impressively handled and closely linked to an engrossing plot and finely drawn, convincing characterisation. The over-riding theme of the novel is Keep Tryst and all the central characters are confronted with the issue of fidelity of some kind, with its breaching or betrayal resulting in an acute sense of loss and/or guilt. The novel well documents the corruption among church officialdom and the blatant misogyny of many of those in positions of power, yet the author handles these issues sensitively. I enjoyed this book enormously and would be more than happy to read it a second time. I'm sure such an accomplished debut novel will enjoy considerable success."

—**Charles Jones FRSE**, *Emeritus Forbes Professor of English Language, University of Edinburgh*

"With style and verve Marie Macpherson whirls us into the world of sixteenth-century Scotland: its sights and smells, sexual attraction, childbirth and death, and of course the ever looming threat of religious strife. Few are the known facts of John Knox's first thirty and more years, but this vivid creation of a fictional life for him not only entertains but raises many questions in the reader's mind about the character and motives of a dominating figure in Scottish history."

—**Dr Rosalind Marshall**, *Fellow of the Royal Society of Literature, research associate of the Oxford Dictionary of National Biography, to which she has contributed more than fifty articles, and author of biographies of Mary, Queen of Scots, Mary of Guise, John Knox, Elizabeth I and Bonnie Prince Charlie.*

THE FIRST BLAST OF THE TRUMPET

The Knox Trilogy
Book One

Marie Macpherson

I

Hallowe'en

The night it is good Hallowe'en
When fairy folk will ride;
And they that wad their true-love win
At Miles Cross they maun bide.
The Ballad of Tam Linn, Traditional

Hailes Castle, Scotland, 1511

"There's no rhyme nor reason to it. Your destiny is already laid doon."

Hunkered down on the hearth, Betsy jiggled the glowing embers with a poker and then carefully criss-crossed dry hazel branches on top. Huddled together on the settle, the three girls drew back as the fire burst into life, the crackling flames spitting out fiery sprites that frolicked their way up the chimney. Betsy wiped the slather of sweat from her flushed face and scrambled up to plonk herself down beside them by the ingleneuk.

"Doom-laden?" Elisabeth queried, her head dirling at the thought. "So where's the use in making a wish?"

"Wishes – and hopes and dreams," Betsy added, "are what keep us going. You make a wish in the hope that it'll come true, but you'll never flee your fate. Now then, my jaggy thistle, when the flames die down, cast your nut into the fire and wish on it," she instructed. "And mind, be wary what you wish for."

Elisabeth delved her hand into the basket and pulled out two nuts coupled together.

"Ah, a St. John's nut." Betsy nodded slowly. "That's a good omen."

"That my wish will come true?" Her ferny green eyes glinted in the firelight.

"Nay, lass, but it'll guard you against the evil eye. Don't fling it, but keep it safe as a charm against witches."

With a doubtful glance at her nurse, Elisabeth slipped the enchanted nut into the pocket of her breeches and chose again. "I will never marry," she began, pausing to savour the astonished gasps before throwing her nut onto the red-hot embers, "unless for love."

"Don't be all blaw and bluster, Lisbeth my lass. It's a wish you've to make, not a deal with the devil. And in secret, otherwise it'll no come true," Betsy warned.

"Then I'll make it come true," Elisabeth retorted.

Betsy shook her head. "You'll have no say in the matter. You maun dree your weird, as the auld saying goes." Then, seeing Elisabeth's quizzical frown, she added, "You must endure your destiny, my jaggy thistle. And never, ever tempt fate by having too great a conceit of yourself. Forbye, if you marry for love, you'll work for silver."

"We'll see," Elisabeth replied, quietly determined that she wouldn't share the lot of those lasses, sacrificed at the altar for the sake of family alliances and financial gain. Leaning forward, her brows drawn tightly together, she glared at the hazelnut, willing it to do her bidding. The nut twitched around the embers before splitting open and spitting out its kernel.

"Sakes me!" Betsy muttered.

"What does it bode?" Elisabeth tugged impatiently at Betsy's sleeve.

"That your peerie heid and nippy tongue will lead you into bother, my lass," Betsy cautioned.

"And that no man will touch a jaggy thistle such as you."

Elisabeth twisted round ready to repay Kate's stinging remark with a sharp nip, but a dunt in the arm from Meg stopped her.

"Even the briar rose has thorns, mind," Elisabeth snapped instead. "Bonnie you may be, but blithe you're not."

"Tsk, tsk," Betsy chided. It made her heart sore to hear her three wee orphans, her bonnie flowers of the forest, bickering. She shook her head as her jaggy thistle, the sharp-witted, spiky-tongued Lisbeth lashed out at fair-haired, pink-cheeked Kate who, like a pawkie kitten, kept her claws hidden until provoked.

Ignoring their squabble, Meg leant forward and cupped her chin in her hands to gaze wistfully into the fire. She lowered her hazelnut gently into the embers where it sizzled and sputtered, before slowly fizzling out.

"Oh, dearie me," she moaned, sucking her top lip over her teeth to stem the tears.

"Don't you fret, my fairy flower." Betsy patted her knee. "That's a sign of a quiet, peaceful life."

"Is it Betsy? Truly?" Meg's watery blue eyes – the shade of the fragile harebell – glistened with grateful tears. Fey, frail Meg had no desire to marry but secretly craved the contemplative life of a nun, sheltered from the hurly-burly of the world behind a protective wall. Let not matrimony and maternity be my destiny, she prayed.

"My turn now." Kate had been rummaging through the basket, picking over the nuts until finding one to her liking. Smooth, flawless and perfectly round.

"We ken fine what you'll wish for," Elisabeth taunted. "And since it's no secret, it'll no be granted."

Kate's eyes blazed in the firelight. "Make her stop, Betsy."

While Elisabeth and Meg were daughters of the late Patrick, 1ˢᵗ Earl of Bothwell, Kate's parentage was vague. An orphan of one of the minor scions of the family –

though tongues wagged that she was a love-child – the "lass with the gowden hair" had been taken in by the earl and brought up with his own daughters at Hailes Castle.

Pernickety and petulant, and endlessly teased by Elisabeth for being a gowk, the cuckoo in their nest, Kate aspired to improve her lowly position through marriage. But, knowing that Kate had set her heart on their brother, Adam, the young Earl of Bothwell, Elisabeth had set her teeth against it.

Taking her time, Kate inspected the bed of embers before deciding where to place her nut. They all bent forward to watch as it hopped and skipped about, before being spat out to land on the hearth. Instinctively they drew their feet back.

"You'll have to throw it back in at once for your wish to come true."

Betsy glowered at Elisabeth, but was too late to stop Kate who'd already picked up the sizzling nut. And dropped it again with a piercing yelp of pain.

"Cuckoo! Cuckoo! Feardie-gowk!" Elisabeth goaded her.

"Sticks and stones may break my bones, but names will never hurt me," Kate recited and sucked on her smarting fingertips to soothe them.

"You were the clumsy kittok for dropping the nut and now your wish is forfeit."

"I don't believe you. You're only saying that because you don't want me to marry Adam. Well, you'll see. I'm no common kittok. I shall be a great lady one day. I shall be the Countess of Bothwell." She flicked back her golden hair and glared at her tormentor.

"Over my dead body, brazen besom," Elisabeth muttered under her breath. She couldn't abide the thought of her cousin becoming her brother's wife and a titled lady, for she suspected that, beneath her simpering mannerisms and ladylike demeanour, skulked a scheming wench.

"While no-one will waste a glance on a rapscallion like you," Kate was saying, "a gilpie no a girl." She tilted her head to look down her snub nose at Elisabeth, clad in her brother's cast-off riding breeches, her copper hair tousled and unkempt.

Seeing her jaggy thistle about to snap, Betsy clamped her hand across her mouth. Only when Elisabeth nodded, to indicate that she'd keep her mouth shut, did Betsy let go.

"Wheesht, wheesht, my fairest flowers," she crooned, "this is no a night for bickering."

"These daft games are tiresome." Kate stood up abruptly and wrapped her shawl tightly around her shoulders. "I'm away to bed."

"Afore the witching hour? On your own?"

Elisabeth's deep menacing growl had the intended effect. Kate glanced round, horror-stricken by the sinister shadows cast by the flickering tallow candles, before stammering, "Well, why not? I ... I ... "

"There's no telling who or what you'll meet on Hallows Eve," Elisabeth continued in her spooky voice, fluttering her fingers in front of Kate's anxious face. "When ghosts and ghouls and boglemen walk the earth."

"Don't you be scaring the living daylights out of her," Betsy chided. "Don't fret, Kate, you'll meet your match soon enough. Come, now, and sing us the *Ballad of True Thomas*." She leant forward to stoke the fire with more logs. "Coorie in my bonnie lassies, and listen."

With a hostile glare at her cousin, Kate tossed her fair curls and began crooning softly in her linnet-sweet voice, which, though she'd die rather than admit it, Elisabeth loved to hear.

> "True Thomas he pull'd off his cap,
> And louted low down to his knee.
> All hail, thou mighty Queen of Heaven!
> For thy peer on earth I never did see."

The girls listened spellbound to the legend of Thomas the Rhymer, lured by the Queen of Fairies to Elfland where he disappeared for seven long years, although it felt like only three days to him. Before he left, she gave him two gifts: a tongue that never lied and the power to see into the future.

"Betsy, have you the second sight?" Meg asked, her whisper breaking the mort-cloth of silence that had fallen over them after Kate's eldritch song. Betsy Learmont came from an old border family descended, so she told them, from this very Thomas of Earldoune, half minstrel, half magician, famed and feared for his sorceries. Betsy stared into the fire for a few moments before answering.

"I jalouse we all have in some way or other. We've all been given a sixth sense, a third eye, some cry it, that sees beyond the veil, but more often than not, most folk pay it scant heed. For where's the use in being able to peer through the dark veil smooring the future with no power to change it? And those who are truly foresighted would say it's more of a curse than a blessing.

"But at certain times of the year, like tonight, All Hallows" Eve – or *Samhain* as the auld, Celtic religion cries it – the thin veil between this world and the next is drawn back. Nay," she said, shaking her head at Meg's raised eyebrows, "not your Christian paradise. Nor thon limbo where the souls of unbaptised bairns and pagans linger for eternity, but the twilight world between heaven and earth where the fairy folk and the unquiet dead dwell."

"The unquiet dead?" Meg murmured.

"Wheessht!" Betsy put a warning finger to her lips, for to mention them risked rousing them. She lowered her voice to a faint whisper. "The restless spirits of folk that have been murdered or have taken their own lives, who roam the earth, looking for unwary bodies of the living to possess." Her chilling words sent a shiver through Meg. "On this night our own spirits can leave our bodies, too. That's why you're able to see the spectre of the man you'll marry."

The blustery wind soughed down the chimney, gusting smoke into the chamber and rattling the shutters. The cold draught at their backs sent shivers skittering down their spines. The girls drew their thick woollen shawls more securely over their heads and huddled in closer together. As the mirk and midnight hour approached, Betsy set about making hot pint. She plunged the scorching poker into a kettle of spiced ale sweetened with honey until the toddy sizzled and simmered merrily, rising to the top in a smooth, creamy froth.

"This will give you good cheer and good heart," she promised.

While they blew on their courage-giving draught to cool it down, Betsy scraped some soot from inside the chimney to rub on their faces as a disguise to fool the malevolent spirits of the unquiet dead. It was nearly time to ring the stooks.

"I'll just bide here by the fire." Kate shivered. "It's far too cold and dark to be wandering about."

"You mean you're too feart. And what will Adam think when he hears the future Countess of Bothwell is a feardie gowk?"

Ignoring Elisabeth's taunt, Kate smeared her pink cheeks with soot and then wiped her clarty hands on Elisabeth's breeches. Betsy deftly stepped in between to foil any reprisal from the jaggy thistle and handed them each a branch from the fairy tree.

"These rowan twigs will ward off evil spirits. Hold on to them for dear life. Or else." She lit the taper in the neep lantern and passed it to Elisabeth. Its ghoulish grin of jagged teeth glowing in the dark would scare the living never mind the undead.

"Now, mind and go widdershins round the stooks," Betsy said, before adding, "and beware of tumbling into thon ditch, my jaggy thistle."

The snell blast as they stepped out from the shelter of the castle walls caught their breath. Hearing the wind whistling and howling like a carlin through the trees, the girls hesitated. Top-heavy pines swayed back and forth in the wind, threatening to fall over and crash down on them. Trees stripped of their leaves were transformed into blackened skeletons with gnarled, wizened fingers pointing in menace. Leaves whirled and reeled madly like hobgoblins at Auld Clootie's ball. Clouds scudded past the furtive moon, casting unearthly shadows. Striving to make no sound that would alert evil spirits, the girls stepped lightly, but the crisp, dry leaves crackled and crunched underfoot.

By the glimmer of the neep lantern they skirted round the ditch filled with fallen leaves until they came to the crossing point. In the cornfield, the harvest straw gathered into sheaves stood like rows of drunken men leaning into each other for support. Kate hung tightly to Meg but kept looking round, convinced that they were being followed.

"Aagh! What's that?" She stopped to brandish her rowan switch.

"Wheesht! You'll wake the unquiet dead with your screeching," Elisabeth growled.

"Look over there." Kate was pointing with her twig. "Isn't thon a bogleman?"

All three huddled together to peer at the eerie shape frantically waving its tattered limbs as if in warning.

"Thon's a pease-bogle, you daft gowk," Elisabeth sneered as the scarecrow keeled over in the strong wind.

Stopping beside the nearest haystack, they bickered about which way to circle it.

"Betsy said mind and go widdershins," Meg said, her teeth chittering.

"The devil's way? Against the sun? Will that no bring bad luck?" Kate shivered.

Meg shrugged her shoulders. "Not at Hallowe'en. For this is the witches" night and we'll vex Auld Nick mair if we go sunwise, says Betsy. Now shut your een and hold your arms out in front. Circle three times and on the third turn your sweetheart's spectre will appear."

"I ... I... I'm no sure I want to do this." Kate was looking round, still certain that some malevolent spirit was stalking them.

"We'll do it together," Elisabeth suggested, for she, too, was feeling uneasy.

Having no wish for a spouse in any form – body or spirit – Meg held the lantern while the two girls, eyes tight shut and arms stretched out like sleepwalkers, began to circle the stook. Willing herself to see the image of the one she loved, Elisabeth squeezed her eyelids tight against her eyeballs until colours flashed and flared in her head.

As they came round for the third time, leaves disturbed by a field mouse or vole rustled nearby. An owl or bat whooshed past her, and then a high-pitched scream rang out, chilling her blood. In the shadows of the trees, Elisabeth could make out two shapes stumbling across the cornfield towards them. As they loomed nearer, she drew back, alarmed to see two bogles, the whites of their eyes gleaming in blackened faces.

"Beware the unquiet dead!" a menacing voice rumbled.

"Or the quiet undead!" another echoed.

When one of the ghouls darted forward to reel her in, Elisabeth turned tail. She flung aside her rowan switch and stumbled over divots towards the ditch.

Suddenly the burn bubbled up and a torrent swept her off her feet. As she was tossed and spun in the murky water, shadowy figures whirled around her. She tried to grab hold of a hand but the rotting flesh fell away from the fingers. A severed head spun towards her, its fronds of hair streaming out behind, its face stripped of flesh. With greenish-black pus gushing through the empty eye sockets and its jaws locked in an eternal grimace, the skull leered at her. The burn water thickened and darkened to blood red, brimming into her lungs. As the whooshing sound in her ears died down, she opened her mouth to gulp down air. From far away she heard an unearthly voice murmur, "She's coming to herself."

When arms lifted her up and propped her against a dyke, Elisabeth snorted to clear the stench of decaying leaves in her nostrils, but as she wiped the glaur from her eyes she let out a yelp. Behind the neep lantern with its jagged teeth, another ghastly head, with soot-stained mouth and bone white teeth, was yawning wide. She jolted backwards but, as she jerked forwards, her forehead whacked the fiend's nose with a loud crack.

"Ouch!" The bogle's hand darted to its face. "*Nemo me impune lacessit.* You're well named, my jaggy thistle. Who'd dare meddle with you? Your snite is worse than your bite. And there was I, ready to bewitch you with a kiss," he mumbled, dabbing at the streaks of sooty blood trickling from his nose. "Pity."

"She hasn't broken anything." Meg had knelt down in the glaur to massage her sister's ankles with fingers cold as the grave.

"What about me?" the ghoul wailed. "Not only my nose but my poor heart is sore."

"She's well enough if she can skelp him like that," Kate hissed, but, seeing the other bogleman approach, she widened doe eyes at him. "Forbye, this spanking wind is whipping the skin off my cheeks," she whimpered.

"Come, then, afore it flays the hide off you." The fiendish Earl of Bothwell was holding out one crooked arm to Kate who, needing no further coaxing, linked her arm through his. But when he offered his other arm to Meg, whose very bones were trembling with cold, Kate's face darkened to a glower. Meanwhile the other ghoul was helping Elisabeth to her feet.

"You ... you ... scared me half to death, Davie Lindsay," she scolded.

"Better not let the cold kill the other half then."

Lindsay pulled her into the shelter of his cloak but the acrid smell of soot from his blackened face began to prickle her nostrils. As she screwed up her nose to stifle a sneeze, he pressed his finger hard against her top lip.

"Squeezing is better than sneezing, my jaggy thistle. And kissing can wait. But keep in mind whose spirit you've seen tonight, otherwise the devil knows who you'll marry."